DIAMOND IN THE ROUGH

by Lori L. Robinett

THREE CREEKS
PRESS

DIAMOND IN THE ROUGH
A Diamond J Romance

By

Lori L. Robinett

Published by Three Creeks Press

Cover Design by JayCee DeLorenzo, Sweet & Spicy Designs

This book is dedicated to my parents,

Dean and Alma Hazen,

for putting up with my obsessions: horses and books.

Acknowledgements:

There are so many people who helped make this book possible. The biggest thanks goes to my critique group: Carolyn Paul Branch, Colleen Donnelly, Ericca Thornhill and Jennifer Bondurant, without whom this story never would have gotten finished. I also greatly appreciate the input of those kind souls who agreed to be beta readers for me: Holly Atkinson (Evil Eye Editing), Patricia Spencer (live long and prosper), and Lynn Simmons. Also, a hat tip to Jon Angell, who helped me through the technical aspects of cattle rustling and sale barns.

Dear Reader,

Thank you so much for taking time out of your busy schedule to read my book.

Do you like giveaways, contests and other free stuff? Swing on over to www.lorilrobinett.com and sign up for my newsletter. All I ask for is your email address, which I will never sell or give to anyone. In return, you'll get exclusive content and special contests!

So . . . pop over to

http://lorilrobinett.com

and sign up now.

Go ahead, I'll wait . . . :)

And you're back? Great! Let's see what's happening at the Diamond J . . .

CHAPTER ONE
The Cowboy

Silver bells jangled as the cowboy pushed through the front door of the scrapbook store. Gina and Midge stopped in mid-sentence. The cowboy was tall, easily six foot, with a broad chest straining against a red plaid flannel shirt rolled up to expose muscular forearms covered with a dusting of dark hair.

Midge was the first to recover. "Welcome to Memories & More!" Her hazel eyes rounded as she took in the visitor.

Gina glanced at her friend. Midge was taller by a couple of inches, thinner by several pounds, and a natural blonde. Gina tugged at her cotton t-shirt. She always felt pudgy and drab next to Midge. "Can we help you find anything?" Gina ran her fingers through her thick hair to smooth the unruly waves. She should've pulled it back today.

"Not yet. Just looking right now." Stubble shadowed his face, accentuating his strong, square jaw. Scruffy boots identified him as a working man. His faded jeans, ragged at the hem, molded to his thighs.

Gina's jaw dropped, until Midge reached over and tapped her under the chin. The two pretended to work as they watched him stroll around the store. Two other customers, both regulars, stopped shopping to watch him. Men weren't unheard of in the store, but they were usually holding bags for their wives. The tall cowboy frowned as he examined the big color wheel posted on the wall.

Dottie, one of Gina's best customers, approached the center island and dropped an assortment of papers on the counter. She tipped her head toward the cowboy. She mouthed, "Who's the hottie?"

Midge shrugged and whispered, "Don't know, but he's fun to look at, isn't he?"

The cowboy strolled closer. Dottie cleared her throat and said in a louder voice, "Did you hear about Frank and Ellie Donovan?"

Ellie was one of the Friday night scrappers. Gina asked, "What about them?"

"Rustlers. Stole every last cow they had." Dottie made a clucking noise. "He was getting ready to send a bunch to the sale barn to make his farm payment. Woke up yesterday morning and they were gone."

"That's awful." Midge let out a huff of air as she rang up the papers. "That's the third one in as many weeks. Bernie & Jo Johnson were hit last week."

Gina shook her head. "I sure hope they had insurance." That kind of thing just didn't happen in Wilder. It was safe. Low crime. Folks left their homes unlocked, dropped their car keys on their seats, walked after dark without fear. But the cattle rustlers were striking a deep blow, hitting the farmers where it hurt.

Midge slid Dottie's change across the counter, which the other woman scooped up. As Dottie walked toward the door, she snuck a peek at the cowboy then glanced over her shoulder and winked.

The telephone jangled on the counter and the two women jumped. Midge snatched the receiver up. "Memories and More, where we help you preserve yours." She listened a second, then scrunched her nose and handed the phone to Gina, holding it like a stinky sock.

Gina sighed as she took the handset. As soon as she heard her ex-husband's voice, she knew the reason for the call and shook her head. "Don't do this, Steve." She fought to keep her tone civil, but her palms hurt where she pressed her fingernails into them. Acutely aware of the gorgeous man standing near the paper racks, she turned away and wandered toward the back of the store. Her eyes closed as she listened to her ex-husband's litany of excuses.

Midge ducked around the paper racks and waved her hands to catch Gina's attention, then mouthed, "Are you okay?"

Gina nodded at her friend, took a deep breath and hissed into the phone, "I have listened to your excuses over and over. Don't walk away."

Her lips pressed together as she listened to the disconnected voice. "I'm not walking away. Sometimes I can't take Toby. This job—" He sounded stressed.

She cut him off. "Steve, please don't. I'll—"

"You'll what?"

She sucked in a breath. What would she do? That was

easy. "Nothing."

"This job'll be finished up this next week. I'll see you soon, sweetheart."

After she punched the red off button, she scowled at the phone and marched back to the center counter. "That man absolutely infuriates me!" She set the handset down on the counter a bit harder than she intended, and winced at the sharp pop of plastic against glass.

Midge touched Gina on the arm. "You okay, Boss?"

Gina ran both hands through her thick hair, then shrugged as she glanced over her shoulder at the only customer left in the store, the cowboy. "I'm fine. It's Toby that I'm worried about. He's been looking forward to seeing his daddy all week."

"And Steve's not coming." Midge rolled her eyes. "Again."

"You got it. Says he's got a job to do. Second weekend in a row." She let out a sigh and stared out the big front window without seeing anything.

Midge stepped forward, stopping beside Gina. Her right eyebrow arched up. "Is it legit?"

Gina shrugged. "Probably not. He always gets mixed up in things he shouldn't." She turned away from the window to look at her friend. Gina continued, "Trouble finds him."

"Like when he was stealing from the distribution company." Midge's forehead creased. "You know, honey, that was a long time ago."

"He let his buddies talk him into stealing beer off his truck." Gina huffed at the memory. "When he got fired for

4

that, I was stuck at home with our baby . . . Not smart. Not smart at all. I couldn't depend on him then. Guess I still can't." He made her so angry. She was over him, but Toby wasn't. It wasn't fair. She walked back to the center island, with Midge trailing behind.

"You're shaking." Midge turned on her heel and walked toward the back of the store again. She called back over her shoulder, "Let me get you a water."

Gina nodded and gripped the edge of the work counter until her fingertips were white, the blood forced from the tips. Why, after all these years, did Steve still have the power to get her so worked up?

They had only been together a year, but that year had been enough. She didn't know if she'd ever trust a man again. She took a deep breath, straightened her back and squared her shoulders.

As she slipped behind the counter, her eyes wandered to a framed layout perched on an easel on the wooden album display case in the front window. All she could see was the back of the picture frame, but the image was clear in her mind. Toby wore his overalls, scuffed cowboy boots and a little John Deere hat, nestled among a heap of orange pumpkins.

He'd been three when the photo was snapped a couple of years ago at the Hartsburg Pumpkin Festival. After Steve had cancelled his weekend visit, Toby'd been heartbroken. She took Toby on a quick jaunt to central Missouri and they spent the day wandering the festival, snacking on all the good food. On the trip home, he insisted she fasten the seat belt over the big pumpkin he picked out. When she looked at her little boy in the rear view mirror, his right hand rested on the pumpkin.

And now he was a big boy going to school, his daddy could break his heart just as easily as he did back then.

"Here ya go," Midge said as she held out a plastic water bottle. Gina twisted the cap off, put the opening to her lips and tipped the bottle. The water stung her teeth, went down cold and wet. It hit her like a jolt, but did nothing to cool her anger.

She slammed the bottle down on the counter, a bit of water sloshing out onto the glass. She yanked a paper towel from the roll under the counter and wiped up the spill with an quick swipe. "That man makes me so angry sometimes."

CHAPTER TWO
Men!

"I never would have guessed." The low rumble of the stranger's voice caught Gina off balance.

She gasped in surprise, turned at the low words, and took a good look at the owner of the voice. She'd all but forgotten the man in the store. He was even taller than she'd first thought, over six feet with broad shoulders. He regarded her with a crooked smile, his electric blue eyes twinkling under the brim of his worn cowboy hat. His teeth were white and straight, except for one front tooth that slightly overlapped the other. Thick dark hair curled around the edges of his Stetson. He tipped it back, leaned forward and rested his elbows on the counter. He slowly rubbed the rough stubble on his strong, square chin as he gazed intently at her.

"Gina?" Midge's voice broke her reverie. For good measure, Midge poked Gina in the ribs. Color crept up Gina's cheeks.

She shook her head and blinked. "I'm sorry. What was that?" She glanced down. He ducked his head and caught

7

her eye. The right corner of his mouth twitched up in a grin, and she caught herself smiling back at him. Her eyes stayed locked with his as he stood straight. He was taller than her ex-husband, who'd been only a couple of inches taller than her. She pressed her lips together, irritated that she still compared every man she met to her ex.

His deep voice wasn't loud, but had a quiet power to it. "I just said that I hadn't been in here before, but hoped you ladies might be able to help me out." He struck her as a gentleman, in spite of his attire, so much different than the brash tones of her ex's voice.

Her first marriage had been the result of a hormone fueled sexual escapade that ended with her pregnant and him trapped. Their divorce was final before Toby mastered the art of crawling. And Gina had been alone ever since, if you didn't count the handful of disastrous dates she'd had over the years.

Gina stumbled forward as Midge's hand pressed into the small of her back. Gina hadn't even realized she'd taken a step back. The cowboy in front of her kept eye contact and winked at her. His eyes reminded her of a deep blue spring sky with lightning streaking across it.

Get it together! She cleared her throat, then spread her hands, palms up, to indicate the store. "Can we help you find something?"

Midge broke in, "Perhaps a gift for your wife or girlfriend?"

The cowboy's grin faded. "No, nothing like that. I'm from the Diamond J Ranch and the boss is wanting to do a big shindig for Memorial Day and wants to send out invitations or flyers or something."

Gina nodded and turned toward the blank cards and envelopes section against the north wall. His boots echoed on the wooden floor as he followed her, and when she stopped, they stopped. For a moment, she stood, aware of him right behind her. She could almost feel his heat radiating toward her, reaching out for her.

She gave herself a shake. Ridiculous. That's what this whole thing was. How could she even think about being attracted to a man, much less some minimum-wage making cowboy? If she ever did allow herself to fall for a man, he would have to be perfect. A solid, respectable man with a good job, who was kind and caring and thoughtful. Someone who could be her partner, a good role model for her son. Preferably good looking.

Granted, this guy met the height and weight requirements.

But he looked dark and dangerous, which she didn't need in her life.

She took a deep breath, gathered her thoughts and pointed to the display. "Here are some blank cards, or you could do something on 8 ½ by 11 paper. Do you prefer cards or flyers?"

He shrugged. She let her eyes wander up and down him one more time. Waves of dark hair peeked out from under his black Stetson, probably permanently curled around his hat. Yes, he definitely had the physical attributes her dream man would have, even the blue eyes, but cowboy didn't fit into her equation anywhere.

She pulled a plastic bag from a hook and held it up. "A

card would be my suggestion."

He took the package of blank cards from her, and his fingertips brushed hers. His hands were rough and calloused, a working man's hands, yet his touch was gentle. The cowboy turned the package over and looked at it from every direction, doubt clouding his tanned features. His hat dipped slightly on his forehead as his dark eyebrows pinched together in a frown. He glanced at her and asked, "What do I do with them?"

She pointed toward the clear acrylic stamps hanging above the cards and envelopes. "You can stamp the invitations. You know, a who, what, when, where sort of thing. Then you can put a square of colored paper on the front, maybe some stickers or stamps that go with the theme of your party."

Midge called out from the center counter island, "Gina is really good at making invitations. She does custom work!"

Gina spun toward her friend and opened her eyes wide in warning, but it was too late. The cowboy had heard the offer and his face brightened visibly.

"Really? You do that?"

Gina shook her head and waved her friend's suggestion off. "No, I don't. I just do them for my friends sometimes."

He stuck out his right hand and she instinctively reached out with her own. He enveloped her hand in his and shook. "Then, we should be friends. I'm Aidan. Aidan Brackston."

"Nice to meet you," she murmured as she stared at their hands. Her hand fit so well into his, and it felt right.

Comfortable. Warm. Strains of Sinatra drifted through the speakers, and it took her a moment to remember the name of the song.

Never Let Me Go . . . How appropriate.

He prompted, "And you are?"

She blinked rapidly. "Right! Sorry! I'm Gina Montgomery."

Midge called out again. "She owns this place."

Aidan continued to hold Gina's hand. She looked at him and he met her gaze, holding it. Finally, her eyes wandered to his left hand hanging at his side, still clutching the bag of blank cards. No wedding ring. No tan line.

"Just Gina," Midge continued. "All by herself."

Gina yanked her hand back as if she'd been bitten. This time, the color raced up her cheeks. She glared at Midge, who casually went back to straightening the baskets of findings lining the counter, sorting all the little metal charms and chains and fasteners, then Gina became acutely aware of how close Aidan stood to her. She took a step backwards and cleared her throat.

Aidan's eyes danced and the corner of his mouth twitched up. Her cheeks burned under his amused gaze. She nodded toward her friend. "Midge also does invitations. Her prices are reasonable and she does good work. Perhaps she can help you." She felt so awkward, so stupid. Good looking men always made her feel like a gawky teenager, and she hated that.

"I'm sorry—" He started to protest.

Gina'd heard enough excuses for one day. Her jaw

jutted forward as she marched toward the back room, disappearing through the swinging door. Once in the backroom, alone, she cursed herself for walking out. For not being strong enough to stand there and take whatever might have come next. What was she afraid of, anyway? She glanced through the tiny Plexiglas window and saw him standing at the center island, one elbow leaned casually on the counter, one foot propped up in front of the other, toe on the ground. Midge leaned back against the post, an easy smile on her face.

That's what she was afraid of.

Having a nice, normal conversation with a nice, normal man. Why? Simple, because there was no such thing. All interactions with men were for one reason and one reason only, for the man to get the woman in bed. Midge gave her hope, though, because Midge was married to a wonderful guy that treated her right. They were partners in life. They had the kind of relationship she hoped to have someday.

But, she reminded herself, Midge and Doug didn't have the pressure of a child. Her own marriage had been doomed from the start. It started with her fat and cranky, with hormonal fluctuations that would have caused the best marriage to form a few stress fractures. Their marriage erupted in an explosion of hate and anger and blame when she confronted him about losing his trucking job. Steve walked out and left her to raise Toby on her own.

Not that Toby was a burden. He wasn't. But having him meant she had to put his needs above hers. She didn't have time to date. She couldn't risk dating someone who wasn't perfect. Toby'd had enough disappointment in his life. If she brought a guy around and Toby started to like him, and then things didn't work out . . . well, that just wasn't something she could risk.

She couldn't run off with every good looking cowboy that caught her eye.

Not even one with deep blue eyes that sent a charge down her spine every time he looked at her.

Gina pressed against the Plexiglas window of the store room again, just as the door swung toward her. The door smacked her face with a sharp POP and she fell backwards, landing on her backside with a thump.

Light silhouetted the dark figure in the doorway, radiating around him like a halo. He bent toward her, hand extended, and the halo turned into a cowboy hat.

Ah, there was that good looking cowboy she was just thinking about . . .

She reached up and took his offered hand, and he pulled her up so she stood mere inches from him. She'd been right about his height. She looked straight ahead at his broad chest. His muscles filled out his red plaid flannel shirt. Dark hairs curled over the shirt where his top two buttons were undone. Her eyes wandered up the curve of his neck, over the strong line of his shadowed jaw, and settled on his lips. They were parted slightly, welcoming, inviting. She looked at those amazing blue eyes . . . which were not focused on her eyes, but staring openly at her chest.

There was a sharp pop as she slapped his face.

CHAPTER THREE

An Invitation

Aidan blinked, his hand flew to his face and his eyes opened wide. Then he frowned and said, "What was that for?"

Midge appeared behind him and chimed in, "Yeah, what was that for?"

Gina's hand fluttered in the air for a moment as if controlled by some invisible string, then dropped to her side. He was checking her out, but she'd been checking him out, too. Equal opportunity ogling.

"Oh, my gosh. I'm sorry." She looked down and admitted, "I don't know what got into me. I shouldn't have done that."

He shook his head and looked at her sternly. "No, you shouldn't have." His lips pressed together and his eyes narrowed.

The words hung in the air. Tension stretched. The clock on the wall ticked the seconds off. Gina swallowed the lump in her throat. It would serve her right if he smacked her back. Or if he walked out of here and told everyone he knew to stay away from the crazy lady at the Memories and More Scrapbook Store. She didn't need that kind of publicity. The poor economy had hit Wilder just as hard as the rest of the country. This store had been a dream come true for her. It allowed her to work flexible hours, to run Toby wherever he needed to go, to be there when he needed her.

Her chest rose and fell as she sucked in a deep breath and prepared to take whatever the cowboy wanted to dish out. She lifted her chin and pulled her shoulders back, ready to take her medicine. Midge caught her eye, looked pointedly at her chest and gave her a thumbs up. Gina's eyes rounded and she shook her head slightly, frowning at her friend.

Her well-meaning, but ill-timed friend.

The cowboy – she had forgotten his name! – caught her look and glanced back toward Midge, who shrugged and tried to look innocent. She failed miserably, instead looking like an impish pixie.

He turned back to Gina and tapped his tanned cheek with an index finger. "You owe me for that."

Gina nodded. "You're right. I am so, so sorry. There is no excuse for—"

"Stop." He held up his hand, palm out, in front of her face. "Words are empty."

"Hey, now." She frowned. "You were checking me out."

His lips split in a wide grin. He drawled, "And you were checking me out, too, darlin'."

She stuttered for a moment, unsure of what to say next. Finally, she continued, "I'm so sorry, Mr., uh—"

"Aidan. The name is Aidan, ma'am."

That term raised her hackles. "Ma'am? Just how old do you think I am?"

His face held firm. No smile, no scowl. "Old enough to know better, I'd say. Now, about that apology." Before she could interrupt, he held up his hand again. "There is something you could do to make it up to me. You know, for slapping a customer in the face for absolutely no reason."

"I'm listening." She regarded him warily.

"My boss, Beth Jameson, needs invitations. You can make invitations." He turned to Midge and involved her in his negotiations. "Right?"

Midge nodded vigorously, then added, "Sounds like the perfect solution to me!"

Gina scowled at her friend, then at Aidan, and then let her shoulders relax. She threw her hands up in surrender. "Okay, you win. I'll make the invitations."

A smile spread across Aidan's face, and his features softened as the tension left them. She looked at him, and wondered how it was possible that a man could irritate her and attract her at the exact same moment.

They moved through the doorway and into the store, Midge in the lead, followed by Aidan, with Gina behind. It gave her a chance to really look at him without fear of getting caught. His jeans hugged his legs, every muscle outlined by denim. Of course, he was wearing Wranglers. What else would a good cowboy wear? She breathed in his scent — freshly cut grass, hay and horse.

They sat down at a work table, side by side. His arm

brushed hers as they looked at the various rubber stamps and patterned papers Midge laid in front of them. She felt every touch. Gina jotted notes on a piece of paper as she quizzed him about the event, details about the barbecue, things about the Diamond J Ranch.

"You know, it would be great to incorporate the name of the ranch into the design of the invitations," she offered. She sketched out a diamond shape.

He nodded his agreement. "Beth would like that a lot, I think, and I know Beau would."

"Good. I think I've got enough to get started then. How many do you need?" she asked as she sat back in the folding chair.

He shrugged, "I don't know. Maybe a hundred?"

Her eyebrows arched. "Must be quite the party."

He nodded. "Yup." The word had two syllables, the way he dragged it out. "Lots of folks come out for this event."

The Diamond J Ranch had been a fixture in Cardwell County for years. A legend. The old timers talked about the old days when the Jamesons would run their cattle the old way, actual cattle drives.

From the time she'd been a little girl, she dreamed of rodeos and horses and, yes, cowboys. And here she was sitting with one. She prodded, "And who are the lucky people on the guest list?"

He shrugged again. "Mostly rodeo folks, and some business people from around here. Beth wants to make an impression on folks and drum up business."

She nodded, "Anyone I would know?"

He looked confused for a moment. "You mean my boss?"

She leaned toward him just a bit, feeling flirty, and let her arm brush against his. "I mean, would I know any of the business people around here who are invited?"

His eyes widened as recognition dawned on his face. "You want to come?"

Midge walked by and observed loudly, "About time. Yes, she wants an invitation."

He grinned and looked down at Gina. "Well, then, absolutely make a hundred and one invitations. Consider yourself invited."

She smiled back, sure Toby would think a day at a real live ranch was almost as exciting as going to a carnival or something like that. "Can I bring someone?"

His smile faded and he nodded once, then scooted away from the table. "How much time do you need to get these done?"

She slid her chair back and followed him as he strode toward the door, worried she'd been too pushy about bringing Toby with her. She walked quickly to catch up with him. "Today's Friday. I can have them ready by Monday. Would you like to come by and pick them up, or shall I deliver them to you out at the Diamond J?"

"I'll have somebody pick them up." He touched the rim of his hat as way of a goodbye and pushed out the door.

"Mmmm-hmmmm, he was yummy." Midge said as she pulled a new pack of Echo Park patterned paper from a box. "You need help with those invitations?"

"No, I can handle it. In fact, I think I'll get started right now." Gina moved to the front of the store and watched out the big front window as Aidan crossed the road. He swung up into a dusty white Chevy pickup. When he reversed out of the parking space, his head swiveled back toward her and she ducked behind a display rack.

Gina shook her head at herself, then returned to the table and sat down. As she experimented with various stamps and designs, she allowed herself to remember how good he looked. Rugged. He had the look of a man who knew what it was to work for a living, well-muscled and tan. He'd smelled of hay, straw, horses, sunshine.

But guys who smelled like that never had two dimes to rub together. She reminded herself she was not looking for a man, but if she were, a ranch hand who probably made just enough to pay for his beer on Friday and Saturday nights was not going to make her dreams come true.

CHAPTER FOUR

Advice

As Aidan drove out to the Diamond J Ranch, he thought about finally meeting Gina. When Beth asked him to order invitations for the Memorial Day Barbecue, he'd jumped at the chance to meet the owner of the scrapbook store. He'd seen her around town, tried to be cool and confident, but his flirting hadn't done any good. She had a boyfriend.

Of course she had a boyfriend, he told himself. She had curves in all the right places, wide blue-green eyes, freckles sprinkled across her nose and that mane of wavy auburn hair was hard to miss. He could imagine how it would feel to have that thick hair tickle his face, while he gripped her hips as she straddled him—

A blaring horn broke his train of thought. He jerked the wheel to the right and put the old truck back in its lane. The green Honda continued on its way and he waved an apology at the driver. Aidan glanced in the rearview mirror and took a moment to appreciate the last few minutes.

Gina was every bit as beautiful close up as she was from

a distance. Dark red highlights streaked her thick hair, usually swept back in a low ponytail, but today it hung loose, spilling over her shoulders. And those eyes. Reminded him of the dark green moss that carpeted the forest floor.

Aidan maneuvered his old truck into his usual parking spot under the big oak tree, put it in park and waited for it to shudder to a stop. The door squealed in protest as he opened it. He slid out and slammed the door. As usual, it didn't shut all the way, so he gave it a kick for good measure.

"Why don't you just shoot that thing and put it out of its misery?"

Aidan looked around to find Beau leaning against the barn door, a piece of hay sticking out of his mouth, bobbing as he chewed on it.

"Nothing wrong with my truck," Aidan said. "I know its quirks."

Beau shook his head. "You know, you could get a deal on a new truck."

Aidan shrugged, "I know. And when I'm ready, I'll go. But for now, this ol' truck'll do just fine."

Beau nodded toward the truck. "You know, you're not fooling anybody driving that old heap."

"Not trying to fool anybody. Just happy with what I got." Aidan waved a hand toward the house. "Is Charlotte inside?"

"Yup." Beau pulled the bit of hay from his mouth and dropped it on the ground.

Aidan started toward the house. "Okay, then. I'm gonna

run in for a minute. You got something you want me to do after that?"

"Yeah, the fence on the yearling pastures needs to be replaced. Why don't you grab one of the boys and work on fence?"

"Can do, Beau. See you later."

"Hey, Aidan!"

Aidan stopped and turned in his tracks. "Yeah?"

"What're you talking to Charlotte about? A girl?" Beau's teeth flashed when he grinned. He waggled his eyebrows. "You know, I highly recommend settling down with a good woman."

Aidan grinned. Beau wouldn't have uttered those words a year ago. He'd been a confirmed bachelor until Beth Jameson came along. Aidan shrugged and said, "We all can't marry the boss."

"Lots of eligible bachelorettes around, and now that I'm taken, they'll have their sights set on you." With a shrug, Beau turned and disappeared into the barn. He called over his shoulder, "You don't know what you're missing!"

His friend's laughter followed Aidan as he crunched across the gravel toward the big house. He tugged the back door open, slipped into the kitchen and the scent of fresh baked bread and roast beef greeted him. He closed his eyes and took a deep breath. This was what he loved about the Diamond J Ranch, about his life now.

Growing up, he was never greeted by scents like that. Here, the crock pot held a big pot roast, potatoes, onions and celery. Back then, the only good scent in the house was a fancy little pot with scented gel. His mother didn't even fill that herself. Juanita, their housekeeper, filled it.

Charlotte lifted a fresh baked apple pie from the oven. "Afternoon, Aidan." She placed it on a cooling rack, then closed the oven and wiped her hands on her apron. Charlotte was a stout woman, with a rounded middle and chubby cheeks that were perpetually pink.

"Afternoon," he replied. He clasped his hands together, then stuck them in his pockets and finally let them hang at his sides.

She glanced over at him, then grabbed the copper tea kettle from the stove and filled it with water. "I was going to make myself a pot of tea. Join me?" Though she'd lived in the States since she was a little girl, her voice still carried a hint of Irish brogue.

He glanced over his shoulder. He held fond memories of afternoon tea with his grandmother, but it wasn't a very manly habit.

She scoffed, "Ain't none of the boys around to see you enjoying a bit o' tea time."

He grinned, scooted a chair back and lowered himself onto the seat. The tea kettle whistled merrily.

Charlotte pulled two cups from the hooks under the counter. "What are you in the mood for today?"

He rummaged through the little basket, located a bright yellow packet and tore it open. "Earl Grey." He slid the basket back across the table.

"What's on your mind?" Charlotte asked as she flipped through the varieties of tea.

One corner of Aidan's lip pulled up in a half grin. "How'd you know something's on my mind?"

She pinned him with her intense blue eyes and said, "That's the only time you're in my kitchen unless you're here to eat."

She sat down across from him, curled her plump hands around the cup and waited. The only sound was the soft tick of the oven as it cooled.

Aidan lifted the cup to his lips, but it was too hot and he sat it down. He sighed.

"So, tell me about her."

The grin was full this time. "Do you know the gal that runs the scrapbook store in town?"

A frown appeared on Charlotte's brow. "Carla something?"

"Gina." Her name felt like warm chocolate on his tongue, rich and sweet.

She grabbed the honey bear from the center of the table and popped the top. After she swirled honey into her cup, she offered it to Aidan but he shook his head. She urged, "Go ahead. Tell me about her."

"I've had a crush on her for a while, I guess. Seen her around town. Went in there today to see if she'd help with the invitations to the barbecue."

Charlotte nodded her approval. He briefly ran through the conversation and events at the store earlier in the afternoon. He finished, "So the invitations'll be ready Monday."

Charlotte steepled her fingers in front of her as she considered the situation. "And you want to know if you should pick them up or have someone else do it?"

"Right." He wanted an excuse to see her.

"And you're worried about her bringing a date to the barbecue."

His shoulders drooped. "Right."

She sipped her tea, her index finger tapping the side of the cup thoughtfully. "Well, I think you should go pick up the invitations yourself. Get to know her a little better before you start worrying about a date that she may or may not bring to the barbecue."

He nodded, took a couple of gulps of his tea, and set the cup down with a thump. "You sure I should go pick them up?" A frown furrowed his brow as he stared down at the half empty cup.

"She's not Tracy." Charlotte's voice was soft, kind.

At the mention of his ex-girlfriend, Aidan felt a surge of anger. "I know." They'd dated for several months before she'd shown her true colors.

"I know how disappointed you were when she started planning how to spend your trust fund."

He huffed out a sigh. His mouth curled up in a wry smile. "She racked up all that credit card debt, and though I'd pay it off for her."

"Don't judge this new gal based on what someone else did."

"I wish I hadn't told anybody about that money."

Charlotte lifted one shoulder. "Your last name is Brackston. That name shows up all over this state. People are bound to put two and two together."

"Thanks for the tea." He scooted his chair back.

He let himself out the back door and headed for the barn to round up fencing supplies and help. He trusted

Charlotte. She and Mr. Jameson had had a strong, steady relationship for years. Theirs was a love that was comfortable and nothing like the convenience that seemed to hold his own parents' marriage together.

He wanted to feel a love that deep someday.

CHAPTER FIVE
Falling in Like

As Aidan and Joe, the other ranch hand, worked on the fence that afternoon, he thought about what Charlotte said. The more the thought about it, the more he thought he would go pick the invitations up himself. If Gina was working, he could chat her up a little, find out a little more about her.

If her friend Midge was working, maybe he'd ask a few questions. That woman was a firecracker if he ever saw one and he'd bet dollars to donuts that Midge would be straight with him. Maybe she'd even give him a few hints and tips. They say the way to a man's heart is through his stomach. Well, he didn't know what the way to a woman's heart was, but her friends were definitely the gatekeepers.

The two men worked hard checking and repairing loose and missing fencing. Much of the woven wire looked good, but they found a section along the north pasture that needed to be replaced. Within a couple of hours of working under the blazing sun, both stripped off their shirts and tossed them on the XRT.

They stopped a couple of times to drink cold water from the thermos, but neither wasted time talking. Sweat slicked their backs, trickled down their faces, burned their eyes.

Aidan swiped his arm across his forehead, then grabbed the post driver and slammed it down on the new t-post. Metal clanged against metal, drowning out his grunts. A loose group of cows gathered around, watching the men work.

Aidan glanced at the animals, then at the fence. Keeping the herd secure was a full-time job. Like most ranchers, they occasionally had a cow get out — usually a young calf. But what worried him the most was the spate of thefts that had plagued the area recently. The entire tri-state area had been affected, but Cardwell County had been hit hard recently. Every animal was at least a thousand bucks on the hoof, probably more.

Keeping the herd safe had become even more important to him since he'd invested in fifty head himself. Beau and Beth allowed him to run his cattle with the ranch's herd, but he hoped to have a ranch of his own soon. Every time he saw one of his bright red ear tags on an animal in the pasture, he felt a surge of pride.

With a grin, he turned back to the task at hand. The sun was hot, and the sooner they got the work done, the sooner they could get back to the house and drink a cold one.

Finally, the last post was driven into the ground and the woven wire attached. The two men tossed their tools into the bed of the vehicle, slung their shirts over their shoulders and climbed onto the XRT, with Aidan driving and Joe in the passenger seat.

Joe yawned loudly and raked his dirty blonde hair back from his face. "Dang, this beats the old days, don't it?"

Aidan looked sideways at his buddy. "Say what?" He peeled his leather work gloves off and tucked them between the dash and the windshield.

"You know, the old days. 'Member when we used to have to make a couple of trips to haul fencing supplies out here?"

Aidan laughed. "I remember more than one flat from driving my pickup out here 'cause you didn't want to make more than one trip. Convinced me that we could drive the truck out here, no problem." He pressed on the accelerator and the XRT lurched forward.

Joe snickered. "Didn't hurt your truck none."

"Guess not," Aidan spun the steering wheel and headed for the barn. "But the thorns from all those danged locust trees did a number on my tires."

The vehicle bounced along the fence row. Joe said, "What'd ya have to do in town this morning?"

Aidan felt heat warm his cheeks at the memory of his visit to the scrapbook store. "Ordered invitations for the Memorial Day party." His mind immediately flashed to Gina, gorgeous, with curves in all the right places and thick, auburn hair that fell in waves past her shoulders. She was a firecracker, too. He touched her cheek with his fingertips, remembering her palm connecting with it.

He grinned. She was a feisty one. Would she be interested in a ranch hand like him? Most women weren't, unless they figured out who his family was.

Then again, Gina was no ordinary girl. She was a business owner, all woman, with a sultry expression that drew him in. Sexy as hell. He hadn't been on a date in ages, and the lack of action left him thirsty as a man crossing the Sahara. And Gina was the oasis shimmering in the distance.

The XRT lurched to the right. The steering wheel jerked out of Aidan's hand. A couple of t-posts rolled out of the bed of the ATV with a loud clatter. Hands grasped for purchase as Aidan aimed his foot at the brake and slammed down. The XRT ground to a stop.

Aidan blinked and stared straight ahead into the stretched woven wire that had passed their inspection earlier in the day.

Joe exploded, "What the hell was that?"

Aidan's mouth opened and closed. Finally, he got out, "I – I don't know. Guess I wasn't paying attention." Damn it! He'd been daydreaming about Gina's curves, her breasts, her hips, what it would feel like to run his hands over every inch of her body.

"Damn right you weren't paying attention. You knew that gully was there. I even warned you we was coming up on it and you flat out ignored me." Joe slapped the dash in a show of exasperation.

"I didn't ignore you," Aidan retorted angrily. He needed a night out worse than he'd realized.

Joe faced him, glaring. "You sure enough did. Have been all afternoon."

"Have not."

"Have, too."

The two sat in silence. The engine of the XRT rumbled quietly beneath them. In the distance, a crow cawed and a horse whinnied. Joe pointed at the fence in front of them. "Looks like we are gonna have to replace this stretch of fence after all."

With a heavy sigh, Aidan reversed the XRT out of the wire, then slid out of the driver's seat and scooped the t-posts up. He tossed them back onto the bed of the XRT with a grunt, then grabbed the fencing pliers and the fence post driver. Without a word, he worked loose the two fence posts that were leaning crazily, placed new t-posts and drove them into the hard ground with ringing ferocity. Joe sat in the XRT and watched, a grin playing the corners of his mouth, arms crossed over his sweat streaked chest.

Aidan returned to the bed of the ATV and pulled a couple of tensioners out of the bed, affixed them and tightened the stretched woven wire. He gave it a few test tugs, wiggled the fence posts and, satisfied the fence was secure, hopped back into the driver's seat of the XRT.

He pulled away, watching his path more carefully this time. Joe held his tongue for nearly a minute. Judging from the muscles twitching in his jaw, that was all he could handle. "OK. Enough. What the hell is going on with you?"

"Nothing," Aidan snapped.

Joe fired back, "Bullshit."

Aidan sighed. He could try to avoid it, but that wouldn't work forever. It's hard to hide something from someone you work and live with. His chest rose and fell again with another sigh. Jeez, he'd been sighing a lot lately. "Okay, here's the deal. I tell you, but you tell nobody, got it?"

Joe nodded.

"I'm serious man. Just between you and me." He punctuated his demand by pointing at Joe, then himself.

Joe looked sideways at Aidan. One thick eyebrow rose. "Yeah, sure, cross my heart and all that stuff. What gives?"

"I met a woman."

Joe hooted and slapped his knee, but Aidan held up his hand in the classic symbol for stop. He said, "When I say I met her, I mean just that. We just met. No date. No nothing. Just met."

Joe rolled his eyes. "Couldn't close the deal, huh?"

Aidan frowned and the ATV sped up. "It's not like that. She's a really nice lady."

"Then why would she go out with you?"

Aidan started to sigh yet again, caught himself, and frowned. He gripped the wheel tighter, his knuckles turning white.

Joe pressed on. "Who is she?"

"Owns the scrapbook store in town." *And she has the most amazing blue-green eyes.*

Joe's eyes widened at this, and he gave a low whistle. "She is hot." He drew out the last word.

Aidan smacked his buddy in the arm. "Don't talk about her like that." She was good-looking, but there was more to her than that. She was different than the rodeo bunnies he'd dated. "Say, do you know if she's seeing anybody?"

Joe shook his head. "Ain't never seen her with nobody.

Ask Charlotte, she'd know."

Aidan nodded, not willing to admit that he'd already talked to Charlotte. "Anyway, that's it. She's on my mind 'cause I met her today. Guess I got a little distracted."

Joe hooked his thumb over his shoulder at the freshly repaired fence behind them and snorted, "I'll say."

They reached the barn and Aidan nodded toward the bed, anxious to change the subject. "Make sure all the wire gets back to the barn? There's been a lot of thefts in these parts lately."

As Joe hopped out of the XRT, he nodded. "Meth heads, probably. Taking scrap to the recycling depot for quick cash."

There was more to it than that. Aidan could feel it in his bones. This area used to be safe, but now anything metal had to be locked up and whole herds of cattle had been taken. Druggies wouldn't be organized enough to pull off the thefts. Aidan left Joe to put the fencing supplies up while he headed for the barn to clean stalls.

Maybe one of the boys playing poker tonight would know something. If the Sheriff had found any leads, somebody at the game tonight would know about it. Word traveled fast in a small town like Wilder.

He pushed away thoughts of rustlers and turned to the task at hand. For once, he was glad that work didn't stop at the Diamond J Ranch just because the calendar said it was the weekend. Beau, the ranch foreman, and Beth, the new owner of the ranch, wanted the ranch in top shape for the upcoming barbecue. The event was a kind of coming out for Beth, since she'd officially become the owner of the ranch earlier in the month. The party was only a week away, and a lot of chores remained to be done to get the grounds and stock ready.

He worked his way methodically through the barn, raking up the old straw and laying down fresh. As he wheeled a cartload of manure out to the compost heap, he swept his arm across his forehead to clear the sweat.

Working at the Diamond J was hard work, nothing like the job he would've had if he'd worked the family business like his father wanted, but he wouldn't go back for anything. The heavy leather gloves were hot, his back ached with exertion, but this was honest work. Again, nothing like the family business.

He emptied the cart and returned to the barn to start on the next stall. Would Gina be disgusted if she knew what he did every day? Or would she respect him for being a hard worker, earning an honest living? He thought about the trust fund his grandfather had left him. He had access to it now that he was thirty, but he hadn't dipped into it yet and had no intention to do so. He was doing just fine on his own.

His brow furrowed when he remembered Gina asked to bring someone with her to the barbecue.

Even so, he couldn't wait to see her again. If she had a boyfriend, so be it. But he wasn't ready to give up just yet. He scooped a forkful of dirty straw, putting his back into it.

The faster the weekend went, the sooner Monday would arrive.

CHAPTER SIX
Crop Gossip

Gina placed an acrylic mask with a paisley design over her sheet of cardstock and spritzed a bit of purple ink with a metallic shimmer, then lifted the template. The resulting pattern was understated and elegant. As she examined the result and considered her next layer, a sharply dressed woman appeared from around the corner of the paper racks and gasped. "That is absolutely gorgeous!"

Gina grinned as she admired her handiwork. "Thanks. Something so easy adds so much to the project."

"Indeed. I'll have to remember that for my next card." The woman scraped a folding chair back and sat down across from Gina. "You going to do a Christmas in July card class this year?"

That class was still two months away, but was already filling up fast. Gina nodded and looked across the table at her customer. She would recognize Christine Dorman anywhere, and never ceased to be surprised at the woman's appearance, which never changed. No matter where she was, what she was doing, or what time of day it was, she looked exactly like her billboards and for sale signs. Her dark hair was cropped close to her head, accentuating her high cheekbones and wide, toothy smile.

Christine pursed her red-stained lips. "Put me down for that class then."

"Will do." Gina held up the pink heat gun and raised her eyebrows. "Do you mind?"

"Go right ahead." Christine's brow pushed together as she watched Gina wave the small gun across the paper.

As Gina dried the spray, her thoughts turned to the good looking ranch hand from the Diamond J. A little tremor of excitement ran through her body at the memory of him.

She glanced at Christine. That woman knew everything and everyone in the little town of Wilder. Before Gina allowed herself to think about him anymore, she wanted to know more about him. After all, she was a single mother and had more to think about than whether or not he made her tingle with desire.

After she flipped the heat gun off, she cocked her head and looked at Christine. "You know a lot of people in this town." She caught her lower lip in her teeth. She felt like a teenager with a crush.

Christine's whitened teeth gleamed when her lips split in a big smile. "Of course. I'm the number one real estate agent in Cardwell County. I make it my business to know the people in this town."

Gina glanced around to make sure no one was listening. Midge had taken the afternoon off since she was working late at the crop that evening. "We were visited by an employee of the Diamond J today, and I wondered if you might know him."

Christine's eyes sparkled at the mention of the legendary Diamond J. "I know several of the folks out there. Charlotte is a dear. And Beau does such a good job of running that place. I thought for sure I'd have a shot at the commission on that place when Jonathan Jameson passed away." She made a clucking noise. "And I hope if and when his daughter gets tired of living out in the sticks and moves back to Kansas City, she'll give me a call."

Gina liked Christine, but the woman was too focused on money. One shoulder lifted in a half shrug. "This guy is just one of the ranch hands. His name's Aidan."

Christine's bright lips pressed together in a tight grin and her eyes slid left then right. She leaned forward and whispered conspiratorially, "You mean Aidan Brackston. He's downright yummy, isn't he?!"

One corner of Gina's mouth twitched up in a grin. Yummy was definitely a good descriptor of the cowboy. She made a rolling motion with her hand. "So, spill. What's the scoop on him?" *Please don't let him have a girlfriend, please don't let him have a girlfriend.*

One perfectly drawn eyebrow arched up. Christine whispered, "You understand, this is all just between you and me?"

Gina nodded eagerly.

"He's had me looking for a place for him for ages. He's very selective. Knows what he wants, and doesn't want to settle. He's not in a hurry. Wants just the right thing, not just whatever happens to pop up."

Gina blinked. "I thought the Diamond J provided room and board as part of the employment?" Why would anyone pay for a place when they had a place to live for free?

Christine said, "They do, but that cowboy wants a ranch of his own."

"Oh?" After a beat, Gina sighed. Her shoulders drooped. "Oh. He's getting married or something."

Christine shook her head and her dangly earrings swung. "Oh, no! I think this was just for him. Never any mention of a woman, girlfriend or otherwise, and he was always alone when I took him for viewings. No woman would ever move into a house without seeing it first."

That was true. "Maybe he's surprising her?"

Christine cocked her head as she considered that, then shook her head. "No. He never used the term 'we' - it was always 'I'."

Gina turned her attention to the supplies in front of her, processing this new information. She placed her pictures on the layout, moving them to get the placement right. He was available. Single. That was a good thing.

But how could he afford acreage on a ranch hand's salary?

Christine tapped her chin thoughtfully. "The thing that was surprising was what he wanted and what he chose. He was very particular about the architecture of the place. Said he'd really like to have something by Frank Lloyd Wright, but you know there just aren't many of those here in Wilder. Closest I could find was the Sondern House in Kansas City. It went up for sale in 2003, so I thought the new owners might be persuaded to sell, but no."

Gina blinked. Why would a cowboy be interested in Frank Lloyd Wright? How would he even know about an architect like that?

Christine continued on, warming to the topic. "But when that sprawling Prairie style house on the west side of town came up for sale, I thought of Aidan immediately."

"Wait!" Gina looked up from her layout. "You mean the house on Grant Lane? With all the windows and the flat roof?"

Christine nodded. "Precisely."

Gina frowned. "That place looks expensive." It was all she could do to afford her little two bedroom, one bath house.

Christine's eyes flared and her head bobbed. "Yes, it is. The commission would've made Christmas very special for my grands this year."

Gina's jaw dropped. That was odd, right? How could a cowboy who worked as a ranch hand make enough money to afford something like that? It made no sense at all.

"Apparently, he's come into some money recently, so I thought he might want to jump on something." Christine sighed heavily and shook her head, then continued, "But he wasn't interested. He's dead set on owning land of his own. At least forty acres."

What was Aidan into that he could afford to buy a house like that? Gina pressed her lips together. She'd made one bad choice. She wasn't about to make another. This called for caution.

"I really need to get going." Christine pushed away from the table and stood. "Wish I could stay for the crop tonight, but I have to show a house."

Gina blinked, still thinking about Aidan. She added absently, "I'll put you down for the Christmas card class."

Christine waggled her manicured fingers at Gina and called out, "Sounds good! See you soon!"

Gina didn't have time to mull over how Aidan could afford a ranch. Not only did she have a hundred invitations to make for the Diamond J Ranch Barbecue, but the store hosted a crop on the third Friday of each month. Women started to arrive about 5:30 that evening, pulling their cars up in front to unload carts and bags and rolling totes.

Gina greeted the regulars and introduced herself to the two new gals who'd heard about the event from Crop Circles, the scrapbook store in Tranquility, about thirty miles to the west, just this side of the Kansas state line.

Gina glanced at the big round clock on the wall. Twenty after six. Getting to know the newbies was important, but she wanted to scoot out as quickly as possible so she could get home to see Toby and relieve Sandy.

Sandy, a retired schoolteacher, had stepped into the role of grandmother shortly after she started watching Toby. She was a widow with no grandchildren of her own and a flexible schedule. Thanks to her dead husband's pension, she lived comfortably. Whenever Gina got stuck at the store, Sandy didn't complain. Just fixed a meal or made up a bed – whatever was needed.

Gina excused herself, then wandered around the crop

tables to mix with the other customers.

Dottie, who had been in the store when Aidan stopped by, patted the table next to her craft mat. "Nobody's sitting here. Take a load off, Gina!"

Gina hesitated, but glanced around and saw that everyone was busy unpacking their supplies or scrapping, so she pulled the folding chair back and sat down. She pointed to the papers and photos spread out in front of Dottie and asked, "What are you working on tonight?"

"I'm making an exploding mini-album." Dottie fanned several pictures out. "My trip to Alaska."

Gina pointed at a package of heavy duty magnets. "How are you going to use the magnets?"

Dottie tapped one side of the album. "One magnet here, behind a picture, and the other under the patterned paper on the front."

Gina nodded her approval. "Smart."

Dottie asked, "How's little Toby doing?"

Just the thought of him lit Gina's face up. "He's doing good. Sandy's at home with him now. Hard to believe he'll be six tomorrow."

"Having a party?"

Gina nodded and raised her eyebrows. "Cowboy themed." Like she needed any more of an excuse to think about cowboys.

"That'll be fun." Dottie said as she swiped her pink glue gun across the back of a photo. "Say, you ought to call Beth Jameson out at the Diamond J. She's trying to get more involved in the community. See if she'd bring a couple of baby farm animals over, like they did for the elementary school last week."

Gina's mouth dropped open. "That is an awesome idea! Toby would be so excited!" And maybe she'd get to see Aidan again, spend a little time with him, get to know him better.

Dottie leaned toward Gina and whispered, "And Steve? What's going on there?"

Gina's left eye began to twitch at the mention of her ex-husband. "Oh, he's fine, I guess. He was supposed to pick Toby up tonight, but couldn't make it."

"I am so sorry." Dottie shook her head. "That boy always was trouble."

Marlene, who had been listening from across the table interjected, "It seems to follow him, or he follows it, I'm not sure which."

Gina glanced across the table at the woman who managed the truck stop out at the junction. Marlene had been only been coming to crops for the past month or two, so Gina didn't know her well. "You know my ex?"

The woman nodded, and her silver streaked curls bobbed. "Steve Potts, right?"

Gina nodded and offered a brief description. "Yeah. Kind of a small guy? A few inches shy of six foot?"

Marlene arched a thin eyebrow and looked a touch irritated. "Yes. Steve Potts. Your ex. Your little boy's daddy. Short, wiry, with blonde hair. Blue eyes. Perpetually tanned. Always in trouble." She shook her head and swiped her tape runner across the back of a photo before adhering it to her paper. A smile curved her thin lips up. "He sure knows how to work that bad boy angle."

That last comment caught Gina's attention, and curiosity burned in her stomach. Steve's bad boy image is what drew her to him back in high school. She narrowed her eyes and looked at the scrapbooker. Marlene was attractive, or would be if she'd quit trying to stay young. Her bony shoulders stuck out in points against her thin t-shirt. Silver highlights failed to hide the gray in her shoulder length hair.

Gina's first thought was Steve's philandering. Was this woman one of his flings? She pursed her lips as she considered the possibility. "That's definitely him. How do you know him?"

Marlene leaned forward, bony elbows propped on the table. "He hangs out at the truck stop all the time." Her husky voice gritted on Gina's nerves.

Gina cocked her head to one side, "Really? And what does he do there?"

The other woman grinned, displaying teeth yellowed by nicotine. "Drinks a lot of coffee. Hangs out at the restaurant, in the trucker section."

Gina knew the section. She and Toby ate out there sometimes – the restaurant was known for their Friday night specials. You could get a plate full of food at a great price, and kids under 12 ate free. The truckers had their own section at the front of the restaurant, with corded phones at every table, a vestige from the days before cell phones.

"Why would Steve be in the trucker section?"

Marlene laughed, which dissolved into a dry, hacking

cough. When she caught her breath, she shook her head and heaved, "Damned cigarettes. Trying to give them up, but this cough just won't go away."

Dottie reached across and patted the other woman on the hand. "I smoked a pack a day for years. Finally kicked the habit, and now my lungs feel so much better. The cough'll go away eventually."

Though Gina appreciated the health implications, she wanted the scoop on her ex. In an effort to steer the conversation, she prompted, "And you say Steve hangs out in the trucker section?"

The other woman spoke slowly. "Truckers are notorious for doing things outside the boundaries of the law. You know, hookers, drugs, black market, selling hot stuff. Anything you can think of that's illegal, it probably happens at a truck stop."

Gina fought the irritation rising within her at her customer's condescending demeanor. Why should she care what Steve was into, as long as he didn't drag their son into it? "I know that, but what specifically is Steve into?"

Marlene shrugged. "Not sure exactly, but since he's not a trucker, he's got to be hanging out with the people he is for some reason. Sure hope your boy doesn't follow in his daddy's footsteps, cause if he does, you'll have your hands full." She gave a dismissive snort.

Gina frowned at that last comment and bit her tongue to keep from saying the first thing that popped into her head. The woman's insinuation hit a nerve, focused Gina's fear that her ex-husband's actions would hurt their son.

Instead, she asked, "Who's he hanging out with? What are they into?"

"I'm not sure." Marlene leaned over and grabbed a clear plastic paper holder out of her bag and set it in front of her. "There's always this one woman who looks like a nut case. Wears bright colors. Like a beatnik flower child or something. And she's older than me!"

Gina heaved a sigh and glanced at Dottie, who arched one eyebrow and shrugged. "Who else does he hang out with?" She fought to keep her irritation from showing.

"There are sometimes a couple of guys with the old lady. Last week, she had on overalls and these bright socks poking out from the bottoms, and had her hair in long pigtails. Looked like frickin' Pippi Longstocking."

CHAPTER SEVEN
Poker Fever

Aidan opened the top drawer of his dresser, reached under the t-shirts and pulled out the sock where he kept a roll of bills. He peeled off a couple of twenties, stuck them in his billfold, then tucked it into his back pocket. It was poker night, and he had been looking forward to it all week.

They played for small amounts of cash, but braggin' rights were at stake every night. There were now five guys, including himself and Beau, and they rotated between three houses each week. This week they were going to be at Bert Winton's house.

Beau banged around in the kitchen, talking to himself and slamming doors. Aidan walked down the hall and stood in the doorway, watching his roommate. Since Beau had professed his love for Beth, he'd been spending more nights at the big house with her instead of staying in the bunkhouse.

Aidan leaned against the doorjamb and watched the other man squat down and peer into the cabinet. "Whatcha doin'?"

Beau turned around, scowling. "It's my turn to bring snacks and I can't find a thing here. I thought I had something, but . . . " His voice trailed off.

Aidan cracked a grin and shrugged. "You talking about the Frito's and jalapeno cheddar dip?"

Beau's scowl deepened. He cocked his head to one side and his lips flattened into a thin line. He said in an accusatory tone, "You ate them, didn't you?"

Aidan nodded, then walked over and opened one of the cabinet doors. He pulled out a big jar of salsa and set it on the counter. "We got salsa and tortilla chips. That'll work."

"But you bought them."

"But I ate your Frito's and cheese dip so how about we call it even?"

Beau nodded and snagged the big bag of tortilla chips from the counter. "Sounds like a plan. Come on, I'll drive."

"You sure?"

"Yeah. I'm not in a drinking mood tonight anyway."

The two walked out and climbed into Beau's four wheel drive pickup. As they turned out of the drive, Beau nodded toward the pasture. "You boys get all the fence checked this afternoon?"

"Got the east pastures checked. Plan to do the west pastures this weekend." Aidan watched the fence posts flash past. He couldn't help feeling cynical, though. "For all the good it'll do. You know the rustlers'll just pull up, open a gate and take whatever they want anyway, right?"

"I know." Beau strangled the steering wheel in his grip. "Beth thinks we need to put padlocks all the gates, start

47

locking them. Your thoughts?"

Aidan lifted one shoulder. "They'll just cut the fence and take what they want anyway." The rustlers made him angry. It was more than mere stealing. They were messing with folks' livelihood.

Beau reached over and smacked Aidan's arm. "Enough of that. You were looking for Charlotte earlier. You meet a girl or something?"

Aidan was thankful his friend's eyes were focused on the road as he felt warmth sweep up his neck and face. "Beth asked me to go to the scrapbook store to get invitations for the barbecue next weekend."

Beau let out a low whistle. "The one with the long hair, kind of a dark reddish brown? Curvy?"

One corner of Aidan's mouth quirked up. "Yeah, she is hot. Long legs, curves. And those eyes . . ." He held his hands up in front of him. "And I bet I could fit my hands around her waist."

"That's what you need, buddy. A woman." Beau lifted two fingers from the steering wheel in salute as they met another truck. "I have to admit, I've never been happier. Beth is amazing. It's nice to go to bed with her, nice to wake up with her. We laid awake 'til almost midnight last night talking about bloodlines."

Aidan nodded. Beau had been noticeably happier since he'd finally admitted he was crazy about Beth. It took him a year to finally ask her to be his girlfriend, then he proposed just two weeks later. Aidan wanted what they had. He was ready to settle down, have more than just a casual relationship.

With that realization, he blinked, surprised at himself. He'd never had a serious relationship. The closest he'd come was his high school girlfriend, and that entire relationship was set up by his father, determined to join the two families. Everything revolved around money, in his father's opinion. She had been a spoiled, entitled little bitch, the daughter of a real estate mogul. His father hadn't spoken to him for a week when Aidan broke up with her.

Then there was Tracy, the local girl who'd expected him to pay her credit card bills after she found out who his family was.

If she only knew the trouble that money came with. His father had been a cruel, distant man, who used his wealth to control everyone around him. He'd been in the news so many times for shady business deals, but the authorities couldn't get anything to stick. The press referred to him as Teflon Teddy Brackston.

He snorted. And Beau and Charlotte wondered why he didn't let people get close. He'd been running from his past for so long, trying to avoid getting caught up in his father's plans -- he'd left that life so long ago.

That was it, he thought. Come hell or high water, he was going to ask Gina out when he picked the invitations up on Monday. If she had a boyfriend, said no, so be it.

CHAPTER EIGHT
Suspicions

The clock on the wall said it was a little after 6. It was time to get home and relieve Sandy. But Gina couldn't resist one last question. "Was he out there today?"

Marlene shrugged. "Just got there when I left."

Gina pushed back from the table and caught Midge's eye as she walked toward the back office.

Midge followed her. "Leaving?"

"Yeah. I'm going to run a quick errand before I go pick Toby up." She tugged her bag over her shoulder and jingled the keys in her hands. It echoed her nerves. She couldn't stop mentally comparing Steve and that cowboy. Aidan looked dark and dangerous with that five o'clock shadow and his black cowboy hat. Why was she drawn to the bad boys?

Midge frowned. "You okay?"

"Yeah." Gina paused in the doorway. "I think Steve is up to his old tricks. I'm going to go find out."

Midge had been a friend for many years, and knew all about Steve and his checkered history. He'd gotten off lucky, as far as Midge was concerned — she'd said as much for years. The local cops weren't able to make anything stick, and since he was a local boy, they didn't try real hard. He'd stolen a couple of cars and went joyriding, and he ran a successful business selling black market cigarettes to underage kids when he was younger.

Midge's forehead creased. "You think it's black market stuff? Or something more serious?" Her lips pinched together.

Gina shrugged. "It's Steve we're talking about here. Hard telling. But I'm going to find out." She pushed through the door and nodded to the scrappers on her way out.

As she walked along the sidewalk, she dug in her purse for the business card Aidan had left with her earlier in the day, then punched the number for the ranch into her cell phone.

An older woman answered the phone, then put Beth on. "This is Beth Jameson."

Gina quickly explained who she was and what she wanted. She added, "If it's not too much trouble, that is."

Beth laughed. "That is a wonderful idea! I can send one of the boys with two calves, how would that be?"

Gina sagged with relief. She hadn't even realized how nervous she was about asking for the favor. "That would be great. I'd be happy to pay you."

"Nonsense," Beth said. "Just be sure to tell folks where the calves are from. I'll have the boys bring along a few panels of fencing to keep the little guys corralled."

They worked out the timing and Gina hung up with a

smile on her face. Toby was going to be so excited at having real farm animals at his party. He'd asked for a pony, but this would be nearly as good.

Beth had said she'd send one of the boys. Gina wondered how many "boys" worked at the Diamond J.

She hurried along the sidewalk. Gray clouds hung low in the sky, threatening rain. The wind had picked up since she'd gone out at lunch.

She reached her battered Toyota Tercel, opened the door, tossed her purse into the passenger seat and slid in. As always, she closed her eyes and whispered, "Please start, please start, please start."

The key, stiff in her fingers, refused to turn. She jiggled the steering wheel and tried again. This time, the key turned in the ignition and the car sputtered to life. The drive to the junction took less than five minutes, but that was plenty of time for Gina to think up at least a dozen scenarios that all ended with her little boy being known as the son of a convicted felon.

In spite of the fact that it was still daylight, the truck stop had a glow about it. Lots of neon in the windows, and the huge electronic billboard added to the illusion. She sat behind a rumbling livestock hauler as she waited for the red light to turn green. Those things, trucks used to haul live animals, always gave her the creeps with those sad brown eyes staring out. Thankfully, this one was empty, but the warm summer air intensified the rank odor.

The wind blew out of the west, so the smell of cattle and manure and sweat wafted right over her car and into the ventilation system. She cranked her window down, which didn't help, but at least increased the flow of air through the small car.

The light turned green and the truck rumbled into motion, the engine struggling to get the monstrous metal beast moving. The semi veered to the left, toward the truck islands and parking. Gina swung right into the parking lot in front of the restaurant, but chose a spot close to the highway, so she'd have a clear view of the restaurant entrance and the truck parking. She put her car in park and switched the engine off.

It coughed twice and died.

She gripped the steering wheel, not sure what she was even doing. Driving to the truck stop had been nothing but an impulse, a gut reaction to Marlene's comments. Steve was her ex. She needed to quit worrying about him.

Her thoughts turned to the cowboy who'd ordered the invitations. He had that dark, dangerous look that she was drawn to, but he was different. He'd been so nice, so pleasant.

Mmmm. The best of both worlds.

A bad boy that's a real gentleman.

CHAPTER NINE

Memories

As they neared Bert's house, Aidan looked out at the pasture, dotted with a handful of white faced black cows. "Looks like Bert has a few head this year. Guess he decided not to get polled Herefords again."

"Too bad. He used to have one of the biggest herds in the area." Beau made a clucking noise with his tongue. "I think it was too hard for him after what happened last year."

Beth had been with them that night. It was right after she'd come to the Diamond J, after her father's death. Aidan said, "Beth impressed me that night. She jumped out of the truck and went right to Bert." It had been so quiet that night. No cattle lowing in the pasture. No snuffling of breath, no munching on grass, no hooves rustling through the weeds.

"It scared her pretty bad."

"When I first saw the gate hanging open that night, I thought his cattle had gotten out." But then he'd seen the dual tire tracks that led right up to the gate. Though Beth didn't seem to hadn't immediately understood the implications of those facts, Beau and he had.

"Damned rustlers," Beau growled. "I'm afraid we haven't seen the last of them."

Aidan swallowed hard as he recalled the worst part of that night at Bert's place. "I don't get why they left that one, though." Those sons-of-bitches had taken the rest of the animals, then killed a heifer. Slit her throat and left her to die.

One corner of Beau's lips curled up in a snarl. "Trying to throw the authorities off, trying to make it look like some sort of ritual sacrifice."

Aidan pursed his lips. "That's right. I did hear that the Sheriff thought it might be some kind of cult or something."

"Enough!" Beau slapped his hand on the dash. After a few beats, he said in a forced tone, "Snap out of it and focus, or you're gonna lose your shirt tonight!"

The memory of that night still felt fresh, even though that had been last summer. Aloud, he said, "You worry about your own shirt – I seem to recall that you still owe me from last week's game."

Beau laughed that hearty laugh of his as they turned into the long driveway. The tires crunched in the gravel, and as they passed over the creek, the lights cut through a light mist rising from the water. The truck rumbled as they climbed a the small hill.

They were almost at Bert's place. Aidan looked across the pasture to the big oak tree. That was where he had buried the heifer.

Beau's cell phone buzzed and he answered it. "Sure, sure. Yeah. We can do that. We've got a handful of hog panels in the barn that'd work, and it'll be good for the calves to be socialized."

When he ended the call, he glanced at Aidan. "Got a job for you to do tomorrow."

Aidan rolled his eyes. "Is it a job I'm gonna want?"

"Beth wants you to take two calves to a kid's birthday party tomorrow at two. She said she'd leave the address on a notepad in the office in the barn."

"Great." Aidan dropped his head back against the seat. Just what he wanted to do. Spend his Saturday with a bunch of screaming brats.

CHAPTER TEN
The Truck Stop

Fluffs of clouds here and there dotted the blue sky. Heat radiated off the blacktopped parking lot, and the big trucks parked at the back side of the lot looked like they were shimmering. A couple of bob-tailed trucks broke up the monotony of the regular semi loads. The livestock hauler she'd followed into the lot slanted into a space next to another 18 wheeler.

The driver's side door swung open and a slight woman climbed down. Gina sat up straight, gripped the wheel and leaned forward. The woman wore bright red leggings, with a flowered skirt over them. Her tie-dyed t-shirt contained all the colors of the rainbow. But the kicker was her hair.

Pigtails.

Gina chewed her bottom lip as the woman slammed her truck door shut, then sashayed across the parking lot toward the convenience store section of the truck stop. The woman walked lightly, hands swinging as if she didn't have a care in the world. Gina glanced around the parking lot, but didn't see Steve's black Ford F-150. The older truck would've been easy to spot, with lots of chrome and a few dents and dings.

Gina watched through the big plate glass window as the woman with the pigtails walked through the convenience store. She paused just inside the door, facing the window. Gina hadn't been in the convenience store for ages – she usually got gas at the Casey's or the Break Time in town – so she had no idea what the woman was looking at, but whatever it was caught the woman's attention. The woman bent down to get a closer look, her frizzy hair disappearing from sight for a moment, then bobbing back up. The pigtails turned to the side and bobbed along toward the heart of the truck stop.

Gina hesitated, keys in one hand and the door handle in the other. She gazed at the truck stop. It couldn't hurt to go inside and have a cup of coffee.

She pushed the car door open, then walked casually across the parking lot. She hoped that she didn't run into anyone she knew. How would she – how could she? – explain what she was doing? She tugged the glass door open and stepped into the artificially cooled air of the truck stop, then looked around. She spotted the odd woman as she slid into a booth in the restaurant. A tired looking waitress refilled the bacon bits on the salad bar.

Gina caught the waitress's eye and pointed to the first booth beyond the trucker section. The waitress nodded and Gina hurried through the trucker section, avoiding eye contact with the subject of her surveillance, and slid into the booth, facing the door. She watched the back of the odd woman. Gray streaked her frizzy red hair.

As Gina expected, the diner was busy. Truckers sat in booths, some alone, some paired off. Behind her, tables and booths were full.

The waitress dropped a stained menu in front of Gina. "Get ya somethin' to drink?"

Gina turned her coffee cup upright in the saucer. "Just coffee, please. Decaf."

"Be right back with it, hon." The waitress walked away from Gina and stopped at the other woman's booth. The waitress hurried past Gina toward the kitchen. Less than a minute later, she returned with a coffee pot in each hand, and poured Gina's from the one with the green lid. She gestured at the cream and sugar, then bustled off and poured coffee out of the regular pot for the crazy lady.

The two women sat alone in their respective booths, surrounded by other people involved in conversations. Gina slowly stirred a sugar packet and two creamers into her coffee.

Gina hadn't been planning to get anything, but she when she saw the chicken fingers on the menu, she changed her mind. Toby loved chicken fingers and that would give her an excuse to be at the truck stop. She ordered a one-trip salad bar for herself and chicken fingers with white cream gravy to go. After the waitress moved on to the crazy lady, Gina walked to the salad bar and filled her plate. She passed the waitress at the end of the salad bar.

Gina caught her by the arm, "Excuse me."

The harried waitress smiled, after the briefest hint of a

frown appeared on her brow. "Whatcha need?"

Gina leaned forward and whispered, "That woman with the pig tails? She looks familiar, but I can't place her. Do you know her name?"

The waitress shook her head no, but added, "Drives one of them bull haulers. Comes in fairly regular."

Gina thanked the woman for her time and walked back to her booth. She had no sooner sat down than her ex walked through the front doors of the truck stop. He exuded that bad boy aura, with a black leather jacket and dark jeans. He pulled off his mirrored sunglasses and tucked them in his chest pocket as he strolled into the restaurant and slid into the booth across from the pig tailed woman.

Gina slumped in her seat as her mind raced. What business could Steve possibly have with that woman trucker?

CHAPTER ELEVEN
The Ex

Gina cautiously raised her eyes. Steve looked over his shoulder, and glanced at the other truckers sitting nearby. His eyes never slid her way, though. She stirred her salad a bit to distribute the dressing evenly, then forked a piece of lettuce and stuck it in her mouth. She couldn't leave before Steve, so she chewed slowly.

Gina strained to hear what was said over the clanking silverware and music emanating from the overhead speakers, but couldn't make out the words. These two obviously weren't going to do anything illegal sitting in the restaurant of the local truck stop.

Spending Friday night sitting at a truck stop spying on her ex-husband was not her idea of a good time. She should be home with her little boy.

Or getting ready for a night out on the town with the ruggedly handsome cowboy from the Diamond J. He was the first man she'd met in ages that she felt a spark of attraction for. Wilder was full of young men straining at the leash, anxious to escape as soon as they graduated high school and, at the other end of the spectrum, devoted husbands and fathers who were already taken.

Her chest rose and fell in a heavy sigh.

Too bad she'd chosen wrong when she was younger. She wondered what she'd ever seen in Steve. His bad boy image had been so intriguing, so tempting, for an honor student like her. He pushed the limit, smoked Marlboros, drank Busch beer, drove too fast and stayed out too late. Their romance was fueled by teenaged rebellion, pure and simple. They'd both been immature. She could see that now.

Again, her thoughts turned to Aidan Brackston. He was gainfully employed, polite . . . and he had the most amazing blue eyes. The chemistry between them had been palpable.

And, boy, did she need some chemistry in her life.

She was being ridiculous though. She'd met the man once. He probably had no interest in her at all.

She sighed and stabbed a chunk of hardboiled egg with her fork.

Though she often told people she didn't need a man, that was a lie. Even though Steve had been immature and foolish, she missed being married. The need for a man, a partner, was like an ache buried deep within her chest. She wanted someone to go out to eat with, someone to go to Toby's football games with, someone to warm her at night.

Wilder wasn't exactly a hotbed of action for a single woman like herself. She didn't go to bars, she didn't want to do the online dating thing. That left her with very few options.

Maybe that was why Aidan Brackston made such an impression on her. He was mature and responsible, if how he completed assignments for his boss was any indication. He had walked into a scrapbook store, generally considered women's territory, asked her opinion and listened to her suggestions. Even though he was totally out of his element, he had been charming and pleasant and carried on an intelligent conversation.

She wondered how he treated his girlfriend. More importantly, she wondered if he *had* a girlfriend. For whatever reason, she couldn't get him out of her mind. Maybe because he was a cowboy. She'd always had a thing for a man in a cowboy hat and boots.

She sighed heavily. Dreaming did no good. Aidan was good looking, and probably had a beautiful girlfriend. Probably one of those barrel racers, with long dark hair pulled back in a braid, skin tight jeans and cowboy boots. Besides, why would he want to have a relationship with a single mother? She had given up on having a life of her own when she decided to file for divorce and raise her son alone.

Though she didn't regret the decision, it was hard to live with sometimes. After all, she wasn't dead. She still had desires. She still felt a stirring deep within her.

She still hoped for a fairy tale ending, wanted to be swept off her feet by a knight in shining armor.

And, though she wouldn't admit it to anyone, even Midge, she still wanted a man in her bed.

No, it was more than want.

It was a primal need.

"Refill?" The waitress looked at her expectantly, holding the coffee pot out.

She peeked at the booth she'd been spying on, just as Steve and the pig tailed woman scooted out of their seats and strolled toward the cash register.

Gina shook her head. "No. Just the bill please."

The woman ripped the ticket off her pad and laid it on the scarred table, then bustled on her way, dodging from table to table, refilling off-white coffee cups at tables and booths as she went. Steve and his companion paid separately, then walked toward the door together, still talking.

Gina slipped her hand into her purse, pulled her billfold out and opened it. A twenty and two singles. She pressed her lips together, pulled the twenty out with a sigh and slid out of the booth. Just as she did so, she looked up to see which direction Steve and his friend went, and saw Steve walking toward her.

Damn it!

She pivoted and hurried toward the restrooms, hoping and praying he hadn't seen her. When she reached the door to the restroom, she chanced a glance over her shoulder. He stood in the middle section of the truck stop, looking at a display of radio headsets. She debated. Go into the restroom and be safe, or hurry out of the restaurant and follow them?

If she lost sight of them, there were three ways they could go. To the left out the front door to the parking lot, straight ahead to the convenience store, or right to the trucker restrooms and back lot.

No, she had come this far. She wasn't turning back now. She turned and headed for the cashier. As she paid her tab, she saw her ex and the pig-tailed woman stride through the convenience store. Gina broke her twenty, hesitated for a moment, then returned to the table to drop a single bill for the waitress.

She walked through the convenience store, pausing for a moment on her way to the door to act as if she was browsing. She didn't want to get to the door too quickly.

"Ma'am! Excuse me, ma'am!"

Gina's heart jumped up to her throat. She swiveled toward the voice and saw the harried waitress hurrying toward her. The woman held up a white Styrofoam container.

Toby's chicken fingers.

Gina returned for them, then was on her way out when she realized she was about where the odd woman had been when she stopped to look at something. She glanced down at the metal boxes that contained newspapers – the USA Today, the Kansas City Star, but the most prominent was the local paper with a headline that blared, "Rustlers Strike Again" over a bleak photo of a farmer with a tear rolling down his cheek. Gina leaned down and squinted at the caption under the photo. She recognized the man. His wife was one of her croppers. He occasionally came in with her, sometimes helped carry her supplies into the store, and bought Christmas gifts for her from the store.

She blinked, stunned at how close the crime hit to home.

She'd heard some of her customers talking about the recent spate of cattle rustling. It sounded almost funny to her at first, like something out of an old western, but it seriously affected people's livelihood. Cattle were a major economic endeavor in Missouri and Kansas. Even worse, a farmer in a neighboring county had been shot dead when he tried to stop the crooks in the middle of their crime. The thieves were getting bolder and more dangerous with each passing day.

She'd imagined outlaws on horseback riding away with a herd of cattle like the old westerns on MeTV, but as she looked out the window, she saw Steve and his new friend standing between two cattle haulers.

She pointed her little car home and drove, wondering how on earth her ex managed to get involved with cattle rustlers.

Was he really, or was her imagination running away with her?

CHAPTER TWELVE
Cats & Dogs

Beau swung the truck around so that it was pointed out toward the road, then shifted into park. They both climbed out, slamming their doors with a double bang that sounded sharp in the relative quiet of the night. A pair of bats swooped through the air, catching bugs drawn by the dusk to dawn light attached to the front of the pole barn. A set of headlights swept across the front of the house. The two turned to watch as another pickup rolled down the driveway and swung around in the gravel to point out to the road, just as they had. A short block of a man hopped down from the driver's seat and landed with a soft puff of gravel dust.

"Hey, there, Stump!" Beau called. Aidan raised a hand in greeting. They waited for the short man to catch up with them, then they all three strode up the steps to the front porch. A border collie raised up slowly from his spot on the porch and woofed a greeting.

Aidan reached down and scratched the dog behind the ears. The dog wiggled happily at the attention. Before they could knock on the door, it swung open and Bert greeted them with a booming, "Howdy, boys! Hope you brought your wallets with ya, tonight!"

The dog stayed at Aidan's side until he reached the threshold. Once there, the dog turned to the porch and returned to his post, his tail thumping on the ground. The others went ahead. Bert looked outside, his eyes swept from left to right, then he closed the door and bolted the dead bolt closed with a solid thunk.

Aidan commented, "Shelby's lookin' good."

Bert nodded and said, "Yeah, she's a good dog. Your old boss did a heck of a job raising those dogs. Always said he could have done just as well with that as with the horses and cattle."

Aidan nodded in agreement and asked, "I thought she came inside with you at night?"

Bert shrugged. "Used to, but after those rustlers took my entire herd of cattle last summer, I figure it's better that she be outside. Maybe she'll bark if she hears something."

Aidan certainly understood the man's fear, but he was also concerned about his safety. "We got another litter of puppies that will be ready to go soon. You want another one so you can have one inside, too?"

Bert laughed and said, "No, one's enough. I got Sam, the Newfie, outside to keep Shelby company, and I got Martha inside to keep me company."

Aidan smiled at that. "OK, Bert. Two things now. Sam is so old, he wouldn't hear a freight train running thru the barn lot and I don't think your wife would take too kindly to being compared to a dog!"

Bert nodded his acknowledgement of that and they all walked toward the dining room. Bert had the best location of all of them for these poker nights. He and Martha had a six-sided dining room table and Martha had given him a folding poker table top for Christmas this past year. The chairs rolled easily on the linoleum, and they were padded, upholstered in red vinyl. Martha had decorated the room with Bert's poker nights in mind. The light hanging over the table was surrounded by glass, like the ones that usually hung over pool tables, with each of the four sides featuring a different suit, all done in red and black. There were plaques on the walls of the various suits from cards, and the highlight of the room was a large print of dogs playing poker, displayed prominently on the large wall with sconces on either side of it to light it and draw attention to it.

Each of the men grabbed a beer from the refrigerator, except Beau who took the token Coke, then took a seat at their regular spots. Bert dealt the cards. Martha appeared briefly to get a snack from the kitchen, then disappeared. Almost immediately, the sound of her sewing machine drifted down the hall.

They talked briefly, in bits and pieces, between making their bets and studying their cards. As usual, talk turned to business. Ranching business depended on livestock, and livestock success depended on everything falling into alignment with weather, the market, health and feed fitting together like puzzle pieces.

The market was always a popular discussion, with everyone complaining that prices were high in the grocery stores, but low when they sold their animals at the sale barn. Weather could make or break a rancher, and it had been horribly dry lately.

Stump added his two cents. "We need one like that night your new boss lady wrecked her car going out to the Diamond J last year."

Bert agreed, and then a dark cloud moved across his features. "We need a soaking rain like that one last summer, the night that my cattle were stolen." His voice broke, then he continued in a voice thick with emotion, "The night that poor heifer was mutilated."

Aidan could feel his blood begin to boil at the memory of that poor animal. "That was horrible. There's been an awful lot of thefts in the tri-state area for the past year. Any leads?"

Bert nodded and said, "Actually, yes, but it's not much of a lead. Ran into the Sheriff at the feed store earlier this week. He said there's talk the cattle rustlers in the area have connections to organized crime." He riffled the cards together.

Beau choked on his Coke and said, "As in the mob?" He cut the deck when Bert tapped it.

Stump answered, "I've always heard that there were low level mobsters in this area, sort of an outlier of the crime families in Kansas City. My sister's friend in college up at Warrensburg got caught up with that crowd. Somebody approached her while she was down on Pine Street one Saturday night and asked her if she'd be an escort for someone to a party. Offered her a thousand bucks for the night."

Aidan let out a low whistle. "That's not chump change." He held his hand on the table to catch the cards aimed at him as Bert dealt them.

Beau asked, "Did she do it?" His jaw muscles clenched and unclenched.

Stump nodded and continued his story, "At first she thought it was a joke, but a sorority girl friend of hers told her it was the real deal. Sort of like dating a celebrity. So, yeah, she did. Wasn't going to at first, but heck, for one night? Got to go pick out a fancy dress with a bodyguard type."

Bert broke in, "Did she get to keep the dress?" He fanned the cards in his hand and frowned at them.

Beau snorted. "Good grief, Bert, that's such a girl thing to ask. Who cares if she got to keep the dress?"

"That'd be important to a girl, especially a broke college kid." Bert defended himself. "Ante up."

Stump said, "Yeah, she got to keep the dress. My sister said the girl told her it was kind of a fairy tale night, where they went to this big fancy house over on the Kansas side. They had a fancy Italian dinner, with all sorts of pastas and lots of wine flowing. Apparently, she was just supposed to sit beside him and look pretty, and then she went one direction with the other women while the men lit up cigars and went out on the patio."

Aidan considered that scenario for a moment, then said, "I bet they were all paid escorts or girlfriends. The mobsters probably left their wives at home while they went to that dinner party to conduct business." His own father disappeared often, to attend business dinners in

Dago Hill.

Stump said, "That's what my sister thought, too."

Bert asked, "Did she ever do it again?"

"Nope," Stump answered. "There was another friend of theirs that ran errands for the mob. One night he left to run a van of stolen goods for them to St. Louis. He never came back. After that, her friend was afraid to get involved, so the next time the guy called and asked her to escort, she told him she couldn't do it."

Aidan asked, "So, was that the end of it? They didn't push it or anything?"

"Guess not," Stump said with a shrug.

Beau said, "That'd be scary getting involved with the mob. People think it's glamorous, or think they'll be different."

Bert asked, "What do you mean, different?"

Beau answered with fire in his voice. "Alive. Dealing with the mob is dangerous, and some of those low level people running stuff for them think they're invincible. They're not. You play with fire, you're gonna get burned."

The other three men stopped what they were doing and looked at him, hands forgotten for a moment.

Bert broke the silence. "Sounds like you're taking this a little personally. The cattle rustlers will pay, regardless of whether they're mob or not."

Beau laughed uneasily, then scowled at his cards, "That's what I'm afraid of."

Bert straightened in his chair, eyes narrowed. "What do you mean by that?" Anger sharpened his words.

Beau glanced around the table. "Nothing. I just mean

that I hope whoever it is isn't involved with the mob. That's all."

Bert's face turned florid. "To my way of thinking, it's awful what they're doing, no matter who is calling the shots."

Aidan added, "And there's no call for mutilating the poor animals." Anger burned in his belly. He hoped like hell his father wasn't involved. His dad had been rumored to have mob connections for years, though it had never been proven.

Stump cleared his throat and said, "That's what bothered me the most about this deal. Did you hear about that ranch up north of here that was hit?"

The other three looked at him and waited expectantly. Finally, Bert prompted with an exasperated tone, "So, what happened?"

"The entire herd was taken, just like Bert's here was, but there were two calves that were killed. They say that both calves were killed, their heads pointing north. Their eyes were missing and all their organs were removed."

The room grew quiet and cold as Stump continued, "And they were each missing an ear. And it happened during the full moon."

The grandfather clock in the hallway ticked off the seconds as they considered what Stump had said. Bert was the first to break the silence. "Now that I think about it, my heifer's head was pointing north too. Think that's significant?"

Stump nodded, "I think that means it's some sort of Satanic cult that's involved. Wasn't your herd taken and your heifer killed during the full moon?"

Bert nodded, but Aidan broke in, "No, there was a crescent moon that night."

"It's all a bunch of bull. Nothing but rumors. Half of it probably isn't even true." Beau took a drink of his pop, then added, "And a full moon doesn't have anything to do with it."

Aidan looked at his friend with a frown creasing his forehead. "What do you mean? Those satanic groups always do things during a full moon."

"That's a load of crap. It's crooks trying to throw the law off their trail." Beau's lip pressed into a thin line and his eyes narrowed as he stared a hole through the cards in his hand. After an uncomfortable silence, he growled, "Are we here to play cards or not?"

The other three glanced at each other uneasily, then all three shrugged. Bert tossed a couple of chips into the center of the table and said, as if nothing had transpired, "OK, Beau, I'll see your five and raise you five."

Beau and Aidan chatted on the way home from the poker game. Aidan was more talkative than usual, his mood buoyed by the small wad of cash in his front pocket.

Something in the ditch caught his eye, flashes of fur in the light of the headlights. He shouted, "Stop! Stop the truck!"

Beau stomped on the brake and the truck slid to a stop. Aidan yanked the handle, swung the door open and jumped out. Three large dogs, two Shepherd mixes and a lab mix jumped around, snarling, darting forward, then retreating. Their jaws snapped ferociously at a small yellow bundle of fur in the ditch. They circled and growled, the fur standing up on their necks. Aidan screamed at the dogs, cursing them.

There was a general impression of Beau behind him, but Aidan didn't know where he was or what he was saying. It was as if he had tunnel vision. His whole world narrowed down to those three big dogs attacking the poor tabby cat. The cat yowled, a harsh, hoarse sound that made his skin crawl. He waded into the dogs, swatting them with his hands, kicking with his booted feet.

The dogs backed away and the cat froze on the ground, its big yellow eyes glowing round as they reflected the glow of the headlights of Beau's truck. It was terrified, unable to move. Its tail was wet with the dogs' saliva, bent at an odd angle. A gash along the cat's left shoulder bled, and the poor animal shook uncontrollably.

Aidan squatted down and spoke soothingly to the feline, asking her if she was okay. He reached out a hand, palm up, and the cat reacted by hissing and spitting. He spoke softly, trying to assure the cat that the dogs were gone and that he meant her no harm. The cat's back arched and her ears pinned back against her head as she bared her sharp teeth.

At that moment, he heard a fierce growl behind him.

He turned slowly, pivoting on one foot. He knew he was in a very vulnerable position. The two shepherd mixes had returned, only temporarily scared away. They inched forward, fur bristling on their backs, their fangs glowing white in the darkness, and he could imagine the saliva dripping from their mouths, frothing in their killing frenzy. He prayed that the cat would stay behind him, quiet and low. The last thing he needed at that moment was for the cat to cause the dogs to charge.

He kept his eyes on the two dogs and slowly raised up. He kept his weight forward, on the balls of his feet, ready to move if either of the animals pounced. The cat panted behind him, exhausted after fighting the dogs off. His heart thudded in his chest. The dogs looked even more menacing in the light of the headlights, like something out of a horror movie. An image of Cujo pouncing at the window of the little car flashed through his mind.

This was not good.

The larger of the German Shepherd mixes took two quick steps forward and then settled his weight on his haunches, ready to pounce. Just as the dog launched himself toward Aidan, there was a loud pop and a thwump.

The scrubby tree on the other side of the ditch shivered in the night. The dogs yelped, tucked tail and ran. Aidan blinked in the darkness, stunned. A gunshot? But who shot?

Beau yelled, "Get down!"

Aidan dropped to the ground, then cautiously lifted his head and peered into the darkness. He spotted Beau, a dark silhouette in the harsh glare of the headlight. Aidan whispered as loud as he dared, "You okay?"

"Yeah. You?"

"Yeah." He'd hit the ground hard and his ribs ached. "What the hell was that?"

Heavy footsteps whipped through the tall green grass.

A voice boomed through the night. "Get up slow and keep your hands where I can see them."

Another voice commanded, "Slowly."

Aidan swallowed hard, placed his hands flat on the ground and pushed to his feet. Hands raised, fingers splayed, he slowly turned to see Beau doing the same. His heart thudded in his chest and his mouth was dry. Alone on a deserted country road. There were only two of them, but how many of the other guys?

The gruff voice softened. "Beau? Aidan?"

Aidan squinted at the two dark shapes next to Aidan's truck and slowly lowered his hands. The muscles in his legs bunched, and he fisted his hands, ready to spring if necessary.

Beau demanded, "Who the fuck are you?"

"Easy now. Calm down." The two figures stepped into the light in front of the truck, the taller one holding out a long gun in front of him with one hand. "It's me, Frank Donovan."

The wider man spoke up, "And me, Dave Murray." The light glinted on the long gun he held at his side.

"You shot at us!" Aidan's temper flared. He clenched his fists so tight they hurt. "What the hell is wrong with you?"

Beau stepped closer and put a hand on Aidan's forearm. "Easy," he whispered. To the men, he said, "What are you doing out here?"

Frank spoke first. "After my cattle were stolen, some of us decided to start a sort of neighborhood watch program. We been takin' turns patrolling the pastures around here."

"I didn't shoot at you," Dave added. His voice sounded

defensive. "I shot to scare those dogs off, 'cause you looked like you was in trouble."

Aidan shook his head, his chest still heaving. "We were fine." He flexed his hands, his fingers aching from being clenched. He peered into the ditch. No sign of the cat. The dogs were long gone.

"You didn't look fine," retorted Dave.

Beau sucked in a breath with a hiss. "Frank, you're better than this. You guys can't go around taking the law into your own hands. Someone's gonna get hurt."

Frank said, "We've already been hurt. Those sons-a-bitches took my whole herd. They took my livelihood and I'm gonna be lucky if I don't lose my farm." The anger gave his voice a hard edge.

Beau took a step forward and it was Aidan's turn to put a steadying hand on his friend's arm. Aidan spoke loud enough for all to hear. "Let's all take a deep breath. We're all feeling tense right now."

Beau gave a quick nod. "Frank. Dave. Be careful. Please." He jerked his arm away from Aidan and strode to the truck. He yanked the door open, got in and slammed it with enough force to shake the vehicle.

Aidan nodded to the two ranchers. "Y'all be careful now." He got into the truck and turned to Beau. "Thanks, man. For stopping to get the cat." His heart still thundered in his chest and adrenaline coursed through his veins.

Beau gripped the steering wheel. "Anytime, buddy. But the next time you decide to run to the rescue of a friggin' cat, think about your own safety, will ya?" His voice was sharp.

It had been a stupid move. Aidan knew that. Hindsight was always 20/20. He still would have saved the cat, but he wouldn't have taken his eyes off those dogs. He admitted, "I know. Not smart." Wasn't smart of Frank and Dave to wander the dark roads armed, either. Vigilante justice wasn't the answer, though he'd been tempted a time or two himself.

Beau sighed heavily. "Much as I hate to admit it, if it wasn't for them two, those dogs would have ripped you to shreds. Then they would have had the cat for dessert."

Aidan barked a short laugh. "What about you?"

Beau's face split into a wide grin. "I would've made it to the truck while they were focused on you and the cat."

CHAPTER THIRTEEN
Lana

Lana Sheedy downshifted and applied the brakes, bringing the big semi to a rumbling halt. She waited as two punks in t-shirts and dirty jeans swung open the two gates. She eased the truck forward and glanced in the rearview mirror to make sure she'd cleared the gates. The truck shuddered as she put it in park and pulled the parking brake knob out. The gates clanged shut behind her, loud in the silence of the deep night. When she swung out of the truck, she was greeted by the two young men, muscled and dirty.

"Howdy, ma'am," the taller one said. His long, stringy hair hung over his face. He reminded her of a rat, with a pointy nose and dark, beady eyes.

She nodded at him, then strode down the length of the trailer and rolled the gate up. The first group of cattle trotted out of the truck and down the chute into the processing area. After the last cow left the back section of the trailer, she swung up into the trailer and tramped through, careful not to slip in the fresh manure, then unlatched the gate to release the next group of cows. Like clockwork, they jostled each other and hurried to the chute. It only took minutes for the front section of the trailer to empty.

The two little pricks watched from the back of the trailer as she reached in and yanked the aluminum ramp free and pulled it out. After the first cow ventured down the ramp, hooves clattering on the metal, the others followed quickly, some leaping the last few feet before hurrying down the chute. It was mostly a quiet process, with only an occasional mooing to punctuate the echoing sound of hooves on the metal floor. The two stockyard employees kept careful track of the animals as they exited the trailer, each holding a clicker to count the cattle as they entered the holding pen.

Lana shook her head as the cattle spilled from the trailer. Poor animals had no idea what they were hurrying toward. When the last cow had clambered down from the upper section, she slid the ramp back into place with a grunt. She swung out of the trailer and reached up for the rope to pull the door down. She secured it, then turned and watched shorter kid shut the gate behind the last of the cattle as they disappeared into the depths of the sprawling metal building.

The shorter kid grabbed a clipboard from the wall and handed it to the taller kid, who peered through his greasy bangs at her. "Name?"

"Sheedy Family Enterprises." Lana gave him the name and address to send the check after the sale. His lips moved as he scribbled on the form.

The kid ripped a ticket off of his clipboard. "Here."

"You remember how this works, right?" Lana snatched the check-in ticket from his hand and leaned close. Her top lip curled up in a snarl. "You never seen me or this trailer, right?"

His black eyes met hers for the briefest of moments, then flicked away. "Never seen nobody."

The shorter kid stared away pointedly, and gave no indication of even being aware of her presence. She glanced down at the form to check his description of the animals. He'd jotted a note about the brand. Circle H. She pressed her lips together to keep from grinning. The boys back at the compound had done a hell of a job with the cattle from the Rockin' H. They'd stripped the ear tags and rebranded every head in a single night.

She turned on her heel and clambered up into her big rig. As soon as they opened the gate in front of her, she grabbed the shifter and the big machine jerked forward, empty trailer rattling. She pulled around the building and rolled to a stop in the middle of the nearly empty gravel lot. She looked around and, when satisfied that no one was paying attention to her, swung down out of the cab and landed in the gravel with a thump. Again, she glanced around, then strode across the lot to the office.

Inside, she found a mousy woman with dirty blonde hair, buck teeth and eyes magnified by Coke bottle glasses. The woman glanced up when the bell over the door tinkled to announce Lana's presence. Her eyes widened briefly and she swallowed visibly. "Can I help you?"

"Delivered a trailer load of cattle." Lana wiped her

hands on her jeans. "Need to use your bathroom before I hit the road."

The woman directed Lana down the hallway. After Lana relieved herself, she walked past the woman without another word and quickly pushed out the door. The family'd been using this sale barn to move stolen cattle for nearly a year now, and they had a valuable ally in Bobby Rafferty, the owner. He was a distant cousin and blood counted for a lot in their circles.

Of course, it helped that they had proof that he'd been moving cattle as "certified" with falsified records for years.

As she walked across the parking lot, she gazed toward the east. Fingers of orange reached into the blue sky, pushing away the darkness. Cows mooed in the paddocks, jostling each other as they jockeyed for position at the feed bunks. She glanced at the open shelter protecting the animals from the harsh rays of the sun that would soon be beating down on them. A flash caught her eye and she squinted.

The shorter kid that had helped her unload her shipment was leaning against the barn. He held something in front of his face, but what? She narrowed her eyes and peered at him. His attention was on her rig. He reached up with his other hand and made a pinching motion. Her lips pressed into a thin line as she realized he was holding a cell phone. She clenched her fists and strode across the lot, her boots crunching in the gravel. His head swiveled toward her and he quickly lowered his phone, then slipped it in his shirt pocket.

He averted his eyes as she stepped in front of him. She poked her bony index finger in his chest. "Think you can take pictures of my rig? Find it that interesting, do you?"

His eyes widened as their gazes connected. "No, ma'am. Just taking a selfie."

She squinted at him, then held out her hand, palm up. "Gimme the phone."

He shook his head and straightened. Red colored his cheeks, and she knew she'd called his bluff. She reached for the phone and snatched it from his pocket. She spun away as she worked at the screen, trying to figure out how to reach the photos that he'd taken, but the crunch of tires on gravel drew her gaze.

A deputy sheriff's patrol cruiser pulled into the lot.

The kid snatched his phone back and vaulted over the fence.

Lana hesitated a moment, looking after the kid, then glanced back at the patrol car that had pulled to a stop in front of the office. It was too risky to stick around. She walked across the lot, forcing herself to stroll as if she had all the time in the world. She reached her rig and climbed up, then wasted no time getting the rig rolling. She glanced in the rearview mirror as she pulled out of the lot and pointed the rig toward home.

She needed to talk to Rondo, but she was pretty sure that their sweet deal at Rafferty's stockyard had just turned sour.

Lana pointed the big rig east and pursed her lips as she considered the situation. Their group had used the northern Missouri stockyard to move a lot of cattle over the past year, cattle they liberated from various ranches throughout Oklahoma, Arkansas and Missouri. They'd even taken a couple of herds from Iowa and Nebraska there. Working in a no-brand state made their business less risky.

The family had done well with Rondo leading them, but Lana turned the rustling enterprise into a well-oiled machine. They raised cattle of their own at the compound, so they could mix legitimate stock with stolen to raise less suspicion. Of course, they'd always stripped incoming animals of ear tags or any other identifying marks. Rebranding allowed her to exercise her creative juices. Over the last year or so, she'd turned it into an art form, utilizing their small collection of basic brands to cover existing brands.

The Rafferty stockyard had been her idea. Bobby Rafferty was her contact. She was the one who cultivated him after she found out he forged certification documents for the cattle run through his barn. She was the one who brought him into the fold, after she found out his mother was a Saunders, a dogleg relative of Rondo's mother.

She chewed her lip as she considered the little prick with the phone. And the Deputy Sheriff. Maybe that was a coincidence, but she had a bad feeling.

And she'd learned a long time ago to trust her gut.

By the time she reached the Cardwell County line, she'd made up her mind. It was time to find a new contact. They couldn't go back to the Rafferty stockyard, and she was pretty sure it would be a good idea to stay out of northern Missouri completely for a while. Maybe it was time to do a little recon and locate other outlets for their stolen stock.

She turned off the interstate and wound south on a narrow blacktop road. Telephone poles flicked past. The corn crop looked good, with strong green stalks poking out of the soil.

The family had tried growing crops but had no luck. Rondo said it wasn't in their blood. Maybe he was right. Then again, the red dirt in their compound wasn't good for growing much of anything, plant or animal.

The unmarked gravel road appeared next to a break in the fence, largely hidden by a stand of pin oaks and scrub trees. She swung the semi wide to make the turn, then rumbled slowly along the road, which was little more than twin rocky ribbons separated by dirt, with grass and weeds trying to take over. There wasn't enough traffic to keep the road clear, and the family was just fine with that.

The scrub trees on either side of the road pushed in, grabbing for the rig. Signs of civilization disappeared as she drove. There were no telephone poles, no electric lines, and the strands of barbed wire strung between ancient posts sagged tiredly. A dozen or so cows, some black, some red, ignored the rumble of the semi as she rolled past. After a few miles, the trees opened and revealed a clearing where half a dozen mobile homes squatted in a semi circle.

Home.

She pulled the tractor-trailer up next to a tin-sided lean to that served as the main outbuilding for the family. By the time she'd rolled to a stop, two tow-headed kids and a young woman with thick dark hair pulled back in a loose ponytail had come out to meet her.

The oldest, a boy just starting to show the muscles he would have as a man, held up a hand in greeting as she hopped down. "Want me to take it to the washout? She can help." He motioned to the girl at his side.

Lana tossed the keys to the boy. "Be careful," she cautioned.

His wide grin showed his crooked teeth. The girl hurried around the front of the truck and scrambled up into the cab, obviously not wanting to be left behind.

Lana turned to the woman. "Rondo here?"

The woman held up a hand to shade her eyes from the bright sun and nodded. "Inside." Without waiting for a reply, she continued on her way, bony hips swaying.

Lana strode across the dusty yard, her short legs eating up the distance in no time. The trailer she shared with Rondo was the newest in the compound, a super-single, ninety feet long and sixteen feet wide. While the other homes had metal roofs that were loud during storms, their home had a shingle roof. It was her favorite thing about the home. The spring storms with pounding hail scared her, though she wouldn't admit that to anyone.

Not even the man she shared a bed with.

She tugged the screen door open and stepped into the air conditioned coolness of the living room. Rondo sat in his oversized camouflage recliner, a beer in one hand and a remote control in the other. His gaze focused on the flat screen television hanging on the opposite wall. Baseball. One glance told her the Royals were playing. She squinted at the screen. They were losing. That wasn't good.

Maybe now wasn't the time to discuss the stockyard and Bobby Rafferty.

His eyes flicked at her, then back to the television. "Another beer." He sat his empty bottle on the wooden end table beside him.

Her temper flared, but she tamped it down. It wouldn't do to let Rondo know he'd irritated her. Not yet, anyway. She snatched his empty up on her way to the kitchen, then pulled two cold beers from the refrigerator. She returned to the living room and handed him one, sat on the sofa and twisted the top off of her own. Her eyes burned from lack of sleep, but she lifted the cold drink to her lips and took a long pull.

She hated making long drives on her own, but Rondo insisted he couldn't spare anyone to go with her last night. Once she sat down, the exhaustion was almost overwhelming. All she wanted to do was go crawl in bed, but she knew if she did, she'd be unable to sleep come nightfall.

Rondo sighed heavily as he twisted the cap off and dropped it on the table. His eyes never left the baseball game playing on the television. "How many head did we end up with?"

"Full load. Just shy of a hundred and fifty head."

"How shy?"

"A hundred forty-seven."

Rondo took a long drink, then looked at Lana. "You shoulda gotten a few more head on there. That trailer'll hold one sixty."

Lana held his gaze for a moment, then looked away.

"That's at total full capacity, and we had some good sized animals in this load."

"When's the sale?"

"Saturday."

He dipped his chin and looked at her through narrowed eyes. "Where'd you tell 'em to send the money?"

Lana felt her hackles rise. She knew this operation inside and out. She knew what the risks were, and how to minimize them. "I gave them the PO Box in Webb City."

Rondo had been a powerful man in his younger years. Though he remained thick and stout, the ruddy skin drooped under his chin. Gray now peppered his dark red hair and his thick mustache was nearly white. His most striking feature was his dark green eyes. He winked at her. "That's my girl. Always thinkin'."

She cleared her throat. "This was my last run to that yard. Something was off. A new kid working the yard."

A muscle twitched under his eye and he stared at her. "Bobby Rafferty is family."

She blinked but met his gaze. "I know. Not sayin' anything against Bobby, but a deputy sheriff pulled in just as I was leaving, and I caught a new kid taking a picture of my rig."

Rondo rocked back in his chair and looked at the television. "You take care of the kid?"

Lana swallowed hard. "Couldn't." Lana shook her head, angry at herself for feeling nervous. "That deputy pulled in and I thought it was best to get out of there."

He stroked his mustache a few times with stubby fingers, then said, "What's done is done. We'll let things cool off a bit there, but I'm not turning my back on Bobby Rafferty. You can take the next load to a different sale barn next time, but then we'll go back to Rafferty's place."

Lana pushed to her feet. It was just like Rondo to sit here like a king, giving orders and issuing edicts while she was the one out there on the front lines taking all the risks. "I'm not going back to Rafferty's."

Rondo snorted. "Oh, yes, you will."

She'd been doing this for far too long. He might think he ran the family, but he didn't. She was the one who took care of everyone. She was the one who scoped out the targets for their missions. She was the one who drove the truck. She was the one that knew where all their accounts were held. All that information was kept in a journal she kept under her seat in the big rig. And if he thought she was going to risk it all because he had some sense of loyalty to Bobby Rafferty, he had another thing coming.

Besides, if she played her cards right, she might end up able to retire to a life of luxury now that Beau had a stake in that fancy schmancy horse ranch, the Diamond J.

But before that could happen, she'd run one more load of cattle. And this time, the check would be made out to her, not Rondo.

CHAPTER FOURTEEN
Toby's Birthday

Gina waved the smoke away as she pulled the cake from the oven. "Damn it!" She dropped it on the hot pad and perched her fists on her hips, then glanced at the clock. Not quite 10 am. She shook her head.

"Good thing you started early."

Gina turned as Midge walked through the door. "What are you doing here? You were going to watch the store for me."

Midge shrugged. "I left Dottie there. She's there so much, she knows what to do. I thought you might need some help here." Her gaze landed squarely on the dark rectangle of cake sitting on the counter, and she scrunched up her pixie nose.

Gina pulled another mixing bowl from the cabinet while Midge rummaged for another box mix. The two worked together, Gina mixing and Midge adding ingredients. The only time they stopped talking was while the beaters hummed for two minutes. After Gina dumped the batter into the pan Midge had greased, she popped it in the oven and set the timer.

Midge picked up a package of red and blue bandanas from the kitchen table. "You decided to go with the cowboy theme?"

Gina nodded and pointed to a roll of baling twine. "Yeah, Toby is still into them. Thought we could drape the bandanas over this, to make a banner to hang there on the wall."

Midge grinned as she reached into her oversized tote. She produced a box with a family of model horses. "I got him a set of Breyers. I was going to wrap it up, but do you want to use it as a centerpiece?"

"That'll be great. I got a couple of little straw bales from the craft store the last time I went to the city. They're in my bedroom on the dresser. Why don't you go get them while I put the tablecloth on?"

When Midge returned, she arranged the miniature bales with the model horses. "So, what did you get the little cowpoke this year?"

"Not as much as I wanted. You know, it's been a tight year, money-wise, but--" Gina's eyebrows rose. "I got him a cowboy hat."

It was Midge's turn to grin. "Red?"

"You know it!"

"I know it's a touchy subject," Midge cleared her throat before she continued, "But did you invite Steve?"

Gina sucked in a deep breath and blew it out slowly. "I did. Despite the way I feel about him, he's Toby's daddy."

Midge unrolled the twine and began folding the crisp new bandanas over it. "Steve's not a bad guy. Just a bad husband."

"Yeah, I know." Gina kept talking as she walked to her bedroom. Her house was so small, with such thin walls, it was easy to carry on a conversation no matter what. "He could be a lot worse. And without him, I wouldn't have Toby. He's such a sweet kid. And he got an excellent report card - the teacher said he was helping the other kids sound out words." She walked back into the kitchen, arms full.

Midge cleared off a spot on the table, then reached into the junk drawer for tape and scissors as Gina spread out the wrapping paper. Midge said, "You're totally responsible for that. Between your genes and the work you've done with that little boy, he's a natural."

Gina pointed to the index cards taped to the front of each drawer and cabinet. "Putting labels on everything was a great idea. Thanks so much for suggesting that."

"It was nothing." Midge shrugged, then leaned forward. "But enough about exes and kids. Have you thought any more about the hottie that came by the store yesterday?"

Gina pressed her lips together and shrugged, trying to appear casual, but felt an ember of heat deep within her at the thought of him. "The guy from the Diamond J?"

"Um, yeah." Midge snapped the tea towel at Gina's butt. "You need to get some ass. And he had a mighty fine one. Mmmm-hmmmm. Did you see how those Wranglers showed off his package?"

"Midge!" Gina exclaimed. Her eyes widened in mock disgust, but she had to admit, she'd looked.

And the package was impressive.

Before she could say more, Toby burst through the front door. "Mommy! I'm home!"

The little boy was short for his age, which gave him a stout, stubby look. His blonde hair curled around his ears, giving a halo effect that was not far from the truth. The boy seemed to take his role as man of the house seriously, and worked extra hard to make sure everything went as smoothly as possible for his mama. His bright blue eyes widened as he took in the scene. Almost immediately, he focused on the Breyer box set up next to the little straw bales, then he held up one finger and said, "Be right back! I forgot to tell Missus Randolph that you're here and I'm okay."

He turned on his heel and darted back to the front door, leaned out and waved. He trotted back into the kitchen and scooted a chair out, then climbed up.

Gina stepped toward him and rested her hand on his shoulder. "Happy birthday, little man!"

The boy wrinkled his pug nose. "I'm six now, Mama. That's too old for you to call me that."

Gina pressed her lips together to keep from smiling and nodded sagely. "Right, of course. Happy birthday, Toby."

Midge chimed in, "Happy birthday, Toby!"

He looked at her, then at the box sitting on the table. "Is that my present?"

Midge nodded. "Yup. And I thought the horses would make the centerpiece better, but I think it'd look better if they were out of the box. What do you think?"

Toby swung his head around to look up at Gina. "Can I?"

Gina nodded. "Go ahead. You'll have other presents to open after your friends are here for cake and ice cream."

While Toby worked to free the horses from their plastic enclosure, he said, "What time is Daddy getting here?"

The timer beeped and Gina turned to pull the cake from the oven before she answered. "He should be here any time."

"Good. Today is an important day. You only turn six once."

Gina leaned to the side and glanced out the screen door at the driveway. No sign of him yet, but she'd told him 2. He still had time.

Gina had just finished frosting the still-warm cake when she heard the rumble of a pickup truck in front of the house.

She glanced out the window and felt a little thrill run through her body when she recognized the dusty white truck. Aidan had come! Had he been forced to, or had he volunteered?

Aidan and a shorter, wider man pulled fence panels out of the truck.

Gina hurried out the door to greet them. "Thanks so much for coming!"

The shorter man only grunted in reply, but Aidan stopped in mid-reach and his jaw dropped. He blinked twice, then a smile spread across his face. "Gina! I didn't realize this was your house. Glad to oblige. Where do you want us to set up?"

"Right around here. I can't tell you how excited the kids are going to be about this." Gina led them around the side of the house and watched as the two men quickly arranged the panels in a slightly irregular square.

Aidan nodded toward the house. "So this is where you live?"

She straightened. "Yes." Her house wasn't as big as the Diamond J, but she was proud of her little place.

"Nice." He said as he helped the stouter man clip the fencing together, leaving one panel open as a door. "So you have kids?"

"One." She swallowed hard and nodded. Well, that cinched it. He'd lose interest now. "A little boy. Toby. Today's his 6th birthday."

He nodded, but she couldn't read his expression under the shadow of his dark cowboy hat. The two men returned to the front of the house and Aidan reached into the back seat of the truck to retrieve two cotton leads. The shorter man swung the trailer door open, then Aidan stepped up and clipped the leads to the calves' halters.

Just as Aidan led the animals out of the trailer, Toby burst out the front door. "Are those for me?" His eyes were big as half dollars.

Gina was surprised it had taken him this long to figure out what was going on, but noticed a smidge of frosting at the corner of his mouth. She reached out and put a hand on his shoulder to keep him from scaring the calves. "They're for your party, not for you to keep."

Aidan handed one lead to his cohort and together they led the young animals to the back yard and put them in the pen. Toby skipped along beside them, barely able to contain his excitement. He pestered the men with questions as they walked.

"Are they boys or girls?"

"What are their names?"

"How old are they?"

The shorter man ignored the boy's questions, but Aidan took the time to answer each and every one. After the calves were safely corralled in the makeshift pen, Gina looked up at Aidan. "You're both welcome to come in for cake and ice cream."

One corner of his lips curled up in a grin. "Thank you, but we'll stay here with the little ones."

"I'll bring you a drink when we come back out, then." Gina nodded to him, then took her son's hand and went to greet his guests. Within minutes, the kitchen was overflowing with sugar-fueled kids devouring chocolate cake and cookie dough ice cream.

As soon as the kids finished the refreshments, they went to the backyard to see the calves. They gathered around the little makeshift pen and pulled grass to feed the babies. The fuzzy red calves were jumpy at first, but put up with the mass of hands rubbing them to nibble at the tender green shoots offered to them.

One little girl tugged on Gina's shirttail. "I need to go potty. Can you show me where the bathroom is?"

Gina glanced around. Midge was still inside cleaning up. Gina looked up at Aidan, eyebrows raised. "Do you mind?"

He looked around at the kids intent on the calves and shook his head. "Go ahead. They'll be fine for a minute."

Gina took the girl inside. The girl went into the

bathroom and hollered for help almost immediately. "My zipper is stuck!"

It took Gina quite some time and a bit of ingenuity to get the girl's pants unzipped, thanks to one of Toby's stubby crayons. Squeals and screams drifted through the open windows. Whatever Aidan was doing with the kids seemed to have them excited. She left the girl to her business and hurried out the back door.

She stopped on the back step, one hand still on the door handle, unable to believe her eyes. The kids pressed against the hog panels, fingers entwined in the wire. The shorter ranch hand stood in the midst of the kids, the lead rope in one hand with a calf contentedly munching on the grass. But it was the man and boy inside the pen with the other calf that caught her attention.

She sighed deeply and smiled. Aidan had let Toby get in the pen with the calf. Her son's eyes sparkled with excitement as he ran his hands over the red hair of the animal. When she'd met Aidan at the store, she'd known he was something special, and here he was, going the extra mile to make Toby's birthday the best it could be.

As she watched, Aidan leaned down and spoke into her son's ear. Toby nodded eagerly.

Aidan grabbed Toby under his arms, scooped him up and deposited him on the calf's back. Aidan stepped back against the fencing. The calf quivered a moment, flipped its tail back and forth then sprang into action. It spun in a circle, put its head down and bucked forward once, twice, three times. Toby hunkered down, his arms wrapped around the animal's neck as it bawled its displeasure at being ridden. Gina watched, rooted to the spot, unable to believe her eyes.

The calf bolted forward, then lowered its head and planted his front feet. Toby tumbled forward over the animal's head and hit the ground with a dull thud.

That sound jolted Gina out of her frozen state. She leapt off the back step and ran across the yard. The crowd of kids parted as she pushed her way through, then she yanked the fence open and shoved Aidan out of the way. She dropped to the ground next to her son. She touched his back as he pushed himself up. He lifted his head and looked at her, blood at one corner of his mouth.

"Oh, my God!" Gina wailed. She ran her hands over his body, down his arms, down his legs, then gingerly touched his mouth. Her blood pounded in her ears. For a moment, she felt as if she might pass out.

He grinned. "Did you see me, Mom? That was awesome!" One of his front teeth was gone.

She took a deep breath, blinked away the tears that threatened to spill and told herself to be strong. She scooped him up and pushed herself to her feet, then spun and faced Aidan, pinning him with her eyes. "You! What the hell were you thinking? You did this to him! I leave you alone with my son for one minute and this is what you do?"

Aidan blinked. His mouth opened and closed like a fish out of water. Finally, he managed to croak out two words. "I'm sorry."

"Yeah, you are." She strode through the crowd of kids, who stared at her with rounded eyes, stunned into silence.

She took Toby inside and sat him in a chair at the kitchen table. She cleaned him up with a cool dish cloth, carefully wiping away the dirt and grass from the scrapes on his arms and face.

The entire time she worked on him, Toby chattered on about how exciting his ride had been. "I want to be a cowboy when I grow up. Aidan says I'm a natural."

Her heart was still racing. "He does, does he?" She worked quickly. She'd left all those kids outside alone with those ranch hands. She needed to get back out there before someone else got hurt.

A knock on the back door sounded. She glanced over her shoulder and saw Aidan looking at her, his face shadowed under the brim of his black cowboy hat. He spoke through the screen. "Is he okay?"

She nodded, then turned back to her task. Damn it. He did sound concerned. "Come on in," she called out, clipping off the words.

He stepped into the kitchen. "I'm sorry." He swept his hat off and clutched it in front of his broad chest.

Toby leaned to the side so he could see around Gina. "That was fun!"

Gina shifted so she was in her son's line of vision. "But it was very dangerous." She pointed to his mouth. "You lost a tooth."

The boy's eyes rounded and his grin widened. "I did?"

Gina lowered her chin and gave Toby the sternest look she could muster. "That's not a good thing. You didn't have any loose teeth." Her heart beat was finally returning to normal. Relief washed over her. Her son was okay.

Aidan stepped forward. "At least there was no harm done. A few scrapes and a lost tooth--"

"No harm done?" Gina held up one hand, cutting him off. She turned, sucking in a deep breath and letting it out slowly. "He could've been hurt badly. Broken an arm. Or worse."

His blue eyes darkened like a Missouri sky during a thunderstorm. "I didn't think--"

She gazed up at him. "That's right. That's exactly right. Now, please, go load those calves up and leave." She stretched her arm out and pointed.

He nodded, settled his hat on his head and shoved it down. He tapped the brim, turned and left without another word.

Gina helped Toby down and took him outside to help gather the kids together. She brought them all inside, leaving Aidan and his cohort to take care of the calves.

She got the kids started with a balloon game and turned to look out the front window. Aidan and the other guy had both calves at the trailer, but the calves balked, not wanting to jump inside. As she watched, Aidan stroked them, rubbed them behind the ears. He bent down and scooped the bigger calf up and lifted it into the trailer, while the other ranch hand yanked on his calf's lead rope to no avail. Aidan stepped down, then gathered that calf in his arms. The animal struggled, feet kicking, then seemed to relax in his arms. He lifted that calf into the trailer. Once the door was secure, he turned and looked at the house.

Gina turned away quickly. She'd been so angry with Aidan, but when her gaze settled on her son as he proudly recounted for his friends what it felt like to ride a bucking calf, she wondered if her temper had flared too hot.

She heard the rumble of a truck again and went to the front door, expecting to see Aidan again. Instead, Steve slid out of his truck and hurried up the walk, arms laden with presents.

At least he'd shown up.

Toby ran to him and ripped into the presents, encouraged by the whoops and hollers of his little friends. Steve beamed at his son as he pulled a pair of red cowboy boots out of a box. The boy whooped, then dropped to the floor. Within a minute, he'd stripped off his sneakers and put on the new boots.

Her ex looked up at her and grinned. He mouthed, "Sorry I'm late."

After Toby opened the last present, he got right up in Steve's face. "I rode a calf today."

"Really?" One of Steve's eyebrows raised. "Do tell."

"Mom's friend, Aidan, brought these two calves over and they put a pen in the back yard and we all got to see them and pet them and feed them."

Gina felt Steve's gaze bore into her. He said, "Mom's friend, Aidan, huh?"

Toby plunged forward, telling his story. The kids around him chimed in, anxious to relay what they had seen, and tell how they'd been involved.

Soon, parents began to show up to pick their kids up.

When the last child left with his parents, Toby stood in the doorway waving.

Steve grasped Toby's shoulder and squeezed. "Happy

birthday, little bud. Hope you had a good one."

"I did," Toby said seriously. "Aidan was very nice to let me ride his calf. That was a once in a lifetime thing."

Gina busied herself cleaning up after the party. After Steve helped Toby put some of his toys away, he returned to the kitchen. "So, this Aidan."

Gina looked at him and arched an eyebrow. "What about him?"

"Why haven't I heard about him?"

"Nothing to hear. Just a ranch hand at the Diamond J that delivered the calves I requested for the party." She ran a hand through her thick hair and pulled it back over her shoulders.

Just a ranch hand.

Who made her heart flutter.

Who put her son on a wild animal.

He'd looked so contrite when he'd come into the kitchen to check on Toby, wringing his hat in his hands, those blue eyes focused intently on her, as if her opinion was the only one in the world that mattered.

CHAPTER FIFTEEN
Fear

Gina'd lain awake the past two nights. Aidan made a bad decision, and her little boy paid the price with a lost tooth. But really, how bad was that? Toby had gone right along with it. What kid wouldn't?

After Aidan had pulled away in his truck, Gina couldn't get Christine's words out of her mind, either. How could a cowboy - a ranch hand - afford a ranch, even a small one? There had to be something more to the story. Where could he have possibly gotten the money? Everyone in town had been talking about the cattle thefts. Was he in on it? He did have an edge to him, an air of danger. She'd seen that firsthand Saturday, the way he'd acted without considering the consequences.

She'd also noticed how different he was from the other ranch hand who had come to the house. Aidan carried himself in a confident manner. He met her gaze, spoke to her as an equal, spoke to the other man like a boss would. His voice didn't have the same country twang as most of the folks in Wilder.

She glanced at the big round clock on the wall. It was nearly eleven. She'd called yesterday and left a message with an older woman at the Diamond J that the invitations were ready, and the woman had said she'd make sure Aidan came by to get them before noon. Ever since, she'd worried about being face to face with him.

Toby hadn't stopped talking about the calf. Maybe she'd been too hard on Aidan.

She was in the back room when she heard the bell over the front door jangle. She pushed her way out of the back room with her arms loaded with boxes of scrapbooking supplies ready to be put on the shelves and a pencil clutched between her teeth. Her eyes met his and nodded at her.

A couple of days had dissipated her anger. What he'd done was stupid, but Toby was okay. In fact, Toby couldn't quit talking about his riding experience. But she didn't want to seem too eager. Aidan could wait a few minutes.

Her back stiffened and she held her head high, chin up. She called out, "I'll be right with you."

He nodded and tapped the brim of his hat.

She strode to the racks and sorted the papers into their respective slots. She considered herself lucky to own her own business. When her job at the water cooler factory closed just a couple of years out of high school, she had taken a job as a receptionist for one of the law firms on the square. Her boss was good to her and was even understanding if she needed to miss work because Toby was sick.

Unfortunately, Milton Proctor suffered a heart attack before she'd even celebrated her first anniversary with the firm. He'd survived, but it changed him. He became focused on family and a couple of pet charities. He didn't have to work, so he didn't.

It scared Gina, the changes that she saw happening in Milton. Without him, the firm wouldn't be able to keep going. Gina was surprised when Milton invited her to lunch over at the Come On Inn grill one day. She expected to be let go. Instead, he handed her a lease. She was confused at first. Thought that perhaps he had taken her to lunch to discuss a difficult client. Then she saw her name on the lease.

Her gaze flew to his face. One dollar rent. She raised her eyes and met Milton's gaze. A huge smile spread across his wrinkled face, breaking the map of wrinkles.

And so her dream of owning a scrapbook store had come true.

She peeked around the paper rack at the cowboy standing in the front of her store. He was tall, easily six foot. His shoulders were broad, his arms well muscled. A pair of work gloves tucked in his back pockets drew her eyes to his butt. Red dust covered his black cowboy hat, and his boots were scuffed.

Yes, she thought, he was a real cowboy, not one of those wannabes that walked around in polished boots made out of some exotic leather like shark or ostrich. He'd been such a natural on Saturday with the calves, but he had no idea how to take care of a child.

She scooped up the box of supplies and hurried toward

the crafting table, eager to drop them off and get up front. She smiled around the pencil in her teeth, hoping it looked like a smile and not a grimace.

Something dark and fuzzy came into her field of vision, from below, right across the top of the box. It was big, and it was getting bigger. Her focus shifted from the cowboy to the thing crawling across the papers in the box clutched to her breast.

Spider!!

Horror didn't even begin to explain the depth of emotion that she felt. Her blood ran cold, her mouth went dry and a shiver ran all the way down her body, starting at her scalp and traveling all the way down to her toes. The spider was hairy, ugly and had a round body at least as big as a quarter. It froze for a moment, then the legs started to move again, first one then another, moving toward her.

She screamed. Not a horror movie scream, but a high pitched girl scream. She pitched the box and the contents flew through the air, papers and envelopes and glue and glitter going every which way. As the papers fluttered to the ground like leaves, Gina's eyes searched the mess for some sign of the spider. She looked down and saw it about two feet in front of her, moving fast across the old linoleum tiles, straight toward her.

She shook and screamed again, then jumped onto the nearest chair, but didn't stop there – she climbed on top of the folding table and squatted there, watching the spider. It moved with her, as if it were drawn to her, and stopped just inches from the leg of the table she was perched on top of. Its two front legs felt in front of it, as if it were trying to find her.

She was so focused on the spider, as if she had tunnel vision, that she didn't see the others. Wasn't even aware that she was not alone in the shop, until she heard Midge's voice.

"Good grief, stop screaming, would you? You scream like a girl."

Gina looked up, trying to fight the shivers that kept running down her arms and legs. Goose bumps pimpled her flesh. And she saw him. The cowboy. In her fright, it took a moment to remember his name. Aidan. That was it. Aidan.

She rolled her eyes, irritation dimming the fear for a moment. He wouldn't want anything to do with her after this escapade. What a frickin' nut case he must think she was!

Midge looked at the spider, then dashed toward the back room.

Gina called out, "Where are you going?"

Midge yelled over her shoulder, "To get the spider spray. Ain't no way I'm going to step on that thing! It'll be gross – guts everywhere!"

She disappeared into the office and from all the clanking and banging, it sounded like she was making quite a mess trying to find the spray she was looking for. Aidan stepped forward and eyed the spider still exploring the floor directly below Gina's perch.

Calm as could be, he walked over, picked up a piece of paper and scooped the spider up. It jerked a bit, then froze. Aidan strode to the front door. Gina stood up on the table and watched as he opened the door, squatted down and tipped the paper. Stunned, she stood and watched. She'd never seen anyone do that before.

Midge burst through the back door, the glossy black can of spider spray leading the way. She stopped and her hand dropped, limp at her side. She blinked, then moved toward the crafting table. She looked up at Gina, then glanced over her shoulder at Aidan, who walked toward them down the center aisle of the store.

Midge mumbled, "What the—"

Gina broke in, her voice incredulous. "He didn't kill it. He released it."

Aidan came to a stop just before he stepped on the blizzard of papers on the floor. He shrugged. "I took him outside. The spider."

"But," Gina frowned as she sat down and swung her feet off the table. "It was a spider."

Aidan stepped carefully between the papers, then reached out for Gina's hand. She hesitated a moment, then placed her hand in his and let him help her down from the table. His eyes were beautiful, so clear and bright and blue, shot through with streaks like lightning, like nothing she'd ever seen before.

Midge broke in, "Don't worry about me, you two. I can pick all this up all by my lonesome."

Gina tore her eyes away from the cowboy and looked down at her friend, who squatted on the floor gathering up the stuff that Gina had sent flying through the air when she freaked out about the spider.

Suddenly, she was mortified at how she acted. She averted her eyes and righted the box that she had tossed aside in her panic. She picked up small boxes of embellishments and brads, and Aidan squatted on his heels beside her.

He picked up a card and looked at it. He said, "Hey, these are the invitations for the barbecue!"

She nodded, feeling her cheeks flush as she realized that she had just dumped the entire set of invitations. She couldn't even remember the last time that she mopped the floor. Last Monday? She picked one up and examined it. She blew on it, to get the dust off of it, then brushed it off. She placed it carefully on the table, then picked up another. Aidan stared at the invitation he held between his thumb and forefinger.

Damn. Her first really good job, almost a real corporate job, and she screwed it up after all the time that she had put into designing and making them.

He flicked it with his other hand and said, "These are the invitations you made for my boss."

She murmured, "I'll redo them." Double the cost of supplies. There went her profit margin.

He scooped up a bunch of the invitations and tapped them together on the floor to straighten them up, then glanced at her. "Why would you do that? What's wrong with 'em?"

Midge said, "She's worried that they're messed up now and you won't be happy with them. Or that your boss won't be happy with them."

Aidan scooped up another handful of invitations, added

them to the stack he'd already started and straightened up. "Nothing wrong with these. They'll be just fine. I'm sure Beth will be thrilled to pieces with them."

He set the invitations on the table and again held out his hand to Gina. She felt herself wilt just a little at the gesture. She hated feeling helpless and for some reason, that was exactly the way she felt at that moment. She wasn't in control of the situation. Didn't present the image of a professional woman. She reached up and took his hand then straightened.

He kept hold of her hand even after she stood. His grip was strong and sure, hardened with hard work. Her instincts had been right. He wasn't a wannabe. He was the real deal. She looked up into his eyes and felt her knees melt.

He spoke softly. "Again, I'm really sorry about your little boy."

"It's okay." It wasn't. Not really. But she had a job to do. "Toby's been telling everybody that he's a real cowboy now."

His blue eyes sparkled and he smiled. A little dimple formed in his left cheek. She hadn't noticed that before. He gave her hand a little squeeze, rubbed his thumb across hers, then released her.

Her body betrayed her. In spite of the fact that he was irresponsible and rough around the edges, he was sexy as hell. If she felt that way just touching his hand, she couldn't imagine what it would feel like to be close to him, to kiss him, to be cradled in his arms. She wanted to run her fingers over her chest, trace the lines of muscles along his abdomen, follow the trail of dark hair down his chest and lower—

She glanced at Midge and she could tell by her friend's face, it wasn't a secret. Desire was written all over her face. No, not just desire. Lust. Her friend was grinning at her, and winked as she picked up the box of embellishments.

Midge said, "You all go ahead and talk about whatever you need to talk about. I'm just going to take these to the back room. To the store room. It may take me a long time to get these things put away. A long time."

One dark eyebrow twitched up as he looked at Gina, then said, "Didn't you just bring these out of the store room?"

Midge answered for her. "Gina is kind of a space case sometimes. I'm sure she didn't add them to inventory, so I'm just going to go back there and check every single one of these little packages to make sure they're on the computer."

Gina felt the blush rise up her cheeks again. Damn it! Why did she have to wear her emotions on her sleeve? It was damned embarrassing. She pointed to the chair on the opposite side of the table, indicating that he should sit, then she sat down at the table in the chair that she had just leapt into a little bit ago. She scooted the invitations toward him.

He reached out to take the cards, and their fingers touched. It was like an arc of electricity flowed between them. Gina felt a tingle run up her finger, through her hand, up her arm and into her shoulder. The jolt went straight to her heart.

She blinked and yanked her hand back. The man across from her watched her, those amazing blue eyes focused on her. She'd felt that tingle when they touched. Had he?

He looked at her expectantly, his eyebrows raised, lifting his cowboy hat up just a touch. He asked, "Well?"

"Uh," Gina fought to gain her bearings, then stuttered, "I-I'm sorry. What'd you say?"

Midge snorted behind her, "He just asked if you were interested in a little passionate entanglement of the legs."

Gina sputtered, but couldn't form a word to save her soul. Aidan grinned, exposing teeth that seemed even whiter against his tanned skin. One of his front teeth had a tiny chip out of it. "So, how 'bout it?"

Gina flashed a warning look at her friend. "Ignore Midge. She's always saying stuff like that." But the seed had been planted. Now she was thinking about it. With him.

Midge cackled in an impression of a witch. "Made you think, didn't it?"

Aidan leaned across the table and whispered conspiratorially to Gina, "Okay, she did make me think about it for just a moment."

Gina blushed and turned to shoot Midge a dirty look. All she got in return was a big cheesy wink. Aidan cleared his throat and she turned back to face him. Her cheeks were flushed, yet his rough-stubbled face showed no sign of embarrassment. His blue eyes were intent on her, and the corners of his mouth curved up slightly.

Finally, she muttered, "Sorry about her. I keep her around for the comic relief."

"She's good at her job." He rested his elbows on the table and leaned forward.

She was drawn forward, toward him. "That she does. Anyway, you were saying?" Gina swallowed hard. This man oozed testosterone.

"I asked if you're still able to join us out at the Diamond J for the barbecue."

Was he asking her out? She wasn't sure. What did "us" mean? She would love to go, but would she make an appearance there only to be embarrassed when he already had a rodeo bunny on his arm?

But if she took Toby, he would have a ball and she would have someone to sit with. That'd kill two birds with one stone. Besides, Toby would be thrilled at the chance to go to the ranch, but this time she wouldn't leave him in Aidan's care.

She nodded once, quickly. "Yes, we'll be there." She shifted in her seat, conscious of the heat building within her at the thought of going anywhere with him.

His dark brows pushed together as he stared at the invitation still gripped between his thumb and forefinger.

"Do you think your boss will be satisfied with these?" Gina caught her lower lip with her teeth.

He tapped the invitation against the table. "I think she'll be more than satisfied. They look great. I'm sure it's exactly what she was looking for."

"Well," Gina said, "You take them to her and get her to look at them. If she isn't one hundred percent satisfied, I'll redo them."

"Hmmmm," he said, with one corner of his mouth

twitching up. "You're pretty confident, aren't you?"

"No," she said, shaking her head. "Just the opposite actually. I'm not sure she'll like them, and I want to make sure she gets what she wants. If she's happy, she'll come back. If she's not, she won't. It's good business, plain and simple."

"I'm sure she'll love 'em." He nodded, then pulled a folded check from his breast pocket and slid it across the table to her. "Here you go."

She smiled and took the check without looking at it. "Thank you. I appreciate the business."

He slid the top invitation off the stack and laid it on the table between them. "This is for you, so you'll have the details. Stick it on your 'fridge at home. I hope you can make it."

She picked the invitation up. "Thanks. We're looking forward to it."

"Right," he said. The smile faded from his face, and he stood up. She wasn't sure what that was about. The invitation had seemed sincere. She pushed back from the table and stood also, then watched as he gathered up the completed invitations.

On the way past the center island, he handed an invitation to Midge. "You're invited, too, and you're welcome to bring a guest." His boots made a rhythmic thunk as he strode toward the front of the store.

Midge called after him, "Thanks!"

He walked out the door, letting in a whoosh of spring wind as he went.

Midge looked at the invitation, then said, "You know,

I've been hearing about the new management out at the Diamond J. We're going to this, right?"

Gina walked to the center counter and leaned against the support post, "Absolutely. After getting to ride that calf, all Toby can talk about is cowboys."

"I can see why." Midge grinned. "Cowboys are yummy."

Gina shook her head, then gazed out the big plate glass window, her thoughts on Aidan. He had such an easy manner about him, yet there was an undercurrent of danger. She asked her friend, "Did you catch that right before he left? Did he seem irritated to you?"

Midge shrugged. "Who can tell with men?"

Gina rolled her eyes as the front door swung open and the bell chimed to announce a customer. One of the Friday night croppers hurried in and pushed the door shut behind her.

Gina pushed aside thoughts of the cowboy and called out, "Hello, Linda! I ordered in that billiards paper to scrap your Vegas trip – let me run back and get it for you."

CHAPTER SIXTEEN
If It Can Go Wrong

As soon as Gina locked up the store, she hurried home, anxious to see her little boy. She brushed aside thoughts of Aidan and focused on Toby. No matter how long of a day she had, he could make her smile -- and today had been long. Her fingers ached from all the inking and stamping she had done, her feet were tired and swollen from standing all day, and her eyes were dry and scratchy from reading the computer screen all day. But she couldn't complain, she had a job that she loved, even if it was hard sometimes.

She heard Toby before she saw him. He was singing, "Pokémon! Got to catch them all! I know it's my destiny! Pokémon!"

She could picture the images of brightly colored pocket monsters flashing across the screen. Toby's voice was much louder and overshadowed the television. His squeals of delight made her heart sing and when he came around the corner from the living room, she wondered if every parent felt this way. At times, she loved him so

117

much it was like a physical pain. She missed him when she wasn't with him, and everything he did brought her joy. He ran toward her, his arms outstretched, and the last step was a leap into her arms. She reached out and caught him, then swung him around which led to squeals of delight – from both of them. Sandy came around the corner. She leaned against the door jam and propped a fist on her hip.

Sandy asked, "Long day?"

Gina nodded, "It's always a long day when I'm away from my little rascal."

She lifted him up and hugged him to her. "Were you watching Pokémon?"

He looked down, suddenly looking bashful. He murmured, "It's a kid show, but I still like it."

She kissed him on the cheek and said, "I'm a grown up and I like it."

"I'm older than both of you and I like it." Sandy smiled and said, "Hate to run out on you, but I need to hustle. I need to stop by and see my neighbor."

Gina looked up. "How's she doing since her surgery?"

"Pretty well. Still moving slow, but that's to be expected after back surgery."

As the older woman gathered up her things, Gina pulled a five dollar bill from her billfold and slipped it into the other woman's hand. "Tell your neighbor to let me know if there's anything I can do. Give her this, or use it to buy her something."

Sandy tucked the bill into her purse. She leaned down just in time to catch Toby as he launched himself at her for a big hug. "Bye, Nana Sandy!"

Sandy kissed the top of his head. "Love you too, my big boy." She slipped out the door.

Toby ran into the living room, where he plopped down and grabbed a toy horse then galloped it across the wood floor. His lips moved as he made whinnying noises. While he was occupied, Gina flipped through the mail. Bills, bills, and more bills. She added them to the basket on the kitchen counter already overflowing with bills. Given that she didn't have much of a life, didn't live extravagantly or shop excessively, the bills sure stacked up. Rent was due, the car payment was due, homeowners insurance was due, car insurance was due, all the friggin' utilities. There was no end to it. A sigh escaped her lips.

She let her head fall back and she stared at the ceiling. Too bad she couldn't find a knight in shining armor who could whisk her away and make her problems disappear. She could sure use one right now. With a huff, she put her Tupperware container from lunch in the dishwasher, then added the other dishes that were sitting on the counter. She added soap then started the machine.

It sputtered, coughed, then made a loud screech. She lunged forward and punched the button to make the machine stop, but it continued squealing like a stuck pig. The sound of water jetting into the machine told her that it continued to fill. Suddenly, there was a horrendous shudder, the machine belched smoke from the front panel and then it was quiet.

Toby ran from the living room, eyes wide. "Sounds like a monster in there!"

Gina could feel herself wilting. There wasn't enough

money in her checking account to have the dishwasher fixed. Definitely not enough money to buy a new one. Her credit card was maxed. And she already owed Bob's Appliance Repair for coming out to fix the washing machine, so she couldn't call him.

Damn.

It made her physically hurt sometimes to be so broke. Thank God for the child support Steve paid. That allowed her to raise her son on the salary she earned at the scrapbook store, but it didn't leave much extra.

Toby, in that little voice that made her heart melt, said, "It'll be okay, Mom."

"I know, sweetheart." She bent down and gave him a hug. "Guess we'll be doing dishes the old fashioned way."

Growing up, she'd been the dishwasher. This wasn't the end of the world. She tousled his hair and said, "Want me to read a book before you go to bed?"

He clapped his hands and jumped up and down, then raced down the hall shouting, "Harry Potter!"

She shot a withering look at the offending dishwasher, then put her hands on her knees and pushed herself upright. She walked down the hallway and turned into Toby's room. It was small, only big enough for his twin bed – his "big boy bed", as he proudly told everyone who came in – a small dresser, a bookshelf and a toy box shaped like a train engine.

Toby tugged his pajamas out from under his pillow, then flopped down on the floor to pull his pants off. He struggled, tugged and pulled, but when Gina tried to help, he insisted that he could do it himself. He succeeded, finally, in pulling his jeans off and heaved a big sigh.

"Good job, Toby!" Gina gushed.

He looked at up at her from under his thick fringe of dark lashes. Very seriously, he lifted his hands up and said, "I'm tired now. Help."

She pulled his shirt over his head and tossed it in the corner with his jeans. Everything about him was perfect. She tickled his tummy, which elicited a round of giggles, then helped him get into his Scooby Doo pajamas on. They were the ones with feet, which he loved, and so did she. It reminded her of her own childhood. Because hers hadn't been the best, she was determined to keep his childhood as carefree as possible.

He tilted his head to the side, as if thinking. "I'm gonna brush my teeth now."

And with that, he ran out of his bedroom and into the bathroom. She could hear water running in the sink. She sank to the floor and leaned back against the bed. It was the first time she had sat down all day. She looked around the room, at the simple furnishings, all cheap pine furniture. It wasn't what she had imagined her little boy's room would look like when she used to dream of having babies, but the creative touches made it special.

Her favorite part of the room was the paint job she'd done. It had been her first try at tackling painting a room anything other than plain old painting. She started with spring grass green below the chair rail, and blue above the chair rail, then hand painted trains running around the room on the chair rail. Little Toby had been fascinated with trains from the time he was a toddler, and his obsession had grown as he'd gotten older. Thomas the Tank had been his favorite television show, making it easy to pick Thomas gifts for every holiday and gift-giving occasion.

And then last year he discovered cowboys and horses.

But she had worked so hard on this room - no way was she changing it.

She could hear him humming Happy Birthday to himself in the bathroom, which made her smile. He was so proud of being able to do things himself, just like his mama.

Her independent streak had definitely been passed down to him. That was a mixed blessing. Though it was nice to have him do things like brush his teeth and get dressed on his own, she knew it was just a matter of time before she wouldn't be able to do anything for him, because he would insist on doing everything himself.

The sound of running water stopped just after he finished humming the song, and a couple of minutes later she heard the toilet flush. Toby marched into the room and climbed into his big boy bed. She tucked him in, then turned to run her index finger along the spines of the books on his bookshelf.

"Hmmmmm," she mused, "What would you like to hear tonight? Perhaps Where the Wild Things Are?"

"Harry Potter!"

"That's too long. What else?"

"Polar Express!" he shouted gleefully.

She smiled at his suggestion and said, "But that's a Christmas story."

"Polar Express!" he insisted. His chubby little face was set, and she knew there was no changing his mind. She pulled the book from the bookshelf and sat on the floor, balancing the book on his mattress.

She started to read, "On Christmas Eve, many years ago, I lay quietly in my bed . . . "

As she turned each page, Toby said something about the illustration and every now and then she turned the book toward him so they could look at the illustrations together. By the time the little boy returned to his house, Toby's eyes were closed and his breathing was deep and even. His cheeks were plump and rosy, and he had that angelic look that little kids have when they sleep.

A smile touched her lips as she quietly closed the book, returned it to his bookshelf, then scooped up his dirty clothes. On her way out of his bedroom, she flicked the light switch off and closed his door, leaving it open just a crack. He insisted he wasn't scared of the dark, but liked being able to see the light from the night light in the hallway if he woke up.

After she dropped his dirty clothes into the clothes hamper in the bathroom, she returned to the kitchen to deal with the obstinate dishwasher. Her legs felt like they were made of lead. It would be nice to get through a single week without something breaking.

CHAPTER SEVENTEEN
Shower

Aidan walked into the house, swept off his cowboy hat and tossed it on the back of the couch. He called out, "Anybody home?"

There was no answer, so he headed down the hallway toward his bedroom. He pulled clean clothes out of his dresser and went to the bathroom, peeling off clothes as he went. His shirt landed on his bed, his jeans on the floor. He cranked the water on, more hot than cold, and let the steam roll. The water coursed over him, soothing his aching muscles and sloughing off the dirt, grime and sweat of the afternoon.

He closed his eyes and held his face up to the spray of water, then reached up and turned the shower head to massage. He turned his back to the water and rolled his shoulders under the pulsating jets of water, letting the shower do the work of unknotting his muscles.

His thoughts turned to Gina. She was so unlike any other woman he'd met, total opposite of the girls he'd dated in high school, the girls his mother approved of.

Those girls all looked the same. Long blonde hair, painfully thin. They drove expensive cars, carried bags with designer labels prominently displayed, and had weekly manicures. They were fake, but Gina struck him as genuine.

And as a mother. She had a son. He had not seen that coming. The anger that flashed in her eyes when she'd come out of the house after her kid fell off the calf had been enough to scare him. Talk about shooting daggers. She'd been like a mama bear, ready to rip him to shreds. He wanted to ask Gina out, but he wasn't sure he wanted to start anything with a woman who had a kid already. That was more responsibility than he was ready for.

He grabbed the bar of soap off the little shelf and ran it over his body, lathering up. In spite of his hesitation, he longed to run his hands through Gina's thick, auburn hair. When he'd left the store, he'd noticed the red highlights that caught the sunlight. Her curves drew his eyes down her body, over her generous breasts, her narrow waist, her hips. He turned slowly, running his hands up and down his body, washing the suds off until he was slick and clean.

He was going to ask her out. If she turned him down, she turned him down. But he was tired of being alone, hanging out with the guys. He wanted a woman to go out to eat with, to go riding with, to go dancing with.

But not just any woman. He wanted Gina Montgomery.

He stepped into his clean Wranglers and tugged them up over his hips, then pulled a clean t-shirt on. It was dollar night at the Come On Inn. He'd go have a drink and put Gina out of his mind.

She was a mother. She had a little boy. He wasn't ready for that.

CHAPTER EIGHTEEN
Broken Things

Gina pulled the handle of the dishwasher and eased it open. A puff of steam belched out of the machine. She waited until the steam dissolved, then opened the door a bit more and let it fall open. Water gushed out of the open door and spread across the floor. She snatched the dish towel off of the stove handle and dropped it on the floor to sop up the water. She grabbed the little half circle kitchen rug and tossed it in the sink. Oh, well, it needed to be washed anyway.

Not like she wanted to do it at night after a long day at work, though. With a sigh, she turned to the task of mopping up the water as the water spread across the linoleum.

"Damn!" she muttered as she sopped up water, then stood to wring the towel out into the chipped porcelain sink.

A whooshing sound behind her sounded. She spun around to see water jetting up from the lower spray arm. She slammed the door shut, but the spray continued. The water needed to be turned off. She snatched the flashlight off the counter and darted out the back door. Clouds obscured the moon, leaving the night dark. The flashlight beam bounced along the concrete block foundation as she searched for the opening to the crawl space. The dark door appeared as a shadow nearly hidden behind the tangle of weeds that had grown up around the shrubbery. She dropped to her knees and tugged on the handle. Dampness soaked through her jeans. The stubborn door refused to budge. She set the flashlight down and used both hands. With a grunt, she finally unlodged the hatch. It swung open and the musty smell of earth and things she didn't want to think about swept over her.

If she remembered right, there was a handle on the main water pipe that served as a shut off for the entire house.

"Hold it right there!" A gruff voice sounded right behind her.

She tried to spin around and push herself up at the same time, but her foot twisted under her, caught on a root. With a grunt, she fell to the side. "What the hell?"

The man reached down, grabbed her upper arm and jerked her to her feet. "Let's go have a chat with the owner of the house."

She snatched up the flashlight up as he lifted and swung the beam up to shine in the man's face. "You," she spat.

"Huh?" He held his hand in front of his face to block the beam.

Anger spiked, sharpening her voice. "Let go of me right now, Aidan Brackston!"

He blinked in the bright light and grunted. "What? Gina,

is that you?"

"What the hell are you doing here?" Suddenly, she remembered what she was doing, the machine spewing water into her kitchen. She jerked her arm away from him and dropped to her knees again. "I don't have time for this."

"I was going to the Come On Inn and saw you out here. " His tone was wounded, yet defensive. "There's been so much crime. All I saw was a dark figure lurking around in the shadows."

Gina sat back on her feet and leaned forward awkwardly, shining the flashlight inside, trying to see the turnoff.

"What are you doing out here?" He squatted next to her, his thigh against hers.

She pressed her eyes shut and took a deep breath. The kitchen was going to be flooded by the time she got this done. "I said, I don't have time for this. My dishwasher has blown up and I have got to get the water shut off." Her fingers brushed the cold metal of the handle. She wrapped her hand around it and tugged, but it refused to budge. She let out a low growl.

Aidan squeezed in next to her and ran his hand along her arm, his fingertips barely brushing her skin. "Let me help." His fingers were warm. His body pressed against hers, his chest against her back as he reached under the house. His mouth was inches from her ear. She tensed as his fingers reached the handle, then released her hold and let him take over.

He pushed the handle up with a grunt, then settled back

on his heels. "Okay, it's off. Now let's go see about this dishwasher." He straightened and held out his hand, palm up. "You home alone?"

Gina reached up, took his hand and let him pull her to her feet. "I'm fine. I can handle it myself." She brushed the dirt and grass off her jeans.

"I'm sure you can, but why? I'm here and happy to help." He smiled at her.

She shrugged. "Suit yourself." She was so used to handling things on her own, it felt odd to accept his offer. She led the way to the back door and opened the kitchen door for him.

He strode in, looked around at the water and settled his fists on his hips. Wet grass stains darkened the knees of his dark blue jeans. "Okay, you got some old towels to sop up the water?"

She nodded, then hurried to the linen closet in the hallway to gather supplies. By the time she returned, he had the door of the machine open and was scooping water out of the basin into the sink with a large plastic cup.

As she sopped up water, she watched him bend over and straighten, time after time. She moved beside him and wrung out a bath towel, then dropped it on the floor and grabbed another. With the two of them working together, they got most of the water cleaned up in fairly short order.

She peeled off her soaked socks and tossed them aside.

He peered inside the machine. "So, what was it doing?"

"It kept filling with water and wouldn't quit. And it made a weird noise."

He shut the door, swept his cowboy hat off, then said,

"Sounds like the timer went out. Without that, the machine doesn't know to quit filling. Do you have a screwdriver?" He set his black hat on the counter.

"Yes." She hurried to the laundry room and returned with her pink tool bag and sat it on the floor next to him. She stole a glance at him without his hat. His thick dark hair curled over the collar of his white t-shirt.

He squatted in front of the machine, running his fingertips over the edge of the door. He glanced at her tool bag. "Pink?"

"So?" She retorted. "At least I've got tools."

One corner of his mouth quirked up. "Guess as long as they work, color doesn't matter." He fished in her bag until he found the screwdriver he needed. "Do you know how to shut off the breaker that this is on?"

"Of course." She didn't tell him that she knew because every time she ran the toaster and the dishwasher at the same time, it threw the breaker. She hurried to the laundry room, flipped the switch and returned. "It's off."

He squatted and sat back on his heels as he quickly removed eight screws from the front panel of the machine. As he removed each one, he dropped it into Gina's outstretched palm.

Her brow scrunched as she watched him pull the panel off the front, exposing the guts of the machine. "You sure you know what you're doing?"

"Yup. Like I said, it's probably the timer." He pointed at a round motor housing, then ran his fingers along the wires extending from it. "You got a label maker? Or some colored tape?"

"Be right back." She hurried to her bedroom and returned with a small white carousel of washi tape rolls. "Will this work?"

He laughed, a deep, genuine sound. "Scrapbooking stuff?"

"Washi tape."

His shoulders lifted in a shrug. "That'll work." He pulled off two short strips of brightly colored chevron tape and wrapped them around the wires before he disconnected them. He pointed at what he'd done. "That'll make it easier to remember how it goes back together."

Smart, she thought. There was more to him than she'd initially thought.

"Don't suppose you have the owner's manual?" He glanced up as she shook her head, then pulled the door open and peered at the stickers on the edge of the machine. "Ah! Here we go."

"What are you looking at?"

"The schematics. To see what the voltage should be. Don't suppose you have an ohmmeter?"

She cocked her head and narrowed her eyes. "A what?"

"A little handheld tool that measures electricity."

She shook her head. "I have a stud finder." As soon as the words left her mouth, heat crept up her cheeks.

He winked at her. "Don't need that. You already found me." He grinned, exposing his dimple.

She rolled her eyes.

"Let me check the toolbox in the truck. I'll see if I've got mine." He walked out the back door and she watched out the window as he jogged along the side of the house. He moved with a natural athleticism. He was probably a jock in high school.

He returned and held up the bright yellow tool triumphantly as he pushed through the kitchen door. "Found it!"

She watched as he hooked the red and black wires to the timer motor he'd taken from the dishwasher. The needle on the ohmmeter moved just a twitch. He made a disapproving noise. She looked at the reading on the tool, then at the frown on his brow. "What?"

He tapped the motor. "It's bad. You need a new timer motor."

"Great," she groaned. "How expensive is that going to be?"

He shrugged. "Not as expensive as a new dishwasher."

Her eyebrows rose. He was right. She chewed her lower lip, then huffed out a sigh. "Don't suppose you'd be willing to replace it if I buy it tomorrow?" She hated asking for help, but a little thrill of excitement ran through her at the prospect of seeing him again so soon.

"You could probably convince me." He turned to face her, just inches between them.

The dark stubble along his jaw gave him a rough look. She wondered what he looked like freshly shaved. Without his hat shadowing his face, his blue eyes seemed even brighter. He gazed down at her and his lips parted slightly. She shifted forward slightly and, after a moment's hesitation, placed her hands on his chest. He grinned down at her, deepening the dimple in his cheek.

She breathed, "How can I thank you for coming to my

rescue?" For the first time in a long time, she felt like a woman, not a mother.

He lowered his head, his blue eyes hooded. "I can think of something." He traced his finger along her cheekbone, then along her jawline. "You are beautiful."

She started to shake her head. "I'm not--"

"You are." His smile faded. "Before we go any farther, I need to know something."

She swallowed hard and breathed, "Anything."

"Is Toby's daddy still in the picture?"

Her heart dropped. Here we go, she thought. Aloud she whispered, "We divorced years ago."

One corner of his mouth quirked up. "Good. I don't share well."

They stared at each other for the longest moment, Then he tilted his head as she stood on her tiptoes. Their lips met, lightly. The first touch was tentative, exploring. She looked up at him and wondered what she was doing. This was unlike her, but she couldn't ignore the attraction that pulled her toward him.

His hands settled on her shoulders, then trailed down her back, pulling her closer. He caressed her as his mouth claimed hers. His tongue flicked against her lips, teasing them open. She felt warmth spread deep inside her, desire taking over her body as her tongue met his. She pressed against him, wanting to be closer, straining up on her tiptoes in response to his deepening kiss.

"Why is the floor wet, Mom?"

She jerked and pulled away, wiping Aidan's kiss from her mouth as she spun away to face her son. Toby stood in the doorway, rubbing his eyes with his fists.

Aidan cleared his throat and stepped back. He swept his hat up and settled it on his head.

Gina rushed forward and put her hand on Toby's shoulder. She spun him around, then glanced over her shoulder at Aidan. "I'm sorry," she mouthed. "I'll be right back."

After Gina got Toby settled back in bed, she returned to the kitchen. She stuffed her hands in her pockets, irritated at the flush she felt on her cheeks. She looked up at him through her fringe of lashes. "Sorry about that."

Aidan shrugged. "No problem. I'm surprised he slept through all that." He motioned toward the exposed dishwasher. "Do you want me to come back tomorrow and finish?"

She nodded, then pulled a pen out of the mug on the counter and scooted a notepad toward him. "If you want to give me your number, I'll call and let you know I've got the part."

He jotted his number down then gestured toward the motor on the counter. "Take that with you to make sure you get the right part." One dark eyebrow raised. "Or would you like me to get it for you?"

She shook her head quickly. "No, I'll get it. I don't want to put you out any more."

He settled his hat on his head. "See you tomorrow."

With that, he was gone.

She watched him through the window and felt all resolve dissolve. It was a good thing Toby walked in when he did, because she would've let Aidan take her right there on the wet linoleum.

CHAPTER NINETEEN
Milton

She'd just crawled into bed, wrapped up in warm memories of being in Aidan's embrace, when the telephone on her nightstand rang, jangling her nerves and making her jump. She snatched up the handset before it could wake Toby up. She glanced at the clock, 9:54, as she said, "Hello?"

Midge's voice came through the phone line. "I'm sorry to call so late."

Good news never came late. "No problem. What's up? Is everything okay?" A sick feeling settled in the pit of her stomach.

"No," Midge sighed. "I heard some bad news tonight. I wanted to get the details and confirm before I called you."

Gina sat on the edge of the bed and gripped the handset tighter, then asked, "What?"

"It's your old boss, Milton. He passed away this afternoon."

Gina felt a chill go down her spine, all the way down her legs. It was as if all the heat in the room had been sucked out. She closed her eyes and shivered, then whispered,

"What happened?" Milton had been like a father to her.

"Apparently he was out in the yard filling the bird feeder and fell over dead. Heart attack."

Gina tried to murmur something, but it came out as little more than a strangled cry. Milton was gone. He was such a good, kind person. Why did the good ones always have to die? Goosebumps raised on her arms.

Gina finally got out a few words, "But he was in good health."

Midge agreed, "Yes, he was. Walked all the time, worked in the garden."

Gina protested, "But he couldn't have been more than sixty!" Tears filled her eyes.

Midge said, "I heard he would've been sixty-nine next month."

"That's not old." Gina swallowed the lump in her throat. She finally managed to string together a few coherent words, "Any idea what the arrangements are?"

Midge said, "No, I don't think so. I'm sure somebody will take Milton's wife to the funeral home tomorrow to make arrangements."

Gina said, "If you hear, would you call me as soon as you know?"

Midge promised she would and said, "I'm sorry, Gina. I know you really looked up to him."

Gina pushed the end button and sat the handset on the charger, tears coursing down her cheeks, one right after the other. Midge had no idea. Milton had been more than a boss, he had been a mentor and her patron, allowing her to rent the scrapbook store location for a pittance.

She hated herself for being selfish at a time like this, but she wondered what effect his death would have on that arrangement.

She laid awake most of the night, worrying about the dishwasher, the scrapbook store, Milton's wife . . . everything.

After a sleepless night, she dragged her butt into the scrapbook store and started flipping on lights. She had just turned the open sign over when she heard the back door slam shut. Midge walked through the door, looking perfect and cute as always. She was the only woman Gina knew who actually looked better as she got older.

When she had turned forty a couple of years ago, she cut her hair into a short pixie cut and bleached it. It was perfect for her, it fit her. And it had the added bonus of making her cheekbones stand out, and showed off her small ears. Gina sighed, irritated at herself for feeling those pangs of jealousy over her friend's looks. Gina was feeling older than her 29 years these days.

Gina called out a cheery, if forced, "Good morning!"

Midge walked to the center counter, a Styrofoam cup in each hand and handed offered Gina one of them. "Got you one, too. Carmel latte, whole milk, double shot."

"Thanks." Gina took the offered drink. The steam warmed her face. She put it down to let it cool for a moment.

Midge's lower lip pooched out. "Are you doing okay this morning? I know Milton was special to you." Her eyebrows scrunched together.

Gina nodded. "More so than you know." A lump in her

throat made the words come out with a strangled sound.

Midge cocked her head sideways. "I know you worked for him before you opened the store. Isn't he the one who encouraged you to open the store?"

Another chill ran down Midge's spine at the memory. "Yes, he did. The law firm wasn't turning a profit and it was going to close. He felt bad about leaving me hanging out to dry, especially with Toby, so he helped me get this place." She spread her arms wide to indicate the store.

Midge asked, "Didn't he represent you in the divorce, too?"

Gina shook her head. "No, but he got Jed Clinkscales to handle it at a reduced fee. Since Jed and Milton were partners, I did all the typing and drafting of documents. Jed just looked over everything and advised me on what to do."

Midge took a sip of her coffee and peered over the top of the cup. "Your eyes are really puffy today. This hit you pretty hard."

The guilt was tearing Gina apart as much as the grief. She should be upset about the poor man's death, his poor widow. For God's sakes, his children and grandchildren. Instead, all she could think about was whether or not she'd be able to keep the store open. She said out loud, "I cried a lot last night, and didn't sleep very well."

Midge offered, "Do you want to take the day off? I'd be glad to work all day."

"No," Gina shook her head. "That's okay. But I'd like to take a rain check on that offer so I can go to the funeral."

Midge said, "Of course."

Gina took a small sip of her coffee. Still hot, but not quite scalding. "I don't suppose you've heard anything about arrangements?"

"No," Midge said as she pushed the power button on the computer tower under the counter. "But there might be something online."

Gina glanced around the store, thinking about all the work she had put into the place over the last year since it had opened. All four walls were covered with white slat board and hooks held everything from templates to adhesives. Long wooden shelves created rows of paper, everything from Bazzill to beautiful patterned papers. Carousels and end caps displayed embellishments of every type.

She and Midge stood in the center of the store, the island that was the business center of the store, the heart of the store, with easels displaying finished works on the counters. The back third of the store was her favorite, though. She referred to as the scrappy area, with several white banquet tables set up in the center with folding chairs so that people could come in and crop. The surrounding walls were filled with kitchen counters that contained every tool a scrapper could dream of.

But how long could she stay open if she had to start paying rent? She froze, cup midway to her mouth, a sick feeling in the pit of her stomach.

What if the building were sold? Would she lose her location?

Midge asked, "What's the matter?"

Gina's chest rose and fell with a heavy sigh. It felt like a physical weight pushing down on her. She and Midge were close, and they discussed nearly everything, but they had never discussed money. She felt it was a burden that she had to carry upon her shoulders, and hers alone.

But now that burden felt overwhelming.

Gina sat her coffee down and stared out the front window, unable to meet her friend's eyes as she told her secret. She whispered, "I'm terrified I'm going to lose this place."

Midge touched her arm. "Oh, sweetie, it'll be okay. I'm sure business will pick up. It's been going well. Your crops are popular and—"

Gina interrupted her, "No, that's not it." She blinked away tears before they could fall.

Midge pulled back and her features softened. "You can cut my pay. Or cut my hours."

Gina shook her head. "You don't understand, it's so much bigger than that." She sucked in a deep breath, then let the words out in a rush. "Milton rented this place to me for a dollar a month."

Midge blinked and whistled. "Wow. That is so generous!"

Gina snorted. "That was *so* generous. And now I feel *so* like a heel for even thinking about it."

Understanding dawned on Midge's face. Her jaw dropped. "Oh! I get it. You're worried that the deal won't continue now."

Gina felt miserable. "I don't see how it could continue. At this point, I'm not just worried about the rent being raised, I'm worried about the building being sold out from under me."

Midge broke in. "And then what will you do?"

Gina cocked one eyebrow up. "Exactly. That is the question of the day, my dear friend."

The front door opened and the bell chimed merrily. Ed, the mailman, came in and greeted them with a hearty, "Good morning, ladies!"

After he handed off the bundle of mail, which consisted mostly of magazines, junk mail and the electric bill, he turned to leave. At the door, he met a customer and held the door open for her. The woman announced that she was working on a John Deere album for a gift, and that set the tone for the day.

Customers were in and out, and neither Midge nor Gina had time to give Milton's passing and the implications of his death another thought until the doors closed that evening.

CHAPTER TWENTY
The Fixer

Though Gina had been distracted with Milton's passing, but she was dying to tell Midge about Aidan and the events of the night before. As the lunch crowd died off, Gina said, "Mind if I run out for a bit? I'm going to have to swing by the hardware store. The dishwasher broke last night."

"That sucks," Midge said as she rearranged a display. "Who are you going to get to fix it?"

"The cowboy from the Diamond J." The memory of Aidan in her kitchen made her knees weak.

Midge turned to look at Gina with a twinkle in her eye. "Do tell!"

A flush crept up Gina's neck. "Aidan was driving past when I was outside trying to get the water shut off. He stopped to help." In spite of herself, she grinned so wide her cheeks hurt.

The telephone rang and Midge held up one finger. She answered it, then covered the mouthpiece as she turned toward Gina. She whispered, "It's for you. It's Jed."

Fear turned into a cold knot in Gina's stomach and her grin faded. She reached for the phone and held it to her ear, then said in as cheerful a voice as she could muster, "Jed! It's been ages! How are you?"

"Fine," came the response, then there was an awkward pause before he continued. "I hate to be the bearer of bad news, but we need to talk. Is now a good time?"

She glanced at Midge, who was pretending to be busy doing nothing, within earshot, but not obtrusive. She turned away from her friend and said, "It's as good a time as any. What's up?"

"I'm sure you've heard that Milton passed away."

"I did. Such horrible news." Her grip tightened on the handset.

"Yes, well, he lived a good life. We were blessed to have him with us for as long as we did." Another awkward pause, then he continued, "As you might have expected, I'm handling the estate and helping his widow handle things."

Before she could stop herself, she blurted, "Not wasting any time." Her hand flew to her mouth, horrified at the words that escaped. Milton had been so kind to her, and Jed was just doing his job.

He cleared his throat. "No. No, she's not. Feeling a bit like she needs to tackle everything head on. Milton had a good heart. He was a kind man. Generous to a fault. And that brings me to the reason for my call."

Uh, oh, she thought, here it comes. She leaned against the counter, her knees trembling. The remainder of the conversation turned into a sloggy mess in her mind, something about the widow being left with a ton of debt, going to be kicked out of her house if she didn't do something soon, the kids were involved and pushing her to do something about some of the generous deals Milton had done for people in the little town of Wilder.

Jed assured her she shouldn't feel bad because Milton had done other deals like hers, rents that amounted to a pittance to help out the tenants. Not only did she still feel bad, there was the added sting that she wasn't special. Jed apologized profusely for having to be the bearer of bad news, but was blunt about the fact that Milton had offered her the store location at a reduced rent in order to help her get on her feet, and she had done that.

The store was doing well and Jed knew it. His wife spent a lot of money there, as did both of his ex-wives and his teenage daughter.

By the time she hung up, she had taken one major point from the conversation that kept repeating in her head over and over, like a warning or a bad dream.

Her rent was jumping by a few hundred dollars a month. She could either accept it, or move. The choice was hers.

After Midge assured Gina she could handle things, Gina left for the hardware store. The thought of losing the cheap rent weighed heavily on her mind. She needed to come up with a way to increase business, fast. It was simple economics. The inflow had to be greater than the outflow, and her outflow was about to increase.

A tiny, nagging voice - that sounded a lot like her mother - pecked away at her. *You should have known rent would go up eventually. You should have been paying rent into a savings account so you'd be prepared for a rainy day. Rainy days always come along.*

Gina sighed. Between extra expenses like the broken dishwasher, her beater of a car and her increase in rent, she felt like a storm was on the horizon. A big, nasty, ugly storm.

She shook the negative thoughts out of her head. It didn't do any good to sit around and whine. Instead, action was needed. She needed to drum up business, get the current customers excited about new techniques and products, and get new customers in the door. Getting folks in the door was half the battle. If she could get them in the door, they'd buy something.

Most of the time.

She had to up her game at the store. The holidays were simple to plan for, but she needed to take it a step further. Her eyes flared as she looked at July. Of course! Christmas in July! She could do a Winter Wonderland crop, complete with fake snow. It'd be the perfect event in the middle of a hot, humid, Missouri summer. And - Bonus! - that would give her two special events in July, which was usually a slow sales month. She could do an Independence Day crop. Again, she felt inspiration strike.

She pulled into a parking space, plucked her phone from her purse and dialed.

"Midge? Gina."

She was greeted with Midge's giggle. "I knew it was you. What's up?"

"Is your neighbor still the president of the parent-teacher organization?"

"Yeah." Midge's voice dripped with suspicion. "Why?"

"And is Glenda Collins still the FHA sponsor at the high school?"

"Yeah," Midge repeated, drawing the word out.

"You got Glenda's number? I'm thinking we need to do an Independence Day crop. All weekend long. We'll provide baby-sitters and—"

"Great idea! I bet Glenda's work out something to give the FHA girls some kind of credit for doing it. Freebie for you!"

"Oh, my gosh! Midge, that's brilliant!"

"I know. You want to call her, or do you want me to?"

"I'll call her, but would you call your neighbor and see if she'd promote it to the mothers in the PTO?"

"Will do."

Gina ended the call and dialed the FHA sponsor. She didn't know the other woman well, but took a deep breath and prepared to grovel. The sponsor's voice came over the line, electronic and not available. Gina left a message. Gina was always thinking she needed to focus on marketing and build the business, but she was so busy, well, with everything. Being a mom. Working. She was so busy making ends meet that she never looked forward.

And now she felt the wolf sniffing at the door.

Paying rent would be difficult, but what were her options? Without a store, what would she do? There wasn't much work available in Wilder. Could she find a job? Just the thought of having to find a job made her stomach churn. Owning her own business gave her the freedom she needed to be there when Toby needed her. If she worked for someone else, she couldn't do that.

There had to be other events she could plan, to build business, to breathe new life into the store, to draw in new customers. But that would have to wait. She grabbed the old motor out of her passenger seat and hurried into the hardware store.

That evening, she stood in her kitchen watching Aidan replace the front panel on her dishwasher. When he'd tightened the last screw, he pushed to his feet and looked down at her. His t-shirt hugged his muscles. Without his cowboy hat, she could see his brilliant blue eyes clearly. She'd never seen eyes like that on a man with such dark hair, and it was incredibly sexy because it was so unexpected.

He swiped his hands together. "All fixed." He glanced at her, then busied himself stowing his tools in his case.

She pressed her lips together and stuffed her hands in her pockets. "What do I owe you?" He looked so natural standing there in her kitchen. Maybe she was ready for a man in her life.

His voice dropped to a husky whisper. "A date." He turned to face her. He gazed into her eyes, then took a step toward her.

She hadn't been on a date in so long, she could barely remember what they were like.

He reached out and cupped her cheek in his hand. "I'd really like to get to know you better."

She swallowed hard, nodded, then raised up on her toes as he lowered his head. Their lips met and she pressed her body against his. Feeling playful, she flicked her tongue against his lips. He groaned and pulled her closer.

"Hey, Mom, I need a drink of water."

Gina stepped back and blinked away the fog of desire. "Okay, sweetie." She opened the cabinet door and pulled out a plastic cup.

She glanced over her shoulder to see Toby staring up at Aidan with round eyes. "You're the cowboy that let me ride the steer."

Aidan's eyes widened and he looked quickly at Gina. Toby still had a band-aid on his chin from the tumble he took. Aidan shifted from foot to foot under her gaze.

Gina handed the cup to Toby. "Okay, drink up, then you need to get back to bed."

Toby tipped the glass up and drained it. He started to put it on the counter, then stopped and looked at the dishwasher and the tools scattered on the countertop. He turned and fixed his gaze on Aidan. "Mom said we can't afford to fix the dishwasher. Did you fix it?"

Aidan nodded. Gina blushed at her son's confession.

Toby frowned, forming twin furrows between his big, blue eyes. "Okay, you can stay." Abruptly, he turned around and disappeared down the hallway.

Gina's mouth dropped open. Life was so simple for Toby. She wished that were so for her, too. She turned back to Aidan and shrugged. "Kids, huh?"

He nodded toward the hallway. "I haven't been around many kids, but he seems okay."

She studied his face. He had to be weighing whether or not to date her, given the fact that she had a child. A relationship with her was more complicated than most.

He swept his hat off the counter and settled it on his head. "I should get going." He glanced at the hallway. "Not keep Toby awake."

She reached out and touched his forearm. It was firm and well-muscled, covered in a dusting of dark hair. "He said you can stay."

Aidan's mouth quirked up. "I know, but he's probably got to get up and go to daycare and you probably have to get up and go to work, just like I do."

She dropped her hand and caught her lower lip with her teeth. He was right. She hoped that was all it was. "I'll see you at the barbecue, though, right?"

His lips parted in a full-grown grin, deepening his dimples. "Absolutely." He bent and brushed his lips against hers, then pulled back and looked deep into her eyes. He took her hand in his and ran his thumb over the back of hers. "I'm looking forward to it."

CHAPTER TWENTY-ONE
Money

Gina'd given Midge the day off, but Midge appeared shortly after 12 noon with a paper bag from McDonald's. She plopped it on the center counter and pulled two sandwiches out, and slid one across the counter toward Gina.

Gina grinned, "What? No fries?"

Midge winked and pulled out two small fries, "Of course I got fries. One for you, one for me. And they are small, off the value menu, so no guilt whatsoever."

Gina reached under the counter and yanked two paper towels off the roll, kept one and handed the other to Midge. As the two caught up, Gina continued to jot notes. Midge reached across and tapped Gina's notes.

"Looks like you've been doing a lot of planning and figuring." Midge arched her thin eyebrows and said, "Well? What's the verdict?"

"It's not good. I've got sixty days and then my rent jumps up to five hundred bucks a month." She shrugged, thinking that the rent might as well be a million dollars a month, even though, as Jed so politely and helpfully pointed out, that included all utilities.

Midge whistled softly. "Okay, so, that means we've got some planning to do."

Gina rolled her eyes, "It doesn't matter how much planning we do. I can't do it. I'm going to lose the store unless I come up with another revenue stream." Her shoulders drooped under the weight of worry.

Midge grabbed Gina by the arm and looked her in the eye. "Listen to me and you listen good. You are not going to lose this store. Not without a fight. We're going to tackle this like we do every other problem that life throws at us."

Gina shrugged. "And how is that?"

"With vodka," Midge declared. "Tonight is Steve's night to have Toby, right?"

Gina nodded, unable to suppress the ghost of a smile that threatened to break out into a real grin. She'd kept quiet about Aidan, afraid she might jinx things by talking about it.

Midge continued with her head held high. "Then tonight we plan. I'll be at your house at 7. You order the pizza."

Gina shook her head, but she couldn't help but be buoyed by her friend's enthusiasm. "Pepperoni with extra cheese?" Perhaps there was a way to make this happen. Maybe, just maybe, she just needed to be a little more creative, work a little harder, expand the store's offerings.

"Just wait and see what I come up with." Midge's blue eyes narrowed and she pressed her thin lips together, then pushed to her feet and walked toward the store room. On her way through the swinging door, she hollered out, "Can you handle the place on your own for the rest of the day?"

She disappeared through the back without waiting for a response, then Gina heard the back door open and close. In spite of herself, a smile curled her lips. How could she fail with friends like that?

The rest of the day was a struggle for Gina. She felt pushy with every customer, and worried she was smothering them with attention. Every sale seemed to carry the weight of the store, and she greeted each customer at the cash register with the refrain, "Do you need any adhesives with this today?"

To her surprise, it worked. Nearly all of the customers said yes. It wasn't a big sale, but every little bit helped. Perhaps she really could do it, if she just took the time to strategize a bit more. This was a simple thing, and it worked. Suddenly, she couldn't wait for the day to end so she could get home, see Toby off and get to the heart of planning and brainstorming with Midge.

When the clock chimed six that evening, there was one customer left in the store. There was a note of irony in that it was Jed's second ex-wife. She was young, had been way too young for him right from the start, and was already seeing someone else. Her new someone else was active in motorcycle racing, the motocross kind of stuff, and she was searching for embellishments for an album she was doing for him. Gina chatted with Sarah for a few minutes as they held up various ribbons and buttons to the dirt track crisscrossed papers that Gina had ordered in special for Sara.

A flash of inspiration hit Gina and she exclaimed, "I've got it!"

She led Sarah to the opposite side of the store where she pointed out some Tim Holtz grunge paper, Distress Inks and some Distress Stickles, all in grungy colors like dark browns and greens. Gina said, "This'll add texture and color to your layouts — it'll highlight the dirt, not cover it!"

Sarah picked up several items from the Tim Holtz line and dropped them into the basket hooked over her arm. She grinned. "Gina, I know I tell you this all the time, but you are so talented! You have such an eye for design!"

Together, the two women walked to the center island with the cash register. Sarah sat her purchases on the counter, then pulled her billfold out of her Michael Kors purse. Gina rang the items up, hesitated just a moment, and asked, "Do you need any adhesive with this?"

Sarah smacked herself in the forehead with an open palm, and pulled two adhesive refills off of the revolving rack on the corner of the counter. She said, "I almost forgot! See, you think of everything! I'd forget my head if it wasn't attached."

They finished the transaction, Sarah left and Gina locked the door behind her. She finished closing out the store in record time, put the cash in the drop safe in the back office then dashed out the back door. She set the alarm and locked the door behind her, then jogged down the alley to where her car was parked on the side street. It only took her ten minutes to get home, one of the advantages of living in a small town like Wilder.

CHAPTER TWENTY-TWO
The Watch

Gina unlocked her back door and walked into the kitchen. Sandy and Toby were at the kitchen table, playing a game of Chutes and Ladders. Toby slid off his seat and ran to greet her, wrapping his arms around her and squeezing with all his might. She felt her heart melt as he whispered in her ear, "I love you, Mom."

Her little boy was growing up. He had stopped calling her Mommy shortly after he started Kindergarten. The good part about him getting bigger was that she didn't worry about him quite as much when he went with Steve. At least she trusted him to call her now if Steve did something inappropriate. At the thought of Steve, she glanced up at the clock on the microwave.

6:42 p.m.

He was late again. He was supposed to have been over to pick Toby up at 6:30. Of course, she was late, too, and given that fact, she was glad her ex was running late so she could have a few precious moments with her son before he left for his overnight with his daddy.

157

As if conjured by her thoughts, the back door swung open and Steve stepped into the kitchen. Toby pulled away from her and ran toward his daddy, then wrapped his arms around Steve's legs in a hug. Steve didn't bend to meet him, nor did he hug his son. Instead, he patted the boy on the back. She knew he loved his son, and for that she was thankful, but wished he was more demonstrative about it. Men showed affection differently, though. She knew that.

But she didn't understand it.

Steve said, "Go get your backpack, buddy."

Sandy scooted her chair back from the table and began putting the game away.

Steve took a step toward Gina, then laid an envelope on the kitchen counter and slid it toward her. He murmured, "Toby told me about the dishwasher. Here's a little extra to help out."

She frowned and took the envelope, then lifted the flap and looked inside. She flipped through a stack of hundred dollar bills and her eyes flew to Steve's. He was grinning that same lop-sided grin that had first attracted her to him. Her eyes narrowed as she looked at the money again, then back at him. A reflection on his wrist caught her eye. He was wearing a watch.

An expensive looking, very nice watch.

Not the crappy Velcro strap thing from Wal-Mart that he usually wore.

"Where'd you get this?" she demanded, pointing at the watch.

"Job I did," he said, the grin fading. He looked away.

She narrowed her eyes and cocked her head. "What kind of job?"

Sandy grabbed her purse off the floor by the coat tree, hurried toward the door, apparently anxious to escape the tension building in the room, and said, "I need to get going. Tell Toby—"

Toby appeared in the doorway and asked, "Tell me what?"

Sandy blew him a kiss and said, "I'll see you Friday, okay?"

The little boy's chubby cheeks turned pink and he waved her kiss off. "Friday."

Sandy stepped out the back door and pulled it shut behind her. Toby walked over to stand next to his daddy. Gina looked at Steve, still clutching the envelope in her hand, but he kept his focus on Toby. He bent down and asked Toby about his day. Suddenly, his little boy was the most important thing in the world. And that made her even more suspicious.

She cleared her throat. "Toby, why don't you go check and make sure your bedroom is picked up?"

He frowned at her. "It is."

She leaned forward, hands on her knees, so she was looking at him face to face at his height and said, "Just go check for me, okay?"

He dropped his backpack on the floor and flapped his arms in an exasperated expression, then stomped off down the hallway. As soon as he was out of the kitchen, Gina cocked one hand on her hip and said, "Okay, spill it, Steve."

He did his best to look innocent, but didn't quite pull it off. Gina had known him too long to fall for that. He said, "What do you mean, babe? I just wanted to help out."

She frowned, but picked up the envelope of money and tucked it into her purse. Given her current financial situation, she couldn't look a gift horse in the mouth.

At least not yet.

CHAPTER TWENTY-THREE
Old Trucks

Aidan stepped on the gas and the old Chevy hesitated, motor revving, but the wheels didn't move. It finally clunked into gear and lurched forward. Beau glanced sideways at him.

Aidan kept his eyes forward, but felt Beau's eyes on him. He worked so hard to do things without relying on his family's money. The last thing he wanted to do was dig into his trust fund to fix his pickup. He could imagine his father's reaction, could hear his father's deep voice. Just go buy a new truck. His chest rose and fell with a sigh. He hadn't dug into his trust account yet, and didn't want to start now, unless it was for something big like his own place.

Gina's little boy had made a comment about Gina not being able to afford to fix the dishwasher. That was rough. He was glad he'd been able to fix it for her. He'd thought about buying her a new one, but she seemed proud. It must be tough to be a single mother, especially running her own business.

He knew he was lucky to have a safety net, but he liked his old truck. It fit him. But like it or not, the thing needed work. Major work. And his salary as a ranch hand didn't allow him to save much.

His thoughts returned to Gina. He felt a strong attraction to her. There had been a definite spark when they kissed. He looked forward to getting to know her better, but he was worried about the instant family. Was he prepared for that, if things got serious?

Beau finally broke the silence, and said, "You know Cletus in town works wonders on automatic transmissions. Bet he could rebuild this one for you for a good price."

CHAPTER TWENTY-FOUR
Girls' Night Out

The evening began with Midge mixing dirty martinis for them, then they moved into the living room, both sitting with their legs curled under them. Midge had brought a legal pad and she jotted notes as they brainstormed ways to improve customer traffic in the store. They came up with some great ideas, including monetizing their blog, setting up a store on Etsy, and having an overnight fundraiser for the 4-H club – that would bring in parents and club members, plus they would get exposure in local media that wouldn't cost the store a dime.

"Smart idea!" Gina exclaimed when Midge explained the idea. She tipped her glass up and emptied it, then held it up to the light. "And so was this!"

Midge grinned, "I know. But I was afraid we might forget some of our great ideas, which is why I brought along this." She pointed to the legal pad in her lap.

"I knew I liked you for some reason," Gina said.

Midge laughed. "You like me 'cause I can mix a mean dirty martini."

"Yeah, you do." Her voice trailed off when she noticed Midge's watch reflect the light. It reminded her of Steve's watch. "Hey, have you heard any rumors lately about Steve?"

Midge's grin faded and her voice grew serious. "What kind of rumors?"

Gina stood up and took her friend's glass, giving herself time to decide how much to share with her friend. She opted to procrastinate. "Here, I'll refill our drinks."

She walked into the kitchen and poured the remaining contents of the cocktail shaker into their martini glasses. She handed Midge her glass, sat her glass down, then went to the kitchen and pulled the envelope of cash out of her purse. She sat down on the couch, opened the envelope and riffled the bills.

Midge's eyes about popped out of her head. She stared at the cash, then at Gina. "Where the heck did you get that? You didn't rob a bank or something, did you?"

Gina muttered, "No, but I'm worried that Steve might have."

Midge's brows knit together and she asked, "Seriously?"

Gina put the cash back in the envelope, tapped it thoughtfully against her hand and said, "No, I don't think he'd ever rob a bank, but I've got to wonder what he's into. He told me the other night that he had a job to do. Then he showed up tonight with this stack of cash for me—"

Midge interrupted, "How much, if you don't mind me asking?"

Gina said, "A thousand bucks."

"Wow." Midge's eyes widened as she took a sip of her martini.

Gina said, "I'm afraid he did something stupid."

Midge narrowed her eyes and looked at Gina, then said, "And?"

Gina sighed and chewed on her lip a moment as she considered what to say. How much to say. She said, "And he was wearing what looked like a very expensive watch tonight."

Midge laughed, then pointed at her purse. "See that? Fake Coach. I picked it up at a flea market off of I-44. And my daddy still has the Rolex that Mom got him when she was in New York City a few years ago – on a street corner for twenty bucks."

Gina blushed and said, "I know. There are fakes all over the place. But this looked real."

Midge pursed her lips and shrugged. "Maybe it was real. He definitely got an infusion of cash from somewhere." She nodded toward the cash in Gina's hand.

Gina stared at Midge's fake designer purse and murmured, "But where?"

Midge pushed to her feet and held out her hand. "Doesn't matter where he got the money."

Gina took her friend's hand and let herself be pulled to her feet. "What do you mean it doesn't matter? It does to me." Her eyebrows pulled low over her eyes as she dropped Midge's hand.

"It shouldn't. He's your ex. It's time to put him behind you." Midge slung her purse over her shoulder, then snagged Gina's off the floor and handed it to her.

"Especially now that you've got that dark, sexy hunk of cowboy sniffin' after you."

Gina arched one eyebrow doubtfully, but took the handbag. "What are we doing?"

"We've done enough work for one night. It's time for a change of scenery." Her eyes sparkled with mischief. "We're going to the Come On Inn for a drink."

Gina started to shake her head, but Midge held up her hand, palm out. Gina sucked in a deep breath and let it out in a whoosh. She had been stressing for days. A break would be good.

A gentle spring breeze ruffled their hair as they walked downtown. The leaves on the trees were beginning to bud, flowers brightened front yards, and birds chirped. Gina took a deep breath, enjoying the light scent of the peonies blooming in the recycled tires in the town square. The last rays of the sun slanted behind them, making their shadows long and thin.

As they passed the cafe, a waitress waved at them through the glass door as she flipped the sign to closed and twisted the lock. A handful of pickups were parked in front of the Come On Inn, but most of the parking spaces around the square were empty.

Midge pulled the door open and motioned for Gina to go first. The two walked across the wooden floor, skirting the little corral that housed the mechanical bull, and sat at a tall table near the bar. It was still early, and the bar was mostly empty. Country music filtered through the speakers.

Fluffy, the owner, slung a white towel over his shoulder

166

and leaned across the bar. "What can I get you girls?" His voice boomed through the space.

Midge held up two fingers and called back, "Chocolate martinis."

The huge, doughy man behind the counter rolled his eyes and muttered, "Girls." He pulled out a cocktail shaker and began mixing ingredients, all the while shaking his head.

The waitress delivered their drinks. Gina reached for her purse, but Midge put out a hand to stop her. She looked up at the waitress. "It's been a rough day. Better just start a tab for us."

As they watched the little brunette return to the bar, Gina sighed. "That girl can't be old enough to serve."

Midge giggled. "They get younger all the time, don't they?"

Gina took a sip of her drink, then rolled her eyes up to the ceiling. "Mmmm. That is really, really good."

Midge took a sip and nodded in agreement. "So, are you feeling better after we figured out a plan of action?"

Gina caught her bottom lip in her teeth. She was still worried, but that was par for the course for her. Even when things were good, she worried, but she pushed those thoughts down. "Yes, I am. The store has always done better than I thought it would."

Midge propped one elbow on the table and cupped her chin in one hand. "So, on to other things. Don't look now, but your cowboy just walked in the door."

Gina's head swiveled around and her eyes immediately focused on the tall, dark man strolling toward them.

Another guy, a couple of inches shorter and a bit broader, followed in his wake. Her eyes met Aidan's and her mouth dropped open. A smile spread across his face and he tapped the brim of his black hat with his finger. He changed trajectory and approached their table.

"Hey," he drawled, stopping right beside her, less than a foot away. She could practically feel the electric charge jumping between their bodies. He tapped the table. "Can I buy you ladies a drink?"

Gina started to shake her head. "No, we're—"

"Sure," Midge interrupted. "We're drinking chocolate martinis."

He laughed, a deep, pleasant sound, then turned toward the bar. He raised his voice to be heard over the jukebox. "Hey, Fluffy! Two more chocolate martinis for the ladies."

The bear of a man behind the bar nodded and went to work.

"Thank you," Gina murmured.

Midge nudged a chair out with her foot and nodded toward it. "Want to join us?"

"For a minute." He slid into the chair then cocked his head toward the bar. "My buddy Joe is on the phone. I'll give him a few minutes to finish. Did you have a busy day at the scrapbook store?" He spoke to both of them, but his focus lingered on Gina.

Her eyes widened as she looked into those electric blue eyes. "Pretty busy." She motioned at Midge. "We've been talking about the store, drumming up business." She closed her eyes and cursed herself. How boring could she sound? It was bad enough that their time together so far had been spent repairing a broken appliance.

He grinned at her. "Bet you don't have any trouble drumming up business. You're a talented woman. Beth loved the invitations -- I think I forgot to tell you that. She mailed them out that afternoon, and had Joe and me deliver a bunch more in person."

"Good. I'm glad she liked them." Gina's breath came in quick little gasps. All she could think about was how it had felt to be close to him, the feel of his heartbeat, his powerful arms around her.

The waitress brought them their drinks, and both women thanked him. With a start, Gina realized that her friend had already drained her first one. She'd been so distracted by Aidan that hers was still half full.

Aidan leaned closer to her. "I'm looking forward to seeing you at the barbecue this weekend."

"Me, too." Gina stared up at him. He winked and she felt her entire body turn to mush. She managed to squeak out, "Looking forward to it."

The other cowboy scooted off his barstool and strode across to their table. He placed his hand on Aidan's shoulder. "Got some bad news, bud."

Aidan pushed to his feet, his smile fading instantly. "What's up?"

"It's Claude Krampton. His whole herd is gone."

Aidan's eyes narrowed and the muscles in his jaw worked. "What do you mean, gone?"

"Stolen."

Gina looked at Midge and raised her eyebrows. That didn't sound good.

Aidan cursed, then glanced at Midge and Gina. "Sorry." He glanced at the other cowboy. "Let's get out there. Maybe the rustlers missed some."

Aidan spun on his heel and took a step, then stopped and looked over his shoulder. He tipped his hat at Gina and smiled. "Sorry to run out on you like this. Can I make it up to you Saturday?"

She nodded and watched as he walked away. A gust of spring air swept into the bar as they pushed out the door.

"You know, usually when I say 'What an ass,' it's not a compliment." Midge reached across and poked Gina in the shoulder. "But with him, it is most definitely a compliment."

CHAPTER TWENTY-FIVE
The Orphan

Aidan stuck the fencing pliers in his back pocket after he'd tightened the last strand of woven wire to the corner post. Claude waved from cab of the tractor as he pulled up. "Thanks for your help! Woulda taken me all night to check this fence. Want a ride up to the house and then I'll run you home?"

"Sure." Aidan grabbed hold of the fender, stuck his booted foot in the metal stirrup and swung up next to Claude. The older man eased his foot off the clutch and the tractor lurched forward. Aidan held on tight and let his body sway with the movement. Claude wheeled the machine around and headed down the hill toward the old white farmhouse. As the bright headlight swept across the tree line, two eyes reflected the light. They were small and close together, about half the height of the woven wire fence.

Aidan grasped the older man's shoulder to get his attention, then pointed into the darkness. He shouted to be heard over the tractor's engine. "There were eyes in those trees. Can you swing back that way?"

Claude slowed the machine and spun the wheel back to the left. The eyes were still there, glowing in the darkness. Bert shouted, "Coyote?"

Aidan shook his head. "Nope. Coyote would've run by now. Stop for a sec."

Claude stepped on the clutch in and the tractor rolled to a stop. Aidan dropped to the ground, then walked cautiously toward the eyes. Mountain lions had been spotted in the area over the past couple of years, but he'd never seen one himself. That didn't mean he took the risk lightly, though. He walked carefully, heel to toe, quiet, but ready to run if the animal lunged at him. The eyes were round and bright. Not narrow like a coyote or a wild dog. They blinked at him, still reflecting the bright light from the John Deere.

As he got close, he heard a sound in the tall grass ahead of him. A low, sad moo.

"Shit!" He hurried forward as fast as he dared, not wanting to scare the creature. If it was what he thought it was . . .

The eyes turned away, then back. He slowed down. Crept forward. As he moved, a dark shape emerged from the shadows, a lump that slowly turned into a body with legs. The big ears swiveled forward and back, barely discernible in the moonlight. The round eyes remained focused on him.

"Easy, there." Aidan made cooing noises and the animal made a bleating sound, almost like a sheep. He reached out and touched the young calf and it cried out, scared to death, frozen by fear. "You all alone out here, huh? Those bad men took your mama, didn't they?"

He scooped the calf up in his arms and lifted it with a grunt. It weighed little more than a full sack of grain, probably not even a hundred pounds. Couldn't be more than a day old. He stepped carefully, and held the calf close. The little thing's heart beat a staccato rhythm against his chest.

Claude jumped down from the tractor and met him when he grew close. "Holy cow!"

Aidan laughed. "Not holy cow - baby cow!"

Claude's yellowed teeth showed as his lips split into a grin. "I've still got a cow."

"That you do."

Claude held out his arms. "Want me to take 'im and you can drive the tractor up?"

Aidan shook his head. "I've got him. He's not heavy at all. Meet you up at the barn."

The calf struggled in his arms, bucking and kicking. One of the little hooves connected with his left knee and Aidan pitched forward into the dirt, dropping the little guy in the process. Aidan was on all fours and tipped his head up. The animal looked him in the eye, opened his mouth and bawled. It began as an angry sound, but ended in a pitiful, mournful moo. The calf blinked one big brown eye, then lowered its head and sighed. Its front legs were braced wide and it shivered, in spite of the warm temperatures. Aidan's shirt stuck to him, but the night breeze was crisp and cool where his skin was slick with sweat.

Aidan gathered his feet under him and stayed at eye

level with the calf. He held out his hand, palm down. The calf snorted, watching him warily, then let out a plaintive sound. The animal took one wobbly step forward. Aidan rubbed the creature's nose, which was soft as velvet and warm to the touch. The calf took his fingers in its mouth and began sucking eagerly.

"How long have you been out here alone?" Aidan asked. He gathered the calf into his arms and straightened his legs, lifting the critter as easily as a sack of grain. He hurried toward the barn, worried that the calf might've been alone for several hours. The way it sucked on his fingers tugged at his heartstrings. The animal continued to shiver in his arms, but quit struggling, which made the trek to the barn easier than the first part of the trip had been.

The big barn door stood wide open, spilling yellow light into the barn lot. The tractor was parked inside, and Claude waited at the open door, peering into the darkness. He brightened and hurried toward Aidan.

Claude held out his arms, "I can take him."

Aidan shook his head. "I got 'im. Where do you want the little guy?"

Claude motioned toward the barn. "Just get him inside for now. We can put him in one of the stalls for now." He slid a stall door open with a squeal of metal on metal.

Aidan stepped into the stall and leaned down to set the animal down.

Claude grabbed a bucket from the hook on the wall and said, "I'll go get him fresh water."

Aidan frowned. The calf was young. Without its mama,

it'd have a tough row to hoe. Claude returned with the pail and offered it to the animal. The calf stuck his nose in it and snuffled, but didn't seem to drink much. It nudged Aidan with its nose.

Claude examined the animal. "It's a girl. Maybe a day or two old. Haven't even had a chance to put an ear tag in yet."

Aidan said, "You got milk replacer to feed her?"

The old farmer shook his head. "Not here. I'll go to town and get some first thing in the morning. Guess the wife and I can take turns feeding her every couple of hours. Too bad she's not a little older. Stronger." His features pulled downward as if the gravity of the situation was too much for him.

The calf stood in the center of the stall, looking very small, with its legs braced wide. Her big ears shook. Aidan reached out and stroked one of her velvety red ears and she made a mewling sound, then turned her head and butted his hand. He ran his hand over her face and she took his thumb in her mouth and began to suck hungrily.

Aidan sighed and looked at Claude. The older man looked miserable. His eyes were sunken and dark, and the corners of his mouth drooped. He ran a hand through his hair, leaving a shock of thinning gray sticking up. Poor man had aged ten years in a very short time.

Aidan turned his attention to the shivering animal in front of him, still sucking on his thumb. He couldn't remember if they had any milk replacer back at the Diamond J or not, but even if they didn't, either Beau or Charlotte would be able to whip something up.

"Listen," Aidan began, "Why don't I take this calf home and take care of her. I'm pretty sure we got milk replacer back at the Ranch."

Claude cocked his head to the side and rubbed the gray stubble on his chin.

Aidan could see his old friend waffling, and assured him, "It's no trouble at all. And you got enough other things on your mind right now."

Claude glanced over his shoulder, in the general direction of the house. He said doubtfully, "The wife hasn't been feeling very good here lately. It'd be hard for us to take care of a bottle calf right now."

Aidan took that as a go-ahead and scooped the little calf up in his arms again. As they walked toward the door, Claude cleared his throat. "Can't tell you how much this means to me. Ain't as young as I used to be. Those middle of the night feedings—"

"It's no trouble at all," Aidan said. He'd been dragging animals home to nurse back to health since he was a kid. A bottle calf'd be fun.

And it'd be a great excuse to invite Gina and her little boy out for a visit. With a jolt, he realized how natural it felt to include her son in the thought. Maybe he truly was ready to settle down.

The calf snuggled in the passenger floorboard of Aidan's old truck. Aidan shivered a bit in the late night air. He'd given up his shirt to wrap around the baby, but it was worth it as he glanced down at those big brown eyes that blinked back at him, curious and trusting.

"No worries, Lil' Bit." Aidan flipped the heat on low. "I

lost my mama, too. You're gonna miss her, but trust me —
you'll be okay."

He pushed the power button and the latest Rhett Butler
song came on the radio. The calf's head wavered a bit, as if
her neck wasn't strong enough to support the weight. Her
large eyes blinked slowly, then she snorted and laid her
head on the hump between the foot wells. He grinned as
he turned his attention to the road and pointed his truck
back toward the Diamond J.

She slept until he pulled into the driveway and parked.
He slid out of the truck and hurried around the front of the
vehicle, then carefully opened the passenger door. The calf
woke with a start and let out a sharp cry as she jumped
and kicked furiously, instantly in preservation mode.

Aidan dodged the hard little hooves and spoke to her in
a low, soothing voice. Gradually she calmed enough that
he was able to stroke her. She swung her head around and
looked at him as he gathered her in his arms. She
struggled weakly, then seemed to accept her fate. She was
surprisingly strong, given her size, but he could feel the
underlying weakness. Adrenalin fueled her, but that
wouldn't last long. She needed nourishment and warmth
if she was going to survive.

He strode across the gravel toward the barn, his boots
crunching in the rock. He ducked into the barn, glanced
into a stall to make sure it was empty, then lowered the
calf to the ground. Horses snuffled and snorted at the
sounds and scent of the newcomer. Before he could slide
the door open, the calf scrambled away, legs going every
which way. Aidan's head swiveled from the getaway artist

to the empty stall, then back again. The little critter didn't know where she was going, but she was determined to go.

One of the horses whinnied shrilly as if urging her on. Her hooves scrabbled in the dirt, kicking up tiny puffs of dust. She bumped into walls, but headed in the general direction of the big open door.

"Damn!" Aidan cursed as he hurried after her. She was surprisingly fast and he broke into a jog. She slowed when she reaching the gaping darkness of the doorway. Aidan took advantage of her hesitation and lunged for her. She ducked away from him, set her feet in the dirt and cut the other direction. He zigged, she zagged. He stumbled and caught himself before he sprawled in the dirt. He looked up just as the calf darted out the door.

He put one hand on the doorway and pushed off as he followed her. He blinked in the darkness and looked around. A grunt sounded to his right and he spun in the direction of the noise. Beau appeared out of the darkness, the struggling calf in his arms. She let out a plaintive moo, obviously irritated that her escape had been thwarted.

A smile split Beau's tanned face. "Does this escapee belong to you?"

Aidan's shoulders drooped and he nodded as he held out his hands to take the calf from his boss. "She was left behind after Claude's herd was stolen."

Beau's grin widened. "And you decided to take her in." It was a statement, not a question. He handed the calf off, then frowned as he leaned close to examine the baby.

Aidan shrugged. "I couldn't leave her there. Claude's already got so much on his mind, and he's too old to be up and down all night long feeding a bottle calf." Aidan hefted the calf in his arms to get a better hold on her. She snorted her irritation as he turned back toward the barn.

Beau fell in step beside him. "At least she looks healthy."

"Yeah, seems to be. She needs milk." Aidan stopped in front of the empty stall. "I was going to put her in here. That okay with you?"

"Sure," Beau said. He moved down the aisle and stepped up on the ladder. "I'll toss a bale of straw down for you."

Aidan stepped into the stall and set the calf down, careful to stay between her and the open door. As soon as she was down, he tugged the door closed to keep her from escaping again. He looked up as Beau appeared overhead.

"Heads up!" Beau called, then dropped the bale down. The calf jumped when the straw hit the ground with a thump. Her eyes widened and she backed into the corner until her hindquarters were wedged in tight.

The calf stood with her legs braced widely as she regarded the offending yellow cube with large, suspicious eyes. He pulled his pocket knife from his jeans pocket, flipped it open and cut the twine to release the straw. He closed the knife carefully and tucked it back in his pocket before pulling the bale apart. He shook the flakes open, creating a soft, warm bed for the little calf.

The door squeaked as Beau pulled it open. He slipped into the stall and handed Aidan a big plastic bottle. "Found this in the tack room. Thought you might be able to use it to feed your little munchkin."

Aidan took the offered bottle. "We got any milk replacer?"

Beau shook his head. "No, but I bet Charlotte's got whole milk in the 'fridge that could get her through the night, until you can get to town to get some real milk replacer. And give her a raw egg. It'll help with the stress."

Aidan nodded and looked at the calf with her huge eyes and heaving sides. She was scared. Her ears swiveled back and forth, quickly, taking in everything around her. "Good idea. Think she'll be warm enough out here tonight?"

Beau nodded. "I expect so. It's a warm summer night. Good thing this didn't happen a couple of months ago." He rolled the stall door open just wide enough for them to squeeze through.

After Aidan slipped out of the stall, the bottle tucked under his arm, he rolled the door shut and glanced in at the calf. He wasn't sure why he felt so responsible for the little critter, but he did. It brought back memories of being a kid, dragging home every stray kitten and puppy he ran across.

His smile faded as he remembered his father scoffing at him. Calling him a softie. Calling him Amy.

That's why he hadn't been home since his mother died nearly a decade ago. If he ever had a son, a boy like Toby, he would be a better father. He blinked as he realized for the first time in his adult life, he could see himself as a father.

With a smile, Aidan fell into step beside Beau and walked toward the big house and stepped through the side door. Aidan flipped on the light above the sink as

Beau said goodnight and strolled down the hall.

Aidan opened the refrigerator and stared at the half empty jug of milk. He pulled the jug out and examined it in the low light. Vitamin D milk. He was fairly certain that was the same thing as whole milk. He shrugged, poured the milk into a large Pyrex measuring cup then put it in the microwave. As he watched the cup spin as the machine whirred to life, he thought about the calf.

And Gina. He couldn't wait to tell her about the baby in the barn. Any excuse to see her again would do. A little thrill coursed through him at the thought of being near her again.

The microwave timer beeped and he quickly opened the door to stop the sound before he woke anyone in the house up. He touched the milk, then poured the milk in the bottle and hurried back out to the barn.

He slipped into the stall and knelt next to the quivering calf. Poor thing wasn't cold. She was scared. Wanted her mama, most likely. Missed the herd. He held out the bottle and offered her the nipple. After a few false starts, she nursed greedily, sucking and bumping and slurping. He grinned as he watched her drink. Not as good as mama's milk, but it would do in a pinch.

Thoughts shuffled through his brain. Gina. He couldn't get her out of his mind. What would she think of him doing this? Would she understand? Think he was soft, like his father did, or be impressed?

The calf bumped against the bottle, reminding him of the rustlers. They were the worst kind of criminals, dealing in live animals. He worried about the treatment the herd would receive. The only thing that gave him hope was that the animals wouldn't be of value if they didn't make it to the sale barn or butcher's. Maybe that would be enough incentive for the thieves to take care of the cattle.

His stomach churned as he thought of the poor animals packed in a cattle hauler. It bothered him enough when he and the boys had to haul cattle from the Diamond J in the stock trailer, and he knew they took every precaution to make sure the animals were cared for properly.

The calf bumped him hard again, drawing him back to the stall. She slurped at the empty bottle. All done. He stroked the calf's soft black fur for a few minutes, hesitant to leave her alone. Finally, fatigue took over as she dropped to her knees and lowered herself into the thick straw. He pushed himself to his feet and slipped out the door. He could fit in a few hours of sleep before she was ready to eat again.

CHAPTER TWENTY-SIX
The Barbecue

The day of the barbecue dawned bright and warm, a perfect summer day. Memorial Day weekend was always sweet, since it marked the beginning of summer, but this year it was more sweet than usual. Things had settled into a nice rhythm at the Diamond J over the past year. The passing of Jonathan Jameson, the founder of the Diamond J had been hard on everyone, but his daughter had proven herself - and won Beau's heart.

Aidan leaned against the back doorway of the barn and watched Beth standing at the corner of the deck. She'd grown into quite the rancher, smart with the horses and fair with the employees.

The night she learned she'd won her father's challenge, just a few weeks ago, Beau admitted his feelings for her. The memory of that night brought a smile to Aidan's lips. He'd been proud of his own contribution to Beth's success. It had been so much fun, the way Charlotte rounded everyone up. The crew had been unanimous in their support of the old man's daughter.

His eyes swept the crowd already gathered in the yard, looking for Gina. It was still early, but he was anxious to see her. He glanced across the yard at Beau, working the big barbecue grill (actually a barrel that they had jerry-rigged into a barbecue grill), and had to suppress a grin when Beth whipped Beau's cowboy hat off and stuck a chef's hat on his head. Instead of reacting with anger or embarrassment, he took it in stride, with a big grin, totally hamming it up.

He let her get away with things that no one else could even come close to getting away with. He even wore the red and white checkered apron that proclaimed in blazing red letters "Caution – Man Cooking" with little fire extinguishers all over it that she'd given him for Christmas.

He stood at the side of the yard on a little hillock, so he could have a full view of the picnickers. While looking for Gina, he noticed Katie, the neighbor's daughter, sitting in a metal chair with the ice cream freezer between her feet. She was bent over, turning the crank, her pony-tail falling to one side of her face and nearly touching the ice. He walked over to her.

Aidan asked, "Home for the summer?"

"Yup." She turned her head and looked up at him, then blew a piece of hair out of her face. She raised her eyebrows and said, "Finished finals up earlier this month."

"Junior year?"

She grinned. "A senior now. Technically." A bead of sweat ran down the side of her face, dripped and landed on the wooden deck.

He glanced around, spotted a few concrete blocks stacked up beside the house. He grabbed a block in each hand, then walked back up the steps. He sat them down in front of Katie and the ice cream freezer.

She looked up at him, her eyebrows pinching together to form a frown. She asked, "What's that for?"

He grinned at her and asked, "Your back hurting?"

She grinned back and said, "Uh, yeah. Duh!"

"Try this." He squatted down and wrapped his arms around the ice cream freezer and lifted it. A light dawned on her face and she scrambled out of her seat and pulled the two concrete blocks into place in front of her.

"Okay!" She pointed. "You can put it down."

As he lowered the ice cream freezer with a grunt, she helped guide it into place, so it settled in perfectly on top of the concrete blocks. She sat back down, then turned the crank. She declared, "Perfect! Thank you!"

He grinned at her and motioned with his hand. "Anytime, Katie. Need me to do anything?"

"Yeah." She nodded in the direction of the side table beside her. "Could you add a little salt to the ice?"

"Sure." He picked up the bag of rock salt. He lifted the towel off the top of the freezer, tilted the bag and shook a little bit of salt in a circle around the metal freezer. "Want me to take over for a while?"

"Nah." She shook her head, then blew a strand of hair out of her face. "I'm good for now. Besides, don't you need to be looking for the gal that runs the scrapbook store?" She winked at him and grinned.

Warmth spread up his cheeks at the mention of Gina.

"How'd you know about---" He stopped himself. "Never mind. Just holler if you need help." He nodded to her, then looked around the group and spotted Charlotte moving among the crowd.

She was carrying a tray laden with bottles of dark brown bottles, most likely beer. He walked down the steps off the deck and onto the lawn, then headed out with an idea to intercept Charlotte and relieve her of one of those frosty beers. As he walked, his eyes swept the group for Gina's auburn ponytail.

He wove through clumps of people from town and loose knots of rodeo cowboys, most proudly displaying their big belt buckles. He nodded to those who he knew, clapped a few guys on their backs in greeting, heading in Charlotte's general direction, all the while scanning the crowd.

It was already hot, especially for late May, probably nearing 90 already and the humidity was probably about the same, and a cold beer would slide down the throat awful easy.

He felt a tug on his shirtsleeve and his heart flipped, hoping it was Gina. He smiled and turned to find a stocky cowboy, one of the team ropers that bought one of the Diamond J mares late last summer. "Hey, Marty, how's it going?" He held out his hand and the other man shook it heartily.

The cowboy's wide face broke into a crooked grin, "Hey, Aidan! It's goin' good! How're you, man?" He was a few inches shorter than Aidan, built like a bulldog, wide and muscular.

"Good, good. How's the mare working out for you?"

Aidan asked.

The man's grin widened. "She's a peach, she is! Works great. It's like she anticipates what I need her to do. Great disposition." He hooked his thumbs in his front pockets.

Aidan matched Marty's grin. "Cali's definitely a good horse. Glad she's working out for you." He'd liked the cowboy as soon as he'd met him, impressed with the man's gentle way with the horses he'd looked at.

Marty's grin faded to a smile and he shook his head, "She's more than just workin' out. Thanks to her we been in the running for the money in every rodeo we've done. Poor old Ghost had gotten old enough, he couldn't keep up. He deserved to take it easy in the pasture for a while. Been team ropin' now for nigh on eight years with Scotty Busch, and Ghost was with me well before me and Scotty hooked up."

"That's longer than you've ever stayed with a woman!" Aidan said, as he clapped the other cowboy on the shoulder. The two men had a good laugh, then Aidan continued, "I saw you and Scotty ropin' at the rodeo down in Joplin last July. You two work together real well."

Marty nodded and said, "That we do, that we do. And me an' Scotty work together pretty good, too." He winked.

Aidan laughed and said, "You and Scotty've been ropin' together a long time. You *should* work together well."

Marty said, "You know, Scotty's real impressed with Cali and his gelding, Buck, is gettin' up in years. Gonna need a new horse soon, and he'd like to be able to get started training a young horse now that could take over for Buck in a year or so."

Aidan nodded his head over his shoulder in the direction of the back pasture. "Come take a look at our two year olds. We got them in this pasture right here."

Marty looked over Aidan's shoulder toward the pasture and nodded, "Yeah, I got time. Let's see what ya got."

Aidan turned on his heel and ran smack into a little boy. He blinked at the sudden impact and exclaimed, "I'm so sorry! You okay?"

"I'm okay." The little boy looked up at him, eyes big and round, then said in a small voice, "I'm tough, remember?"

Recognition dawned on Aidan as he noticed the Band-Aid on the kid's chin. "It's Toby, right?" Aidan looked around. The boy was adrift in a sea of people. "Where's your mom?"

The boy shrugged. "Dunno."

Aidan and Marty traded a look, and Marty shrugged. He muttered, "I ain't never seen him before."

"I know his mom." Aidan said, then squatted on his heels and squinted at the boy, eye level with him. "I bet your mom is worried about you. How's your chin?"

"Fine," declared the boy proudly. "Mom says I'm gonna have a scar."

Aidan smiled at the boy's demeanor. He was cute, for a kid -- and he was all boy. He'd begged to ride the "steer" like a real cowboy at his birthday party.

A woman's voice cut through the murmur of voices, high pitched and frantic. "Toby! Toby!"

Aidan put his hand on the boy's shoulder and stood up, searching the crowd for Gina. He spotted her thick auburn ponytail moved through the crowd like a bobber on the lake. He felt a little thrill at the sight of her and waved his hand in the air, then shouted, "Toby's over here!"

She stood on her tip-toes to see over the crowd. Several heads swiveled toward his deep voice. Their eyes met and hers widened in recognition. She hurried toward him, pushing through the crowd, her chest tight with worry. She should have been watching her son more closely. As soon as she reached easy shouting distance – close enough that he could hear her with her voice raised, but not quite at a shout, she asked, "You found Toby?" Her eyebrows rose.

He nodded and pointed down.

She reached them and immediately bent down to hug Toby. "I told you to stay right beside me!" Her heart still pounded in her chest from the rush of losing him in the crowd.

"I tried, but I wanted to follow the kitty!" He explained. He started to point then looked around and shrugged, "The kitty's gone."

She raised up and glanced at Aidan, "I'm sorry." He'd been so nice to include them in the event. "I hope Toby didn't get in the way or anything. He was right beside me and then--" Her voice trailed off.

He spread his hands apart, palm up and said, "Nothing to be sorry about. I'm easily distracted, too. Glad to see you made it."

She looked up at him, her eyes still bright from the rush of losing her child momentarily in the crowd. "Thank you again for inviting us." She felt a tingle of excitement at seeing him again.

He glanced behind her, "Did you bring a friend?"

She shook her head no, but Toby was the one who answered, "Mom didn't know if this was a date or not."

They both looked down at him then back at each other. Her cheeks heated. Aidan raised his eyebrows and cocked his head to the side, "So, is this a date?"

She frowned at him, then tilted her head and squinted up at him, "No." She raised her hand to shade her eyes.

Marty elbowed Aidan in the ribs and said, "Aren't ya gonna introduce me to the pretty young lady?"

Aidan blinked quickly and stammered for a moment, then said, "Yeah, sure. Marty, this is, uh, Gina, uh, Gina from the scrapbook store in town. And Gina, this is Marty."

Gina stuck out her hand and said, "Nice to meet you, Marty."

Marty took her hand and shook it slowly, holding her hand longer than he should have, as he drawled out, "And it's very nice to meet you, Gina from the scrapbook store in town."

Aidan frowned at the cowboy and said, "You can let go now, Marty."

Gina withdrew her hand and let it rest on Toby's shoulder, "I hope Toby didn't interrupt anything or get in the way."

Toby swiveled his head and looked up at her, and said, "They're real live cowboys, Mom!" He pointed to their dusty boots as proof.

Marty jerked his head toward the horses in the back pasture and said, "We was just gonna go look at some of the two year olds. Want to join us?"

Toby piped up and protested, "I'm too old to play with two year olds!"

Aidan bent down, his hands on his knees, and said, "You can't really play with these two year olds anyway. They've got four legs and a tail!"

Toby's eyes widened and he said incredulously, "Really?"

Marty shifted so he stood next to Gina, then said, "They're horses. Wanna go look at 'em?"

Toby nodded, his eyes bright with excitement. The four walked toward the back pasture. Gina glanced over and saw Toby wrap his little fingers around Aidan's index finger. Aidan glanced at her, then looked at Marty on the other side of her. Marty inclined his head toward her, talking about the importance of bloodlines and early training in rodeo horses.

As they walked, Aidan kept glancing at her, then at Toby, whose little legs pumped in order to keep up with the adults' longer strides. Aidan had a bemused expression on his face. He opened his hand and Toby pressed his palm against Aidan's, then wrapped his fingers around Aidan's hand. His little fingers didn't reach all the way around, and Aidan's hand swallowed the boy's hand.

He looked over Toby's head at her. A man like that, showing his softer side, was sexy as all get out. The cowboy, with his black Stetson, long hair curling over his collar, and five o'clock shadow, made her go weak in the knees.

She felt her strappy sun dress swing around her legs as her hips swayed back and forth and hoped he noticed. The top — Midge's idea — was fitted, snug around her breasts, cut just low enough to highlight her generous cleavage. As they walked, she saw him steal a glance at her chest and quickly ducked her head, embarrassed. When she raised her head, he met her gaze and those electric blue eyes sizzled with heat. Her mouth went dry and her lips parted slightly.

"Look at the horses, Mom!" Toby exclaimed as he pulled his hand free from Aidan's and pointed at the horses grazing in the pasture. Gina blinked rapidly, quickly gathering her wits about her. The trio arrived at the fence just behind Toby, who was already scrambling up. He got up to the second rail before she grabbed his waist from behind.

"That's far enough, little man," she said. "You can watch the horseys from here."

Toby shook his head and looked over his shoulder at her. "They're called horses, Mom."

Aidan looked down at her, barely suppressing a grin. He propped one foot on the lowest rail of the fence then rested his forearms on the top rail and laced his fingers together. He gazed out at the crop of two year olds and a small smile curled his lips.

She watched him and realized it was pride that lit up his face. She said, "They're beautiful animals." She felt Marty's eyes on her, but she shifted closer to Aidan.

He nodded. "I've supervised the training and I think this is the best crop of youngsters we've had. We'll find out for sure at the auction end of next month." He glanced at Marty. "Of course, they're all for sale right now if someone doesn't want to wait for the auction."

He pointed out a leggy bay with a particularly long forelock and mane. His forelock hung down nearly to his nose, and his mane nearly to his knees. "See that bay colt right there, Marty?"

Marty tore his eyes away from Gina, glared at Aidan for a beat and then looked at the colt. He admitted, "He does look good."

Aidan scoffed, "Of course he looks good. He's out of Uhura by Enterprising Young Man."

Marty pursed his lips and regarded the colt a little more closely. His eyes narrowed. "And how's he working?"

Aidan said, "Real well. Under saddle, he's a pleaser. He'll do anything for you. All you have to do is ask." He took that opportunity to glance down at Gina and wink. She felt the tops of her ears turn pink. She caught her bottom lip with her teeth and breathed in his scent, fresh and clean, like sheets that had been hung out in the summer breeze.

Marty said, "Scotty might be interested in 'im. Whatcha asking for him?"

Aidan said, "Got him priced at fifteen." He shifted slightly so his arm brushed against hers.

She swallowed hard, her heart fluttering in her chest. Twitterpated. Yup, that was exactly how she felt.

Marty whistled.

Aidan pushed the sale. "He'd be a money maker for your team. Already showing promise in working cattle.

Scotty can finish him out like he wants. This colt is fast as the wind."

Marty cocked his head and squinted at the colt. Aidan held out his hand and whistled. Four of the two year olds stopped grazing, raised their heads and looked at him, their ears pricked in his direction. He whistled again, four notes, two high, two low, and the bay colt trotted over to them. The horse nuzzled Aidan's hand and Aidan rubbed him on the nose. The horse snorted and shook his head. Aidan glanced over at the boy. He was at full alert, eyes wide as he stood on the fence.

Gina took in her son's reaction. He would thrive in the country. If only she could afford it. Her chest rose and fell with a heavy sigh. She wasn't even sure she could afford their house. If things didn't improve, the poor kid might end up living in the back of the scrapbook store.

Aidan stuck his hand in his pocket and produced a peppermint. The horse whinnied and Toby jumped, eyes wide. Gina kept her hands on his waist, steadying him. She used the focus on her son to keep Marty at arm's length. The attention was flattering, but she wasn't interested. She stole a glance at Aidan as he unwrapped the candy.

Him, she was interested in.

He offered the peppermint to the boy, who started to pop it in his mouth, but Aidan stopped him and pointed to the horse. He said, "Hold your hand out flat, like this."

He held out his hand, flat, palm up, and Toby mimicked him. "Like this?"

Aidan nodded. "Now put the peppermint on the palm

of your hand and hold it out to him."

"Will he bite me?" Toby followed Aidan's instructions, but his eyebrows pushed together in a frown. His voice was doubtful. Gina tightened her grip on her son, concern niggling at her, but she trusted Aidan.

"Yes, now keep your hand flat and hold it real steady so the candy doesn't fall off." Aidan said, cautioning the boy. He smiled reassuringly at Gina, and she smiled back. Seeing him with Toby gave her a little thrill of excitement. She rarely dated and, when she did, dealing with babysitters or introducing her son to them was awkward. Toby had taken to Aidan immediately, without reservation. In spite of Aidan's initial hesitation, he seemed to be a natural with her son.

Toby reach out and the horse snuffled his hand, eliciting a giggle from him as its lips curled around the peppermint candy and sucked it into his mouth. Toby watched in wide-eyed wonder as the horse crunched the candy. The actions involving candy caught the attention of the other horses and three of the others joined the bay colt at the fence. Gina kept her hands on Toby's waist as he stretched across the fence, reaching out to touch the horses' faces and pet them.

Marty stepped away a few steps and had his cell phone out of its holster and up to his ear.

Gina glanced up at Aidan and asked, "Did you just say this horse is for sale for fifteen hundred dollars?"

Aidan grinned, shook his head and said, "No, fifteen thousand."

That was more than a new car! Gina's eyes bugged out,

she looked at the animal with an admiring eye and murmured, "Seriously?" Ranching was more profitable than she'd realized.

"Yeah," he continued, "We raise registered American Quarter Horses here at the Diamond J Ranch, and train them, some for working ranches, some for rodeo cowboys like Marty over there, and some for people who just like to ride."

Gina shook her head, amazed. "I can't imagine that people could spend that kind of money for a horse to ride just for fun."

"Some do." He shrugged, "Mostly, the high dollar horses are destined for the rodeo. Marty is a team roper – you know what that is?"

She shook her head.

"That's when you see the two cowboys go racing after a steer. One ropes the head – that's what Marty does – and the other ropes the back legs – that's what Marty's partner Scotty does. They call him a heeler." Aidan nodded toward Toby and said, "I bet he'd like to go to a rodeo sometime. They're lots of fun for kids."

"Yeah, Mom," Toby twisted around to look at his mom. "I would like to go to a rodeo."

Aidan tapped Toby on the nose. "Well, then, I'll have to make sure you get to one sometime before winter gets here."

Toby's eyes widened. He asked, "Can we, Mom? Please?"

She nodded. Her heart warmed that Aidan thought to include her son in future plans. Aidan reached out to rub the colt on the forehead at the same moment that Gina did, and their arms touched. She felt a thrill at the tickle of dark hair against her bare skin. She glanced up to find him looking at her with an electric intensity. Her lips parted and she took a deep breath as she felt his fingers touch her shoulder then trail down her arm.

"Pull your head outta yer ass, Aidan!" Marty's voice yanked them out of the moment. "I'm talkin' to ya!"

Aidan jerked his hand back, and Gina caught Toby staring at her through narrowed eyes. For a six year old, he was aware of the adults in his life. She pointed to the horse, redirecting his attention, but felt her cheeks burn with embarrassment.

Aidan's Adam's apple bobbed in his throat as he swallowed hard. He looked over Gina's head at Marty. He asked, "What'd you say?"

"I said Scotty's interested in that colt. Wants to come out tomorrow and take a gander at him, if that's okay with you." Marty frowned at Aidan, then moved a step closer to Gina and said, "I'm sorry I had to step away for a moment there, sugar."

Gina raised her eyebrows, lifted her son off the fence railing and turned around. She looked up at Aidan and said, "Excuse us, please. We're going to go see if the food is ready." All she wanted to do was escape the awkward situation. How could Marty miss the attraction between her and Aidan? Toby certainly hadn't . . .

With a toss of her hair, she hurried off, her son's hand clutched in hers.

CHAPTER TWENTY-SEVEN
Strangers

Aidan watched her walk away, the sensual swing of her hips still as mesmerizing as the first time he had seen her. The flimsy material of the sun dress swirled around her legs. The thick auburn ponytail cascading down her back highlighted the freckles sprinkled across her pale shoulders.

Then he remembered how quickly she had left. Was it him? Surely it was Marty. She had left as soon as Marty called her sugar. With a frown, he turned and looked at Marty.

"What the hell did you have to go and do that for?" he demanded.

Marty protested, "Do what?"

"You called her sugar and she obviously didn't like it." Aidan said. He looked after her as she walked toward the deck where the barbecue grill and serving table were set up, then she abruptly changed direction and headed away from the cluster of people. Dang it. Marty must have scared her off good.

He sighed, figured he could at least get some business taken care of while he was here, and said, "Okay, so I guess that was Scotty you were talking to?"

Marty rolled his eyes and said, "Duh. Yes. I told you that already. He wants to come out tomorrow to look at the bay colt."

Aidan nodded as he turned back to search the crowd for Gina and her little boy.

Marty said, "Am I intruding on something with that little gal? You got dibs on her or something?"

Aidan waved the cowboy off. "Not yet." He glanced at the deck where Beth and Beau stood together, Beau's arm casually draped over Beth's shoulders. As he watched, Beth turned her face up to Beau's and smiled. He wanted that — the easy togetherness. He wanted someone to love him the way Beth loved Beau.

He'd always imagined finding a woman to spend his life with, but he had pictured them as a couple, not a family. Gina's boy was growing on him though. It seemed natural to include him.

Marty nodded sagely. "Gotcha. You just ain't had the guts to make a move yet. Well, you'd better hop to it before some other guy does make a move. Like me, for instance."

Aidan frowned, as irritated with himself as he was with Marty, and motioned toward the crowd. "Let's get back to the barbecue. Beau's been cooking up hamburgers and brats and hot dogs, and Charlotte made her special bourbon barbecue sauce."

The two men walked toward the crowd in the yard.

When they reached the serving table – easy to spot because of the bright red gingham table cloth -- they found the table laden with food. The platter of hot dogs and brats already had a sizeable dent in it. There was a noticeably empty spot at the end of the table, though.

Marty asked, "I thought you said there was gonna be hamburgers an' cheeseburgers, too!"

Aidan looked up at the barbecue grill Beau had been tending when he last saw him. The chef's hat and the apron were laying on the table next to the barbecue tongs. Beau wasn't there, but Beth was. She stared off into the distance, a frown between her brows and her eyes narrowed. Her arms were crossed across her chest.

Aidan turned to follow her intent gaze and saw Beau at the edge of the crowd, talking with his Aunt Lana.

No, talking wasn't right. Beau looked angry, flat out angry. Not that Aidan could blame him. He'd have a hard time being patient with the woman. Sure, she was family, but she was a nut case. At least she seemed that way to Aidan. Every time he saw her, she looked flat out weird and today was no exception.

Her lime green high top tennis shoes reminded her of those basketball players wore when Aidan was a kid, Converse or something like that. A long flowing skirt that looked like it was made up of a bunch of tie dyed handkerchiefs – hopefully sewn together and not pinned together with safety pins – swirled around her like a cloud. Her top fit closely, basically a giant elastic piece of fabric that highlighted her sagging breasts that had been allowed to hang free for too many years.

The only saving grace of the blouse, which was kind of see through, was that giant white daisies polka dotted it strategically.

Her bright red hair was wild as ever, a mass of curls gathered together like a bird's nest on top of her head. That was apparently her idea of dressing her normal look up, an improvement in Aidan's opinion, to the pig tails that she normally wore that always reminded him of Pippi Longstocking.

Jack Brooks walked up and clapped Aidan on the back. "You decided to come and see me about a new truck yet? I'll give you the best trade in I can on your old Chevy pickup!"

Aidan grinned but shook his head no. "Sorry, Jack. Can't afford a new truck just yet."

Jack lowered his chin and looked at Aidan over his wire rimmed glasses and said, "Now, you can be straight with me. I know you could afford it if you wanted to."

Aidan frowned at the man. Typical car dealer, with his light suit, narrow tie and slicked back hair. He regretted letting the man know the truth about his trust fund.

It had seemed innocuous enough at the time, when he was considering buying a new truck. He hadn't even been seriously considering, just went in to check out the end of season deals to see if it would be worth trading. Jack had started talking about all the financing options, had even placed a call to one of the local bankers trying to get paperwork started for a loan.

To get him to stop, Aidan told him he had a trust fund and that any vehicle he did choose to buy would be paid for in cash, so he wanted the best cash price on the vehicle. That had clearly been a mistake, because Jack latched onto that tidbit of information like a dog with a bone.

Aidan shook his head, made an excuse about looking for someone and moved away. To his relief, Jack turned his attention on Marty. As Aidan walked away, he heard Jack say, "Hey, Marty, I got just the truck for you. Just got it in on trade. Real nice dually, be perfect for hauling your horse trailer around to the rodeos. Diesel . . . "

He could see Beau and his Aunt Lana still talking, only now Beau had his aunt by the arm. He glanced up at Beth, still staring at the two. She was chewing her lip, a sure sign she was anxious. He turned to make his way through the crowd, to see if there was anything he could do to help ease the tension.

Seeing the ranch manager man manhandling his frail-looking aunt wasn't doing the ranch any favors, and Aidan didn't want to see things get out of hand between the two of them. He wasn't sure what the history was there, but there was definitely more to it than a typical aunt-nephew relationship.

He'd just about broke through the crowd when a man caught his arm. The man was short, barely coming to Aidan's shoulders, and wore dark pants – not jeans – and a white dress shirt with a dark jacket.

The man stood there, peering up at Aidan through his tiny glasses. He blinked and looked expectant.

Aidan blinked and asked, "Can I help you?"

The little man said, "I certainly hope so. I am looking for a woman."

Aidan suppressed a laugh, but the corners of his mouth twitched upwards in spite of himself. He drawled, "Aren't we all?"

The man frowned and his dark, thin eyebrows pinched together to form a "V". He stepped forward half a step and said, with a slight English accent, "I am seeking a woman by the name of Nadya Svetlana Sheedy."

Aidan shrugged and stepped back, then said, "Sorry. Can't help you there."

The man's nostrils flared and he said, "She may be going by the name Lana."

Aidan blinked. The man stepped even closer, and spoke in an accusing tone, "You know this woman."

It was a statement, not a question. Aidan shrugged and stepped back, "I don't know. The name sounds vaguely familiar."

The man's eyes darted around from face to face around them, and demanded, "Where is she?"

Aidan recovered his bearings and stiffened. "Who's asking?"

The man's nostrils flared and his chest puffed out visibly. He declared, "I am Mr. Ian Woon. I represent the Tri-State Cattle Consortium, and am investigating the theft of several members' property. We seek to interview Ms. Evans."

An investigator? A cattle consortium? Aidan arched his eyebrows and said, "I don't believe we've met."

The little man stuck his nose in the air and said in that haughty accent, "Of course we haven't met yet, as there has been no reason for us to meet."

Aidan rolled his eyes and walked away from the little man, leaving him behind in the crowd. Very odd. A private investigator? Guess the Consortium didn't think law enforcement was doing their job. The conversation left him anxious. He needed to talk to Beau. Could Lana be involved in the thefts?

When Aidan neared the edge of the crowd, where straw bales were set up in semi-circles for seating, he looked around for Beau and Lana. He spotted the two underneath the oak tree next to the gate into the front pasture. Beau's face was flushed red and he gestured wildly with his hands, obviously making a point about something. Beau stood over his aunt, looming over her. Lana looked all wide eyed and innocent, not the least bit intimidated by her nephew.

Aidan strode toward them. Beau glanced at Aidan, then closed his eyes, pressed his lips into a thin line, and made a shooing motion with one hand. Lana flounced away from him, following the fence toward the house, either oblivious to Beau's anger of flat out not caring. Beau turned to face the horses grazing in the pasture.

Aidan joined his boss at the fence and said, "Everything okay, boss?"

Beau made a snorting noise, but no answer.

Aidan glanced over his shoulder, but didn't see Mr. Ian Woon among the clumps of people sitting on the bales or at the picnic tables. He said, "There's a man here looking for your aunt."

Beau's head snapped around and he focused on Aidan with a laser intensity. "Who? Why? What's he want?"

Aidan held up both hands in a gesture of innocence, and said, "Said his name is Mr. Ian Woon. Said he's with the Tri-State Cattle Consortium. Wants to talk to Lana." He paused a moment, searching his memory. "He called her by some big long name, Svetlana something?"

The muscles in Beau's jaw worked furiously. "What did you tell him?"

Aidan let his hands drop and shrugged, then said, "Nothing. Name means nothing to me. No idea who he is. So, I didn't tell him anything. Just walked away."

Beau turned to lean his back against the fence. He propped one foot against the rail and leaned back, elbows resting on the white wooden railing. In spite of the casual pose, tension oozed from him. "You left him wandering around?"

Aidan glanced at Beau and said, "Yeah. You didn't invite him?"

Beau shook his head.

Aidan continued, "He's an odd duck. Little man. Round. Had an accent. English, I think."

Beau's eyes scanned the crowd, darting from face to face. Aidan frowned at his friend. "Do you know who he is?"

Beau shook his head no again.

Aidan nodded, but didn't understand. There was obviously more to Aunt Lana than just a relative who happened to be passing through. He'd suspected that from the start, because Beau changed, grew more wary and guarded, when she had arrived at the ranch in her big yellow semi last summer.

But Beau wasn't much of a talker or a sharer, even though he was probably closer to Aidan than anyone else on the ranch – perhaps with the exception of Charlotte – he hadn't said anything to indicate why he was nervous about her being there.

To Aidan, she was just flat out weird. He'd never met anyone at ditzy at she was. Like a flower child leftover from the 70's, a gypsy-like wanderer, she didn't seem to have a home base and essentially lived in her sleeper cab, occasionally mooching off of friends and relatives like she was currently doing with Beau. Aidan couldn't put his finger on it, but something was off with her, though. He didn't think she was nearly as ditzy as she pretended to be, and that wide-eyed innocent act that she had just played with Beau was just that – an act. He was certain of it.

Aidan nodded in the direction of the crowd and said, "You think we should go mingle?"

Beau nodded and looked up toward the house and said, "Guess I need to get back to the barbecue grill."

Aidan followed his gaze and saw Beth standing on the corner of the deck watching them, arms still crossed over her chest. Even from here, he could nearly make out the concern on her face. He said, "You want some help with the grilling?"

Beau shook his head no and said, "I got it under control. Why don't you go chat up some of the rodeo cowboys, get a feel for what they're looking for, what they think of our stock."

Aidan nodded. "Will do, boss."

They started to walk toward the crowd and Beau said, "And if you see the mysterious Mr. Ian Woon again, let me know."

Aidan nodded as the two split up. He walked up and joined a clump of cowboys sitting on the straw bales, each with a brown beer bottle in his hand. "Howdy, boys. I think the burgers are about ready. Want to go fill your plates?"

As he walked toward the serving table, he scanned the crowd, but didn't see Gina, her little boy, the mysterious Mr. Ian Woon, or Aunt Lana.

There was a funny feeling in the pit of his stomach that he just couldn't escape.

CHAPTER TWENTY-EIGHT
Confrontation

Gina marched away from the two cowboys, irritated at the crassness and forwardness of that guy named Marty. Nothing ticked her off more than a man who assumed that he could be overly familiar with her right away, like he expected her to swoon all over him just because he showed a little interest in her.

Men could be such jerks.

She glanced over her shoulder at the two men, who had turned back to look at the horses. Her irritation at Marty was more about Aidan than anything Marty had done, she admitted to herself. She'd been looking forward to spending some time with him, getting to know him, in a social situation. Though it had been nice to have him around earlier in the week, fixing a dishwasher wasn't exactly quality time.

Toby tugged her toward a big long table covered with food. He exclaimed, "Hot dogs, Mom! I'm hungry! Can I have two hot dogs?"

Her frown faded, replaced by a smile. She said, "Let's

start with one and then you can go back for another if you finish the first one."

The sound of his voice was all she needed to improve her mood. She let him lead her toward the table, where she helped him fill his plate and then filled her own. They wound through the crowd looking for a place to sit, but all the tables were full.

He looked at some hay bales and she could almost see the gears working in his mind as he looked at people sitting on the bales. She said, "Want to sit here?"

"Yes!" he exclaimed as he hurried toward a group of bales where no one was sitting, near the edge of the lawn. He sat down and she sat beside him, then she opened his soda and showed him how to hold it between his legs to keep it from spilling. A few people nodded and said hello in greeting as they passed by, but no one stopped to sit with them. Gina was used to that, but she still struggled with loneliness. Being a single mom left her feeling isolated more often than she cared to admit.

She made a concerted effort to make eye contact with some of the other guests. At Midge's insistence, she had several business cards in her back pocket. She should take advantage of this situation, with so many people from the community in attendance, it was a good opportunity to meet new people and perhaps encourage new customers to stop by the scrapbook store.

Aidan caught her eye as he walked through the crowd. She hoped she hadn't offended him when she left abruptly. It suddenly occurred to her that he might not have picked up on the fact that it was Marty that irritated her and not him. She started to scoot over a bit to make room for him, then stopped herself.

Could she settle for a ranch hand? She glanced at Toby. She had a son to think about. What could Aidan offer her? He couldn't support her and her son. She'd seen the old Chevy pickup he drove. He could barely support himself, much less a family. Was it worth it to start a relationship that didn't have a chance of going anywhere. She wasn't getting any younger.

Then again, he struck her as gentle and patient, not to mention sexy as hell.

And he could fix household appliances.

As she watched Aidan speaking with a short, rotund man, she considered she didn't bring much to the table either. Aidan had a pretty good life now. He lived on a ranch, had a good boss (or seemed to anyway, from the looks of things today), probably enjoyed the single life.

What was there to not enjoy? He ate when he wanted, when he wanted, drank when he wanted, came in when he wanted. He had no one to answer to, no one to nag him. Why would he want to go out with someone with as much baggage as her?

"Why you frowning, Mom?" Toby asked through a mouth full of hot dog.

Because I'm too young to be alone. She reached up and rubbed her forehead in an effort to erase the frown lines and said, "Nothing, little man. Just thinking."

Gina spotted an older woman making her way through the various clumps of people, from table to table, from bale to bale. She carried a large tray laden with bottles and cans. She approached them and said, "Can I offer you a drink?"

Toby tipped his soda back and drained it in one gulp, then grabbed his mother by the arm and said, "Can I have another, Mom?"

She tilted her head and frowned, "I think one's enough, little man."

The older woman lowered the tray to a straw bale and pointed to a short can, her soft green eyes on Gina. She offered, "We have some little cans of root beer and orange drink. Perhaps your mom would let you have one of those?"

Gina put her index finger to her lips and pretended to think it over while Toby pleaded his case. Finally she smiled and said, "Okay, a little can."

As Toby carefully selected his drink from the tray, the older woman whispered to Gina, "I understand completely. Don't want a caffeine fueled child running around 'til all hours of the night, do we?" She had a slight Irish brogue.

"No," Gina said, emphatically shaking her head, though it really wouldn't matter for her. It wasn't like she had anything else on her Saturday night schedule. "I'm Gina Montgomery."

The older woman's eyes sparkled under arched brows. She lowered herself to a straw bale across from the trio, next to her tray of drinks. "Well, hello, Gina! It is a pleasure to meet you, child. I'm Charlotte."

Gina looked at the woman, but couldn't place her. Apparently she worked for the Diamond J. Or perhaps she was friends with the ranch's owner. Gina's mind spun, wondering how the women knew her.

Charlotte gushed, "You did a wonderful job on the invitations!"

Of course, the invitations! Gina blushed at the compliment and murmured, "Thank you. I enjoyed making them."

"Well, you did a heck of a job." The older woman leaned forward. "Miss Beth was so impressed, she sent a few to her fancy friends up in Kansas City."

Gina blushed at the compliment. "Stop by the store sometime and say hello. Let me know if there's anything I can ever do for you." She hoped it sounded less desperate out loud than it did in her head.

Charlotte looked at the card, then tapped it with her index finger as a mysterious smile spread across her face. She said, "So you're *the* Gina."

Gina felt herself pull back, her smile fading as confusion caused her to hesitate. She asked, "I'm sorry?"

The older woman leaned forward conspiratorially and said, "You certainly caught Aidan's eye. He's quite taken with you."

Gina felt off balance, not sure how to respond. Toby declared, "I'm done. Can I go throw my stuff away?"

Charlotte pointed to the end of the row of straw bales. She offered, "There's a trash can right down there."

While Charlotte asked questions about the scrapbook store and the invitations and cards she made, Toby proudly walked back and forth to the trash can, delivering each piece of trash and throwing it away, glad to have a job to do. As he returned from his last trip to the trash can, Gina saw him pause and squint into the crowd. He hurried back to her and said, "Mom! Dad's here, too!"

She blinked and shot to her feet. "Where?" Her eyes swept left, then right.

He clambered onto the straw bale next to her, scanned the crowd and then pointed, "Over there! With that clown lady."

Her gaze narrowed as she spotted her ex walking away from the crowd with a woman dressed rather oddly. Even without the pig tails, Gina was quite certain it was the woman from the truck stop.

Charlotte said, "Is everything okay?"

Gina pressed her lips together as she considered what to do. Charlotte stood and stepped close. "If you need to go talk to him, I would be glad to have your little boy help me with the drinks for a few minutes."

Gina chewed her lip as she considered her options. Steve and the wild haired woman were nearing the fence, and if they continued to walk they would soon be in a stand of trees. She looked at Toby.

There was no doubt something going on that Steve was involved with that she certainly did not want Toby to be involved in or exposed to in any way shape or form. She looked at the older woman, who reminded her of Aunt Bea from the Andy Griffith Show. Though she seemed trustworthy, Gina hesitated.

Charlotte assured her, "Go right ahead. He can help me hand out sodas. We'll be right in this area." She motioned to the half circle of straw bales.

The desire to find out what Steve was up to outweighed her suspicion. She helped Toby slide off the straw bale and said, "You stay with Miss Charlotte here and do what she says, okay? You help her hand out sodas to these nice people. Can you do that for me?"

"Yes." He nodded sagely. "I'm a big boy."

"Yes, you are," she said, then gave him a quick hug. She hurried off toward her ex-husband and the crazy lady he had become entangled with. She wove in and out of clumps of people, mostly cowboys, but some were business people from town that she recognized. A few of the women she recognized from her store, and a handful of them stopped to ask her about things like upcoming classes and new products that they were hoping she was going to get in. She stopped, not wanting to be rude, but kept an eye on her ex-husband.

It was easy to do – his new friend's hair was nearly neon, easy to spot. She excused herself and headed for them. A handful of people stood at the edge of the yard, looking out over the pasture. She walked up to the fence as if looking at the horses grazing in the pasture. She shifted along the fence every few moments, alert to Steve and the woman.

They were deeply engrossed in conversation, their heads close together, ignoring everyone else. One of the horses walked up to the fence and she reached across to pet the horse's muzzle. She was glad. It gave her a reason to be standing there and she didn't feel like as exposed. The horse dropped its head and grazed a few feet to its right, then lifted its head over the fence. Perfect.

She shifted with the horse, closer to the two people she was interested in. This continued a couple more times and at last, she could make out bits and pieces of the conversation.

His voice, " . . . sale barn . . ."

Her voice, scratchy and gravelly, like a woman who had smoked all her life, ". . . sacrifice . . ."

His voice, ". . . out of town . . ."

Hers again, ". . . honor the family . . ."

His again, " . . . strip and rebrand . . ."

At that moment, someone chose to fire up the sound system and strains of Miranda Lambert singing about her hometown drifted across the lawn, effectively smothering the bits and pieces of conversation.

The horse nickered at her and nuzzled her hand, and she realized that she had turned toward Steve and the woman, focusing all her attention on them.

Obviously she wasn't good at sneaking up on people and spying on them.

The odd woman drifted back toward the group at the barbecue, not in any hurry, stopping to pick dandelions along the way. Steve faced away from her, his cell phone to his ear. Gina approached him, no longer sneaking, but didn't announce her presence either.

Once in earshot, she paused and listened as Steve spoke into his phone. "We're on for tonight. Meet me at the Petro at 11:30. It'll take us about an hour to get there."

He listened for a moment, then said, "We're taking them to the sale barn up in northeast Missouri." He nodded, listening, then, "The sale is Monday night."

He flipped his phone closed and turned around. Gina stood ready for him, arms crossed across her chest, lips pressed together, jaw set. She was so angry, she felt like she could spit nails. She sucked in deep breaths, trying to control her anger, not wanting to make a scene within sight of the crowd at the barbecue.

She spat the words at him, "You son of a bitch!"

His eyes were wide and he feigned innocence as he spread his hands apart, palms up, and said, "What was that for?" He glanced over her shoulder.

She glared at him. "I knew you were up to no good. I've seen you with that woman before, at the truck stop."

He shrugged as his eyes slid side to side. "There's no law against talking to women." He waved his hand at her. "Keep your voice down."

She wagged a finger in his face and hissed, "There is a law against cattle rustling."

That got his attention. Suddenly his eyes darted from her to the crowd and back. He spoke through clenched teeth. "I don't know what you're talking about."

She pointed up the hill at the crowd gathered on the lawn and said, "Your little boy is up there. He looks up to you. You are his hero. Level with me right now and I won't embarrass you in front of him."

He started to turn away from her, but she grabbed him by the arm. He jerked it away and said, "You don't know what you're messing with here. Keep quiet and mind your own business. Please."

She could feel a vein pulsing in her temple. "Don't you get it? I don't want our son to be forever known as the son of a criminal. Whatever you are doing, whatever you have planned, it is not worth it. Get out of it before it's too late."

"This is not what you think." He leaned close. "You need to forget what you saw."

Her nostrils flared and she could feel the blood pounding in her veins. She said, "Don't you tell me what to do."

He frowned, his face dark and stormy as he said, "You're messing with something you don't want to mess with."

"Why are you doing this?" she demanded.

He snorted and shook his head, then reached out as if to touch her.

She jerked back. "I'm warning you. You get out of whatever you're into. I will not let you hurt my son."

He turned away from her and began walking toward the vehicles parked along the long driveway. He looked over his shoulder and left her with his parting shot, "He's OUR son."

She stood there, shaking with fury. They brought out the worst in each other, and she hated herself for feeling petty, for losing control of her emotions. Steve was better than this. Sure, he'd had a bad boy reputation when they were young, but he wasn't a common criminal. Somehow, he'd gotten in with the wrong crowd, and he was in serious trouble.

The women in the scrapbook store told that their husbands and sons were taking things into their own hands, setting up patrols, tired of being victims, frustrated with the cops for not putting a stop to the wave of cattle rustling. Too many people had lost too much, and someone was going to get hurt before it was all over.

CHAPTER TWENTY-NINE
Misunderstandings

"Hey, there!" a deep voice called out from behind Gina. She turned to see Aidan striding toward her. She smiled at him and struggled to get a handle on her warring emotions, worried that she might burst into tears.

He continued toward her but let his gaze rest on Steve, walking away from them. He nodded toward her ex-husband and one dark eyebrow rose. "Friend of yours?"

She shook her head, considered how much to reveal, then shrugged and said, "Not exactly. Ex-husband."

His smile faded and he nodded. "Oh, I see." He pressed his lips into a thin line and his eyes narrowed as he watched the other man get into his truck and drive away, tires spinning in the loose gravel.

They stood there awkwardly for a moment, the silence stretching between them like a taut string. The horse nickered again, breaking the silence. She cleared her throat and raised her chin. "Thanks so much for inviting me and Toby to the barbecue. It's very nice."

He smiled and his whole face lit up. He inclined his

head, so his mouth was inches from her ear. A shiver went up her spine when his breath tickled her ear. He whispered, "Want to know a secret?"

Butterflies danced in her stomach. She sucked in a deep breath and nodded.

He whispered, "I was worried you had a boyfriend."

She blinked and pulled away to look at him, shocked. "Why would you think that?"

He straightened and shrugged, "That day at the scrapbook store, when I asked if you wanted to come to the barbecue, you asked if you could bring a guest." He looked at her with those intense blue eyes, as if he were staring into her soul. A hint of red tinged his chiseled cheeks.

Her eyes widened as she realized what he had thought. She said, "Ah, and you thought I was bringing a guy."

"I wondered, when I found out you had a son, if that was who you were bringing, but I still worried about your guest." He grinned again, displaying nearly perfect white teeth. "I didn't expect your date to be under four foot tall." One dark eyebrow quirked up.

She grinned up at him and said, "And not of an age that he couldn't legally partake of an alcoholic beverage."

He nodded and touched the tip of her finger with his nose. "Exactly."

It was such a casual movement, yet so intimate.

He sat up straight. "You know, all I know about you is that you are a talented invitation maker, you own your own business and you don't have many tools. Maybe we should get to know each other a little better."

She shifted her weight from one foot to the other, and nodded. "Agreed. What do you want to know?"

He laughed. "Everything. I want to know everything about you."

Her smile faded. He didn't want to know everything. He just thought he did. "Not much to tell. Divorced. Single mom." That pretty much squelched any passion he might feel for her. No glowing coals, just dying embers.

"I pretty much figured that part out." He looked into her eyes, as if she were the only person there. "How long have you been divorced?"

"Four years. Since Toby was a baby." The crowd around them disappeared and the world shrunk down to them and only them. "How about you? Ever been married?"

He snorted. "No. No time for that."

She gazed up at him. "Maybe you just haven't found the right girl yet."

He took a step closer to her. "Maybe I wasn't looking in the right places."

Only inches separated them. He bent his head, his eyes focused on her lips.

The rest of the world faded away. Her lips parted, seemingly of their own accord, and all she could think about was kissing him. She wanted him to claim her, for his lips to cover hers, for his tongue to tease hers.

A boy shouted in the distance, drawing her back to reality. She blinked and drew back. She laid one hand flat against his chest and murmured, "I'm sorry."

His chest was hard under her touch. It wasn't until he let his hand drop that she realized he'd been holding her. He winked at her. "I'm not."

Her mouth opened and closed, then she yanked her hand back as if she'd been burned. Her chest rose and fell as she stared up at him. Those electric blue eyes smoldered with intensity.

She shook her head and turned away. She couldn't do this. Not now. Her son was here.

Oh, jeez.

She'd left her son with a stranger. She needed to get back to him.

She turned to scan the crowd, and spotted the older woman, Charlotte, standing near the deck, just below the barbecue grill. She glanced up at Aidan and said, "Shall we go rescue Charlotte?" She felt as giddy as a schoolgirl around him. Her cheeks hurt from smiling so much.

As they turned to walk toward the house, he briefly placed his hand on the small of her back. She stiffened momentarily at the touch, then relaxed. The warmth of his light touch steadied her. Again, casual, yet intimate.

As they wove through the crowd, several spoke to Aidan, calling him by name. Several then nodded at her, and she caught the jealous glance of more than one woman.

As they walked up to the deck, she became aware of the tension in the air. The older woman, Charlotte, stood on the next to the top step with Toby on the step one down from and behind her. The woman leaned forward, resting her weight heavily on the railing. She was huddled with a man and a woman. Gina had seen both at the barbecue earlier. The woman was cute and perky, slender with red hair and a porcelain connection. Her fiery hair was pulled up in a messy bun, with fine tendrils curling around her face. The man wore Wranglers (what is it about a man in Wranglers, she thought) and a denim button down shirt. A straw cowboy hat shaded his face and an apron was slung over his shoulder.

Aidan put his hand on her shoulder and whispered, "Something's going on. Wait here."

She caught him before he could go up the steps and said, "Who is that?"

"That's Beau, the ranch foreman – my boss – and Beth. She's the big boss lady. Owns the ranch." He jogged up the steps to join the huddle.

Gina reached out, then let her hand drop to her side. "But my—" Gina stood there for a moment, unsure of what to do. Perhaps she should just take Toby and move on, but she wanted to wait for Aidan.

She stepped forward and tapped Charlotte on the shoulder, just as Toby turned around.

Toby said proudly, "Hi, Mom! I helped Miss Charlotte hand out drinks. That is a very important job on a hot day like today."

Charlotte turned toward Gina, hesitation in her movements, then glanced back at the trio on the deck. She shifted her attention back to Gina and smiled as she patted Toby on his head. She said, "Your son is adorable, absolutely adorable. He was a big help."

Gina smiled and nodded her agreement. "He always helps me at home. Thank you for taking him for a bit."

Charlotte said, "Not a problem at all."

Gina looked up at Aidan, decided not to let the opportunity pass her by. She would thank him for the invitation, perhaps make arrangements to see him again. She placed one foot on the bottom step, but Charlotte suddenly stepped down, blocking Gina's way.

Charlotte inclined her head. "Give them just a moment."

Gina blinked, then nodded. Just as she was about to excuse herself, Beth and Beau went inside and Aidan jogged down the steps. He grinned at her, exposing those deep dimples, when he reached the bottom step. He put his hands on his knees and bent down so that he was eye level with Toby. The little boy narrowed his eyes and tucked his arm around his mother's leg, suddenly shy. Aidan said, "I've got a special secret in the barn I'd love to show you."

The kid hugged Gina's leg tighter and glanced up at her. She grinned down at him and nodded her encouragement. He studied Aidan through narrowed eyes, then asked, "What?"

Aidan grinned. "Have you ever seen a baby cow?"

Toby nodded his head. "At my party."

"How about an itty-bitty baby cow, even littler than the calves I brought to your party?" Aidan straightened and held out his hand. "You want to come to the barn and see one?"

Toby looked at Aidan's hand, but made no move to let go of his mother's leg.

Gina put her hand on her son's shoulder and said, "It's OK. I'll go with you. I want to see the baby cow, too."

Toby let his hand drop. Aidan turned and motioned.

The little boy still looked suspicious. On a whim, Aidan took Gina's hand in his. She hesitated, but after a moment squeezed back and then grabbed her son's hand. The three of them walked through the crowd and slipped into the big red barn.

It took a moment for their eyes to adjust to the dimness after the glaring summer sun. The sounds of the barn surrounded them. Horses snuffled, and a three-legged cat trotted up to them, meowing his welcome.

Toby pointed at the cat. "That's the kitty I saw earlier." Aidan said, "That's Tripod."

"What happened to him?" the boy asked.

Aidan shrugged. "Don't know. He showed up like that."

Aidan stopped in front of the calf's stall and held one finger up to his lips. "She's a baby so we have to use soft voices while we're in there."

Toby nodded solemnly. Gina placed one hand on his shoulder and reminded him gently, "We'll use an inside voice, right?"

Aidan slid the door open just wide enough for them to slip inside. He went first, followed by the boy and, finally, Gina. He glanced back at her.

Toby's eyes grew wide and he dropped to his knees in front of the black calf. She stepped toward the boy, then looked at Aidan and snorted. Her fuzzy ears swiveled back and forth and she nodded her head.

Gina leaned down and grabbed her son's shoulders, looking down at the straw. Aidan quickly assured her, "I cleaned the stall right before I came and got you. It's okay." She released her grip and her shoulders relaxed as she dropped to her knees beside Toby.

Aidan squatted next to the boy. "Here. Hold up your thumb, like you are going to suck your thumb." He demonstrated by holding his thumb up.

Toby's eyes narrowed. "I'm a big boy. I don't do that no more."

Aidan grinned. "Neither do I, but she does." He jerked his thumb toward the calf.

Gina took hold of her son's hand and gently turned the thumb toward the baby. The calf sucked his thumb into her mouth and sucked eagerly, which elicited a burble of giggles from the boy.

Aidan said, "You keep her busy for a minute and I'll be right back." He slipped out the door. In a couple of minutes, he returned with a large plastic bottle filled with milk. He held it out the boy.

Seeing how excited Aidan was about showing off the baby just about melted Gina's heart.

Toby took the bottle and pointed the nipple toward the calf. "It's warm," he said.

"That's how she likes it, and it's easier on her tummy," Aidan said. "Hold on with both hands. She's pretty strong for a baby."

Toby giggled as he grasped the bottle tightly. The calf bumped against him and slurped away, as if she were starving, even though Aidan had just fed her two hours ago.

Aidan stepped back. Gina felt the glow of love as she watched her son. She laughed and encouraged him, asked him what it felt like.

Once Toby seemed confident in what he was doing, Gina pushed to her feet and stepped back, letting Toby enjoy the moment. She turned to Aidan and looked up into his amazing blue eyes. The irises were shot through with dark blue. She whispered, "Thank you."

He grinned back. "I knew he'd like it."

She said, "He's always loved cowboys and horses and this is like a dream come true for him."

"Living here is like a dream come true for me, so I know how he feels." He shifted his weight to the leg closest to her. He inclined his head toward her and whispered, "I'm happy you were able to come to the party."

She smiled. "So am I."

They stood side by side and watched Toby with the little calf. Aidan let his hand brush against the smooth skin of her arm, and she made no move to shift away. It didn't take the young calf long to drain the bottle. She suckled and bumped the bottle, trying to get the last drop of warm milk.

Aidan took the bottle from the boy. "All done. Now that her tummy's full she'll probably take a nap. Let's leave her alone for a little bit and let her sleep."

Toby's shoulders drooped and he huffed out a big sigh. Gina took him by the hand. "Aidan is right. Let's leave her alone. She's a baby so she needs lots of sleep."

Aidan slid the door open and the three of them slipped out. The calf bawled her disgust at being left alone.

As they exited the barn, Gina prompted Toby. "What do you say?"

Toby looked up at her and his eyebrows pushed

together in a look of intense concentration. His eyes rounded and his whole face brightened, then he swiveled his head to look at Aidan. "Oh, yeah! Thank you very much, Mr.—Mr.—"

Aidan grinned. "Call me Aidan."

"Thank you, Aidan."

"Yes," Gina echoed. "Thank you, Aidan."

Toby tugged on Gina's hand. "Can I go play in the straw maze again, Mom?"

She released the boy's hand and waved him on. "Yes, just remember to take turns and be polite."

As Toby ran ahead, Gina adjusted her path ever so slightly, so she was walking right next to Aidan. Their arms brushed against each other with every stride. She glanced up at him. "You made his day, you know."

"I hope so. I remember how excited I was about stuff like that as a kid."

"Did you grow up on a ranch?"

"No, but I was around calves sometimes because of my father's work." His voice held a hard edge.

She raised her eyebrows, encouraging him to continue. "Tell me."

His mouth went dry. "My mom died right after I graduated high school. My dad was busy building his own business. When I made it clear I didn't want to be a part of that business, he had no time for me."

She frowned. "Then you understand how important it is to spend time on you, to take time for your own family, not to get so focused on work."

He warmed to the subject. "That's just it. This place isn't

work. It's home. The people here are my family."

She cocked her head. "But what about your father? He's still alive?"

"My father is nothing like Beau and Charlotte and the others here. He was — is — a cold, cold person who cares about nothing more than making a buck." His voice cut through the spring air like a blade.

She reached out and touched his forearm. The muscles were corded and tight, tense and she massaged gently, as if trying to relax him. "You're not cold."

He sighed, then took her hand in his. "I hope not. I don't want to be anything like him. That's why I left as soon as I could."

She trailed her fingers down his arm, letting them rest on the back of his hand. "So you've been on your own since then?"

"Yes," he murmured. "I couldn't stay with my father. Couldn't stomach how he earned his money. Hated the thought of what he did, and didn't want any part of that."

She pulled back and frowned, suddenly wary. "Is he a criminal or something?"

He barked a laugh, a harsh, humorless sound. "Not exactly. He owns a huge meat processing company. And he's never been caught doing anything illegal." He emphasized the word caught with a shake of his head.

The furrows in her forehead deepened. "But that's what you do here at the Diamond J, right? It's all farming and ranching, right?"

"No." He turned toward her and gripped her forearms. "We raise and train cutting horses. We raise cattle. Yes, we raise livestock, but it is nothing like big corporate farms or the giant meat processing plants. The animals here are treated with respect and care."

His grip was strong. She blinked rapidly and her mouth hung open in astonishment. "But that doesn't happen at your father's business?"

He snorted derisively again. "It is a factory, where living creatures are mercilessly processed in the cheapest, fastest way possible."

She wiggled under his grip and he quickly released her. "I'm sorry," he murmured, then he turned away and rubbed his face roughly with his hands.

She reached out and rubbed his back gently as he took deep breaths in and out.

"I'm sorry," she said. "That sounds horrible."

"It is," he mumbled through his hands. "You have no idea how horrible."

She'd seen undercover videos taken by animal rights activists. Those images were horrible and disgusting. They had been enough to make her consider going vegan.

But surely his family wasn't involved in something as horrible as that. "You are nothing like your father." She continued to rub his back, running her hand in lazy circles over his broad shoulders.

He took a deep breath and said, "My family owns Brackston Meat Processing."

Her eyes widened in recognition "You mean THE Brackston Meats? Like the beef and pork we buy at the grocery store? The family that owns the football team? The family rumored to have organized crime ties?" She clamped a hand over her mouth. Good grief. That family was larger than life. Always in the news.

He nodded and ducked his head. When he left home, he hoped to never hear that name again, but it seemed impossible to escape. The name held nothing but memories of pain and horror for him.

She blinked at him. "That's a huge business. I've heard a lot about it." She looked a bit green around the gills.

He snorted as he thought of the sprawling metal buildings, the crowded feed lots where animals stood in filth and mud while awaiting their final trip to the kill floor. The stench hung in the air, covering the animals like a blanket.

It was nothing like the warm smell of the Diamond J, hay and cattle and horses and grain, all mixed together. Here, the animals were treated with dignity and respect.

But he didn't want to think of the past today. For the first time in his life, he was ready to stop running from his past. Instead, he had a clear vision of what he wanted his future to look like. He glanced down at Gina, smiled and took her elbow. "Enough of that. None of that matters. What matters is me, you, your little boy, and this party."

They reached the crowd and he motioned toward the deck, suggesting they get a drink. Bottles of beer and pop prickled like a porcupine out of a shiny galvanized metal water trough filled with ice. Aidan pulled two beers out and twisted the tops off, then offered her one. She hesitated a moment, but accepted it and took a long drink.

She closed her eyes for a moment and sighed, a look of complete satisfaction on her face. He stared at her openly.

She was beautiful, there were no two ways about it. Being here, with her and her son, he could actually imagine being a member of a family, a real family.

Beau, standing by the barbecue grill, caught his eye, looked pointedly at Gina, then gave him a thumbs up. The corner of Aidan's mouth quirked up.

Folks stopped and talked to them, and several women from the community caught Gina and asked about the scrapbook store, upcoming events, and all sorts of gadgets that meant nothing to him. She lit up when she talked about her craft, talking with her hands as much as her words. He found himself smiling, even though he didn't understand all that was being said.

As she spoke, he watched her full lips move. Every now and then she caught him watching and smiled at him, her blue-green eyes dancing with delight. When she turned, her hair caught, falling over her shoulders. He followed the waves that led to her generous breasts. The material clung to her, showing every curve. He couldn't wait to cup them in his hands, feel their weight, tease her nipples with his tongue.

It was torture to be so close to her, surrounded by all these people. His erection grew, pressing against his jeans. God, he was ready to explode just thinking of her.

All that mattered was being with her, and he intended to do it right. He wanted to court her, wine and dine her, show her he was more than a simple cowhand. He wanted to be with her.

In every way that mattered.

CHAPTER THIRTY
Toby

Toby crawled through the straw maze as fast as he could, but bumped into dead ends more often than not. The prickly straw scraped at his sides when he turned corners, and he kept his head low so it wouldn't get in his hair. He didn't like that creepy feeling, as if fingers were reaching for him.

Once he slowed down and thought about where he was going and where he had been, he made it all the way through the maze. When he exited, a young girl met him with a big grin and lots of clapping. She held out a plastic bucket full of prizes and told him to pick one. After he pawed through the goodies, he selected a big bouncy ball, which he tucked carefully in his jeans' pocket.

The second time he went through the maze, he went slower. At each turn, he considered his options and chose which way to go instead of just plowing ahead. Other kids pushed past him, but he let them go and concentrated on his path. And it worked! The opening appeared before him and he scooted out, very proud of himself. He stood up and swiped the dust from his jeans.

The girl held out the bucket for him again. "Didn't I see you already?"

He grinned, "Yup."

"Then, I think you deserve another prize."

He peered into the bucket and spotted a model horse, with real hair for its mane and tail. He pointed at it. "Can I have that horse?"

She nodded and he snatched the toy from the bucket. He jogged over to the straw bales they'd sat on earlier and pretended to run the horse across the top of them. He made the horse fly off the bale, pretending it was jumping off a mountain and across a meadow full of very tall grass. The horse leapt over a stick and then another. After a while, Toby grew tired of playing with the toy horse and his thoughts turned to the calf.

He looked around for his mom and Aidan, and saw them next to the barbecue grill. He hurried over to them to show them his bouncy ball and his horse. After he showed off his prizes, he said, "Can we go see the baby cow again?"

Aidan shook his head and said, "No, she's probably taking a nap right now. But why don't you and your mom come back tomorrow night and you can help me feed her again? I'll make dinner for us."

Toby's eyes widened and he spun around to face his mother. "Mom! Did you hear that? Can we? Can we, please?"

His mother glanced at Aidan, who looked at her with

raised eyebrows. After a moment, she nodded. "Yes, I think I'd like to come back tomorrow night." She smiled really big.

Aidan offered, "Why don't you two come by tomorrow about 6 or so and I'll grill something after we feed the calf?"

Toby nodded. "What's her name?"

Aidan tapped his stubbly chin with one finger. "I haven't named her yet. Would you like to help me come up with a name for her?"

Toby let out a whoop and spun around, too excited to stand still. He took off, racing his toy horse along beside him, leaving the adults behind.

CHAPTER THIRTY-ONE
A Real Date

Gina was as excited as Toby as they got ready the next day. She'd had such a good time at the Diamond J barbecue. For the first time all week, she put aside her fears and worries about the scrapbook store and money and Steve and let herself enjoy the day. And why shouldn't she? Steve was probably off doing God knows what, without giving her or Toby a thought.

She caught herself.

That wasn't fair.

Steve was a good dad. He never forgot Toby's birthday, made a big deal out of holidays that were important to the boy, and had even gone to the parent-teacher conference with Toby's teacher. He loved their son.

As if on cue, Toby ran into the room, his little cowboy boots thumping on the hardwood floors. He slid to a stop and propped one foot out, toe pointing up. He bent over and wiped off an imaginary speck if dirt, then looked up at her. "These boots Daddy gave me really came in handy yesterday."

Gina nodded sagely. "Yes, they did. And he even got them in the right size." She had heard so many women at the scrapbook store complaining about the fact that their husbands had no clue what size clothes their kids wore.

Toby perched his hands on his hips. "They'll come in handy tonight, too. I been thinking about that baby cow. She needs a name."

Gina turned back to the mirror and leaned close, swiveling her face from side to side. Her skin was losing the glow of youth. Tiny crow's feet accented her blue-green eyes, but they were framed with a thick fringe of dark lashes. She pushed her hair back from her forehead.

Was her hairline receding? She leaned closer. No, surely not. She raked her fingers through her thick hair then shook it. It fell in loose waves around her shoulders. She frowned, afraid that might look like she was trying too hard. After a moment's hesitation, she grabbed an elastic band from the basket beside the sink, then brushed it back into a low ponytail.

She started to leave the bathroom, then spun back around and rummaged through the drawer that held her meager supply of makeup. She opened a tube of gloss and ran it across her lips, then smacked them together.

That was better.

She found Toby waiting anxiously by the back door. Both hands were perched on his hips and a deep frown furrowed his forehead. "We're going to be late, Mom."

It still caught her off guard when he called her Mom. Not Mommy, Mom. She swallowed the lump in her throat and hooked her purse over her shoulder. "No, we'll be right on time."

Her cell phone buzzed. She fished it out of her handbag and looked at the display. An 816 number. She didn't recognize it. She swiped the screen and put the phone to her ear. "Hello?"

"Is this Gina Montgomery?" It was a woman's voice.

"Speaking." A frown settled on her forehead and she felt instantly worried.

"I'm calling from Signet Enterprises. Do have a moment to talk?"

"I'm getting ready to go out." She didn't have time for some silly survey by a party store company.

"I'll keep this brief, then. Beth Jameson forwarded me an invitation she made for her, which led me to your blog."

Gina froze in her tracks. "Okay." Her heart pounded in her chest.

"We're very impressed with your party-planning ideas, and we'd like to offer you a consulting job with our creative department."

"What?" Gina reached out for the car and sagged against it. "I can't move--"

The voice cut her off. "Oh, no. This isn't a full-time position. It's part-time, remote. We think your retail location is a plus. We'd like to partner with you, but we don't want to take you out of your creative space."

"I don't know what to say."

The woman on the other end of the line laughed. "You don't have to say anything now. We can discuss details later, if you're interested."

Gina's mouth opened and closed. She thought of the

rent she had to come up with. "I hate to ask, but how much money are we talking?"

After she got her answer, Gina sank to the ground. They talked a little more about hours and a general overview of the position, then the woman promised to send a complete package detailing the offer.

After she hung up, she sat in the driveway with her legs curled under her. Gradually, she became aware of the gravel cutting into her flesh. It was real. She wasn't dreaming.

Toby stood in front of her with his fists perched on his hips. "Are we gonna go or what?"

Gina pushed to her feet as Toby tugged the rear car door open. He climbed onto his booster seat and tried to buckle himself in. She reached in and helped, then slid into the driver's seat, and they were off. The car started first try, which she took as a good sign. Her spirits were buoyed by the offer she'd just received.

Her store was saved!

She debated calling Midge, but decided to wait until she'd received the offer in writing. Plus, she wanted to do it in person. News this big deserved a celebration!

They turned into the driveway to the Diamond J, and Toby let out a jubilant whoop. As soon as they reached the parking area, Aidan stepped out of the barn and waited for them to park.

He was dressed in dark blue jeans molded to his legs. The sleeves of his red plaid shirt were rolled up, exposing muscled arms covered in a dusting of dark hair. His black hat shadowed his face, but she felt those electric blue eyes focused on her. Her body warmed under his gaze, responding to the animal magnetism that drew her to him.

Gina closed her eyes, took a steadying breath and a shiver ran down her spine. When she opened her eyes and glanced around, she realized that nearly all the vehicles there were black and shiny and new. Her battered blue Toyota stuck out like a sore thumb, just as Aidan's rusty white pickup did. With a grin, she realized that the offer from Signet might give her the opportunity to buy a new car.

As soon as Toby was released from his booster seat, he slid out of the car and ran toward the barn. He glanced back and yelled, "Come on, Mom!"

Gina slammed the car door and followed her son. Aidan took a step forward, into the sunlight. She smiled and felt her heart give a little flip-flop at the sight of him. She had nearly convinced herself that this wasn't a date, that this was just a nice guy being nice to her little boy. But with every step toward him, she hoped it was more than that.

She caught her lower lip with her teeth. "Hello!" she called out.

Aidan's lips split into a grin. "Howdy!"

By the time she reached him, Toby had grabbed Aidan's hand. Her son didn't know a stranger, but he wasn't usually this friendly. Aidan looked down and said in a very serious voice, "Toby, would you rather go eat first, or feed the calf first?"

The boy didn't hesitate. "Feed the baby!"

Aidan met Gina's gaze over the boy's head. "That okay with you?" he asked. His eyes danced with . . . What?

Excitement? Desire?

She nodded and followed as Aidan led Toby into the barn. He told Gina and Toby to go on ahead into the stall while he got the bottle ready. For the next fifteen minutes or so, it was all about the calf. Toby took his job very seriously, and Gina and Aidan leaned back against the smooth wooden wall.

Gina caught Aidan looking at her a few times. Each time she looked up, he unabashedly met her gaze. His eyes reminded her of a spring sky with lightning dancing across it. Barely contained. There was an undercurrent of danger there, but she was intrigued by the energy it promised.

When the calf sucked the last drop of milk from the bottle, Toby's shoulders drooped. He handed the bottle back to Aidan and sighed. "I guess she's done."

Aidan accepted the bottle. "Why don't we go roast some hot dogs, and then maybe we'll come back later and say goodnight to her?"

Toby nodded, but made no move to leave until Gina took his hand and said, "Her tummy is full and she'll probably want to take a nap."

The three of them left the barn and Aidan led the way around to the back of the big house. It was an amazing home, a huge log cabin with a wraparound porch. Gina counted three chimneys growing out of the high peaked roof.

The backside of the house was just as impressive. They rounded the corner and a huge flagstone patio curved along the back of the home, flanked by low benches and huge potted plants. The centerpiece was a stone fire pit ringed with Adirondack chairs.

Gina sat in one of the chairs while Toby ran around the patio, checking out every nook and cranny. Aidan had already started a fire, which now burned low, perfect for hot dogs. The sun hung low in the Western sky, rays of sunlight poking through the thick dark clouds. The warmth of the fire was welcome in the cool evening air. It smelled like rain.

Gina was impressed with how well prepared he was. She hadn't noticed the outdoor kitchen at first. A built in grill took up the majority of the space, with a sink set into the stone countertop next to it. He pulled out a package of hot dogs out of the small refrigerator and pushed two of them on a long metal fork.

He motioned to Toby. "Want to help me roast hot dogs for you and your mom?"

Toby hurried over to him, then rubbed his hands anxiously on his thighs. "How—?"

Aidan held the fork out and showed Toby how to make a fist around the handle, then he wrapped his own hand over the boy's chubby fist. Together, they held the hot dogs close to the glowing red coals. Aidan glanced up at Gina. "Help yourself to a hot dog. There's another fork over there." He nodded toward the built in grill.

As Gina roasted her own hot dog she watched Aidan work with her son. Men usually did one of two things. They either pretended her son didn't exist and ignored him completely, or they spoiled him in a blatant attempt to impress her. Her eyes narrowed as she watched Aidan curl his arms around Toby as they roasted the hot dogs.

Aidan looked up at her and his grin faded. "What's the matter?"

She waved the question off, then turned away to get her hot dog. She returned to the fire pit and squatted on her heels, holding the hot dog close to the red hot coals. She could feel Aidan's eyes on her.

He ducked his head to catch her eye and raised his eyebrows. "Is something wrong? Did I do something?"

She sucked in a deep breath and blew it out. "No. You didn't do anything wrong." Yet. Things were going so well, she just knew the other shoe was going to drop.

Toby jerked his hand back and yelled, "Fire!"

Aidan pushed the boy back with one hand as he pulled the stick holding the flaming hot dog out of the fire, then puffed his cheeks out and blew. Only one hot dog had caught fire, but both were well done.

One corner of Aidan's mouth twitched up and he looked at Toby. "How 'bout you grab me a couple of buns off the table?" He glanced over the fire pit at Gina. "Are you laughing at me?"

"Maybe." She hadn't even realized she'd been smiling. She shrugged. "Hope you like your hot dogs crispy."

Toby returned with a bag of hot dog buns. Aidan showed him how to use the bun to pull the hot dog off the fork.

Toby looked doubtful, then looked at Gina. His eyebrows arched over his big blue eyes. His lower lip pooched out just a bit. "I don't like plain food."

Aidan pushed to his feet and strode over to the little

refrigerator. He returned with a bottle of ketchup and the boy brightened. Aidan said, "I don't like plain food either. Everything needs ketchup."

Toby giggled. "Not everything!"

Gina waited until her own hot dog was crispy and bubbly then joined Aidan and her son in the chairs. The crickets chirped happily, and a bullfrog sang his deep song in the distance. Gina felt herself relax as Aidan and Toby wolfed down their food and roasted two more hot dogs.

She rested her head against the chair back and looked up at the velvet black sky. Stars twinkled like diamonds between the clouds, and she began to recognize constellations. A sliver of the moon was visible just above the oak trees along the back fence line.

Tension slid from her body. Her money troubles were over, and she'd met a cowboy that seemed nearly perfect. Toby was too excited to sit. Instead, he stood next to her, leaning against her leg.

Aidan pushed up out of the chair and went to the outdoor kitchen. He returned with a package of graham crackers, a bag of big puffy marshmallows and a handful of chocolate bars. Gina smiled and tilted her head to the side as she looked up at him in the orange glow of the fire. He had thought of everything. Maybe this wasn't an act.

By the time they finished their s'mores, all three of them had sticky fingers and chocolate smiles. Gina couldn't remember the last time she'd enjoyed a treat like that. Toby stood with his hands out, fingers spread wide.

"We can go inside and wash up." Aidan stood and looked down at her. He held out his own hand, fingers splayed, palm out. "I'd offer you a hand, but I'm kinda sticky myself."

Gina pushed herself out of the chair, using the heel of her hands to avoid spreading the marshmallow stickiness any further.

Together, the three of them walked across the flagstone pavers and through the back door of the house. Gina's eyes widened when Aidan flipped on the kitchen light. It was a bright, airy kitchen decorated in buttery yellow and white. A huge wooden farm table anchored the room, topped by a crock filled with sunflowers.

She washed her own hands, then helped Toby wash his. As he dried his hands on the towel Aidan offered, Gina noticed how droopy her son's eyes were. It had been a big day for him.

Aidan caught her eye and smiled. His eyes were so blue, startling in contrast to his dark hair. They were kind and intelligent, not hard like some men's. His face was deeply tanned, his jaw square and strong, shadowed with stubble. When he smiled, a dimple formed in his right cheek, and she longed to reach out and touch it.

Toby yawned, drawing her back to reality. Her hand dropped to her side and she blinked rapidly. Good grief, she'd actually been about to touch his dimple! What was wrong with her? She was acting like a love sick teenager.

Aidan said, "Would you like to go for a walk down to the pond? It's a beautiful night."

Toby drooped against her leg. She looked up at Aidan. "Looks like Toby's beat. Maybe another—"

Toby pushed away from her leg and looked up at her.

His eyebrows pushed together like a couple of inchworms. "I am not," he protested.

Aidan offered, "Maybe you'd like to watch TV while your mom and I go for a walk?"

Toby's eyes narrowed as he regarded the man seriously. "Do you have Scooby Doo?"

Aidan grinned, his white teeth brilliant against his tanned skin. One slightly crooked tooth overlapped another, but other than that, his smile was perfect. "We do have Scooby Doo. Several movies, actually." He turned his attention to Gina. "Would it be okay if Toby watched some TV while we go for a walk?"

Doubt niggled at her. Was he doing this to get rid of her son? Or was he being nice? Did he just want to get her alone? Her own body betrayed her, with a warm feeling spreading throughout her body, centered deep within her.

She might be a mother, but she was also a woman with needs, who longed to be held by a man, to feel his lips on hers, his hands on her hips, his weight on top of her.

Toby looked up at her, his hands clasped together. "Please?" he pleaded.

She threw up her hands in mock surrender. She trailed behind Aidan and Toby into the living room. Massive furniture and impressive Western art filled the cavernous space. Aidan opened a heavy armoire to expose a large television. Moments later, the Scooby Doo theme filled the air. Gina glanced around. Where was everyone? She knew Beau and Beth lived here, and the housekeeper, Charlotte?

Aidan pulled a large turquoise cushion from beside the couch and dropped it to the floor in front of the television.

Toby promptly flopped on it, chest down, face cradled in his hands. Aidan swept his hand toward the kitchen. "Shall we go for a walk?"

She looked quickly at him. Shall we? This cowboy was a real gentleman, full of surprises. Gina looked at Aidan, eyes wide, eyebrows arched. She motioned toward the hallway. "Are you sure this is okay? He won't wake anyone up?"

"No. Beau and Beth are out tonight. They went to a movie, so they won't be home until late. Charlotte is in her room, but I already asked her if it was okay if I brought Toby inside to watch TV. She said it was fine." Color crept up his face and the words rushed out of his mouth. "All we have in the bunk house is a little TV, and I didn't think he'd be as comfortable out there. It's not as nice as this. And Charlotte is here if he needs anything."

Gina examined his face, his cheeks showing a hint of color. His apparent embarrassment was endearing.

Aidan reached down and touched her shoulder. She closed her mouth. He was right. She'd given Toby plenty of instructions, and he was already engrossed in his movie. With Scooby Doo on the screen, he'd be nearly catatonic for the next hour or so, at least.

She followed Aidan through the kitchen and out the back door. The crescent moon had risen above the trees and offered enough light for them to see as it peeked through the clouds.

As they stepped off the flagstone patio, Gina noticed the ribbon of white that curved ahead of them toward the pond. Aidan's boots crunched on the graveled path.

The Diamond J was a working ranch, legend in the little town of Wilder and beyond. While here, she felt like she'd been plucked out of Missouri and dropped into the West. She glanced at the cowboy walking beside her. She'd dreamed of finding a cowboy as a young girl, and here she was.

But was she wasting her time? Could she really have a future with a man who made his living on horseback, who lived in a bunkhouse with other hired hands? She glanced over her shoulder at the dark hulk of the log home - cabin didn't begin to cover it. But that home wasn't his. It belonged to his boss.

Did that even matter? With the new offer from Signet, she felt more secure. It wasn't like she needed a man to take care of her financially.

Images flashed through her mind. He'd been so patient with Toby even though Toby kept touching his hot dog to the coals. And he'd saved that poor little calf. Aidan was a good man.

Aidan gently threaded his fingers through hers, and a spark of electricity jolted through her body. She'd never been so attracted to a man so quickly. If she had a reaction like this, she could only imagine how explosive sex would be with him.

It had been far too long since she'd been with a man. Was this the first step? Was he going to make his move, now that her son was safely distracted?

Aidan glanced down at her. "Is this okay?" He wiggled his fingers against hers.

She nodded, sucked in a deep breath and let it out

slowly. She needed to slow down, quit overthinking things. He was holding her hand, not groping her. His hand was rough and calloused, and hers was nearly lost in his gentle grip.

The path curved slightly to the right, following the edge of the lake. Cattails swayed gently in the breeze, and a startled frog jumped into the water with a splash.

Aidan pulled her forward slightly and dropped her hand. He touched her back lightly with one hand and grasped her elbow with the other as he guided her to a wooden bench that she could just barely make out it the darkness. She sat, and he sat next to her, their thighs touching lightly. The thin cotton sun dress pulled up slightly, so the rough denim of his jeans brushed against her bare skin.

She gazed out at the inky darkness of the water. The moonlight created a shimmering path across the surface. They sat in comfortable silence, listening to the bullfrogs croaking and insects chirping. An owl hooted in the distance. Cows mooed, and a horse whinnied.

Suddenly, a high-pitched yipping sounded nearby. Gina jumped at the sound and pressed closer against Aidan. He curled his arm around her shoulders and pulled her close, the hair on his arm tickling the sensitive skin on her neck. He turned his head and murmured against her hair, "Just a coyote. Nothing to worry about."

She shivered. "But don't they go after calves?"

"Sounds different when they're hunting. That one is just singing to the moon."

She nodded once, quickly, glad he was with her. He

seemed to be content out here in the darkness, with nothing but the crescent moon lighting the landscape. She leaned into him, enjoying the safe feeling. She hadn't felt that in a long time. Most of the time, she was the one in charge, she was the one comforting Toby. She glanced at her watch.

He said, "Do you need to be somewhere?"

She shook her head. "No, just wanted to make sure I don't leave Toby for too long."

He smiled, his white teeth gleaming in the pale moonlight. "He seems to be a big Scooby Doo fan. I don't think you have to worry about him going anywhere for a while."

She swallowed hard. She hadn't been alone with a man in a long time. Hell, she hadn't been on a date in over a year. Midge had reminded her of that just hours before while they were picking out her outfit for the date. What was she supposed to do? What did Aidan expect? Desire stirred deep within her.

Her brain might not remember how things worked, but her body knew.

As if he'd read her mind, Aidan shifted to face her. He brushed a stray strand of hair from her face, then ran his index finger over the curve of her cheek. "You're beautiful," he whispered.

Her face warmed, and she was glad it was dark. She gazed up at him and wished she could see his eyes. He lowered his face to hers and kissed her gently on the lips, then pulled back. "I can't stop thinking about you." His voice was low. Husky.

She pressed her lips together then opened her mouth slightly and leaned forward, running her hand up his muscled chest as she pressed her lips to his. He pulled her close, his arm curled around her back. She ran her fingers through his hair, then cupped the back of his neck and let herself enjoy the feeling. Warmth spread through her body and she shifted closer, pressing against him. They explored, his tongue gently touching her lips then probing deeper. She flicked her tongue against his, playing, teasing. Her heart thudded so hard in her chest, she was sure he could feel it.

What was she doing, making out in the dark like a teenager stealing kisses?

She pushed the nagging voice away.

The sexy stubble on his chin rubbed lightly against her skin. His hand moved slowly over her back, fingers splayed, pulling her to him. The rough edge of the bench dug into the back of her leg. The sensation was good, grounding, reminded her this was real. Not a fantasy.

She shifted, putting her leg over his, acutely aware of the generous bulge in his jeans as her leg brushed against him. She let her hand roam over his muscled chest, dipping her fingertips between the buttons of his shirt to brush across his thickly curled hair.

Their kiss deepened, both desperate with need. Her hand moved lower. She traced the chiseled abs and felt them tense as she dropped her hand to his waist, then down even further. He groaned, then sucked in a breath as she rubbed against him, feeling him grow.

How she longed to feel him inside of her.

His fingers traced lightly over her shoulders, along her breastbone, then down her side. Her own breathing grew ragged when he touched the curve of her breast. He cupped one breast in his hand. His thumb gently teased her nipple and she moaned as it tightened, responding to his urging.

The sensation of his touch through the thin cotton of her dress nearly drove her out of her mind. All the pent up desire she'd felt over the past week washed over her, drowning her doubt and hesitation. She shifted to press closer to him.

He dropped his hand and she gasped at the sudden loss, but quickly forgot when she felt the pressure of his hand against her the sensitive skin on the inside of her thigh. His calloused hand was gentle on her bare skin as he massaged her, working his way up. She swallowed hard and felt a chill ran down her spine as his fingertips brushed her skin.

Their kiss grew more frantic as they explored each other. His hand moved to her mound, teasing through the thin satin that separated them until she threw her head back and moaned, giving in to the sensation. One finger slipped under the satin, then two fingers. He found her sensitive spot and her pulse quickened as he began moving in a circular motion.

Her breath came in ragged gasps and her whole world became centered on that one tiny spot, that little bud that he found and explored and . . . Oh, God, it was almost more than she could take! She trembled under his touch and his arm behind her was all that kept her from collapsing. He leaned forward, kissed her neck and flicked his tongue along her shoulder. She moved against him as his fingers circled faster and faster, their rhythm in perfect harmony.

She pressed her eyes closed and shuddered as the waves crashed over her, over and over, until finally she collapsed into his embrace. Her breath came in gasps and she shivered, aftershocks still rocking her body.

His hand rested on the curve of her hip as her trembling subsided, then his fingers slid along her skin, tugging her panties down.

She swallowed hard, struggling to regain her balance. She pressed one hand to his chest and pushed slightly. He pulled back and looked at her, his eyes dark with passion. He shifted the satin fabric lower, but she pushed harder.

"No," she murmured. "We can't. I can't." She sucked in a deep breath and let it out slowly.

He gazed into her eyes, opened his mouth and sucked in a deep breath. They were so close she could feel his heartbeat, felt his chest rise and fall.

Finally, he leaned back against the bench and let out a low groan. "I'm so sorry. I shouldn't have—"

"No." She put one finger up to his mouth and gently touched his lips. A breeze floated over the lake, cooling her sweat-slicked skin after the fire he'd stoked within her.

"You're killin' me." He stared up at the sky, his chest rising and falling as his breathing returned to normal, then put an arm around her shoulder and pulled her close. "You know I want you."

She nodded, then swallowed hard. "I know. But Toby—

"

"I know. I know." He smiled down at her, still holding her tight against him. She nestled her head against his shoulder and basked in the attention. He caressed her shoulder and kissed the top of her head. "I'm sorry."

She tilted her head back and gazed into his eyes. "You have nothing to apologize for."

"Oh, but I do." He lowered his head and kissed the tip of her nose. "I just pleasured you on a bench. You deserve to be wined and dined, to be courted."

A giggle bubbled up. "Courted? You are an amazing man, Aidan Brackston." As the blush of pleasure faded, the realization that she had forgotten about her son for the briefest of moments was a sobering thought. Her head jerked around and her eyes settled on the yellow light shining from the kitchen of the big house.

Aidan touched her chin with his finger and turned her face gently back until their faces were inches from each other. "I'm sorry I got carried away."

She nodded. "So did I."

Boy, did she. Her chest rose and fell with a deep sigh. Her whole body felt limp, satisfied, happy. She rested her head on his shoulder.

He kissed the top of her head. He whispered, "I'm falling hard for you."

Her heart swelled with happiness. "Me, too."

They gazed out at the inky darkness of the lake. His fingers traced lazy circles on her bare shoulder.

Gradually, she became aware of a dog barking in the distance and cows mooing. A sharp cry shattered the stillness of the night. She jerked up straight and swiveled her head left and right, trying to determine the source of the sound. Her heart raced. Every nerve in her body tingled. Her ears pricked up and she was on high alert.

Aidan pulled her closer. "It's okay. That was a screech owl."

She sagged with relief.

Suddenly, Aidan stiffened and his eyes widened.

"What—?" Gina asked, but he clamped a hand over her mouth. She blinked in surprise.

Then she heard it.

Cows mooing. Hooves stomping in the dirt. A dog barking. The clank of a metal gate.

And a big truck roaring to life.

CHAPTER THIRTY-TWO

Rustlers

Aidan jumped to his feet and turned slowly in a circle, his head cocked to the side, his eyes narrowed in concentration.

"What—?" Gina's eyes widened as she pushed to her feet. Sound carried out here. She couldn't tell which direction the noise was coming from. The sound of mooing had stopped. The only sound was the slow rumble of an engine, a big engine jerking to life.

"Oh, no! No, no, no—" Aidan grabbed her hand and took off running. She struggled to keep up as he ran through the field. Weeds and tall grass whipped at her arms as her legs pumped madly. He dropped her hand and plowed ahead.

She squinted in the darkness, trying to keep him in sight. She could hear him crashing through the brush, cursing and breathing hard. Suddenly, a sharp pain sliced into her shin and she pitched forward, landing with a grunt.

Aidan spun around and shouted, "You okay?"

She waved him on. "I'm okay! Go! Go!"

She got to her feet and brushed her hands together. Her palms stung, but she swiped them down her thighs and hurried after Aidan. She found him at the edge of the road, hands dangling at his sides, breathing hard. He stared at two sets of taillights disappearing into the night. A semi and a pickup truck, by the looks of it.

He pointed to the side of the road without turning. Gina followed his finger and deflated when she saw the metal gate swinging freely in the breeze.

"Damn," she groaned. She stepped forward and placed her hand on Aidan's shoulder, panting from the run through the pasture. Rain drops began to fall, pelting them as they stood along the side of the road.

He nodded and spoke tersely. "Cattle rustlers. They hit this area last summer, but hadn't been a problem again until just the last few weeks. That's how I ended up with that little calf. Thieves stole the whole herd from Claude's place and left that baby behind."

Gina frowned. She'd assumed the mama cow had died or something. The thought of thieves being so callous as to rip a mother from her baby twisted her heart. How careless. How cruel. Her gaze swept the darkness. "They took the whole herd?" Shivers shook her body as the cold rain began to fall harder.

"Yup." Aidan pointed at the tire marks in the dirt by the gate. "Pulled the semi trailer right up there to the gate and loaded them up in minutes."

"I'm sorry," she murmured. "Are you insured?"

"Of course Beau and Beth're insured, but that doesn't

help the cows or me now, does it?" He scowled at her. "My cattle were in that pasture, too."

She blinked rapidly, stung by his words. She opened her mouth to apologize, then closed it. Lightning bolted across the sky. A breeze ruffled her hair and cooled the sweat on her neck. A shiver ran down her spine. Thunder shook the ground.

He took a step toward her, then gathered her in his arms. "I'm sorry. I'm upset."

She snaked her arms around his waist and squeezed. He seemed genuinely upset. She has to admit, it surprised her. She'd thought a man like him would be hardened to the fate of animals. Then again, he'd surprised her several times in the little time they'd spent together.

"Come on," she urged. Let's go back to the house, get out of this rain."

He released her and twined his fingers with hers. "Right. I need to call the Sheriff."

They walked along the fence and soon reached the driveway. The front of the house was illuminated with uplighting placed strategically behind shrubs and dwarf trees. As they got closer, the outline of the door became visible, spilling light from inside the home.

Aidan glanced around. "That's odd."

Gina said, "Maybe Charlotte heard something and came out to check."

Aidan dropped her hand and took the porch steps two at a time. He ducked his head inside. Suddenly, Gina felt her stomach clench.

Toby.

Oh, God, she'd been so focused on Aidan—

She raced up the steps and through the open door. She heard Aidan's boots pound down the hallway as he shouted for Charlotte and Toby. She looked at the television, which was nothing but blackness. The DVD case sat on the floor, open and empty. The cushion Toby had laid on was rumpled, still indented from his weight.

She spun around and yelled, "Toby!"

No answer.

Panic curled around her heart and squeezed as she fought to keep control of her emotions. She wouldn't do him any good running around like a chicken with her head cut off. The kitchen. Maybe he went to get something to eat or drink. She ran to the kitchen, her wet shoes slapping against the wooden floor, then flipped the light on. Empty.

Think. She had to think.

She flew out the back door to the patio, shouting his name. Her little boy. He was alone. He was scared. He was in unfamiliar territory. Where would he go? Looking for her, most likely.

Aidan appeared in the doorway and stepped out. "Did you find him?"

"No!" Gina's voice wavered. Sanity was hanging by a thread.

"The boy is missing?" Charlotte appeared in the doorway, pulling her bathrobe belt tight. "I'll stay here and search the house. The two of you look outside." She waved them away.

Gina nodded and swallowed the lump in her throat.

Right. Maybe he was playing hide and seek. Could it be that simple? Oh, please, please let it be, she pleaded with any power that might be listening. She spun around, unsure which direction to go.

Suddenly the area jumped to life and Aidan appeared from beside the house. He'd flipped on lights, which lit up the patio area, but created sharp, disorienting shadows. Lots of places for a little boy to hide.

He strode to her and placed a large black flashlight in her hand. "I'm going to go look by the lake. Maybe he followed us down there."

She gulped and swiped the rain from eyes, hoping her son hadn't followed them. If he saw them kissing — or doing other things — what would he think? Embarrassment burned her cheeks. Why hadn't she stopped Aidan? Would Toby be angry?

Maybe that's why he ran. The thought horrified her. She shook her head. No. He liked Aidan. He wouldn't have run. He might've been confused, scared even, by what he saw. But it was dark. He couldn't have seen much. She shook the worry away. There was no time for that - she had to find her son.

Maybe he took cover when the rain hit.

Her eyes widened as it hit her. The calf! She flipped her own flashlight on and skidded around the side of the house and toward the barn. Aidan pounded behind her, the beam from his flashlight bobbing along in front of them just like hers. The big sliding door was open a bit, a slash of black against the red siding. Hope buoyed her along.

She was right! He was out here, she knew it. She hurried down the aisle and slid to a stop in front of the calf's stall. She jerked the door open and swept the light through the stall. The calf bawled angrily as she jumped to her feet, eyes wide with fear.

No Toby.

Gina dropped to her knees, water dripping from her rain-slicked hair.

Aidan squeezed her shoulder. "Don't worry. We'll find him."

CHAPTER THIRTY-THREE
Kidnapping

Rondo jumped into the truck, threw the transmission in drive, then stomped on the gas. He kept right on Lana's tail as she pushed the semi hard. He glanced in the rearview mirror and saw a man in a cowboy hat standing on the edge of the road. Thank goodness they had a head start. Even if that guy went back to get a vehicle to chase them, they'd be long gone. Rondo grabbed his cell phone off the seat and punched in Lana's number.

As soon as she answered, he said, "Somebody saw us."

She scoffed. "All anybody could've seen was a couple of trucks. No way they could'a seen more than that."

Lana was reckless, and he had to put a stop to her insolence. "They saw a semi and a pickup." He gritted his teeth. He'd deal with her back at the compound.

Her voice was muffled for a moment, then she was back. "OK, instead of going all the way to a safe sale barn, let's go to Brackston's place."

Rondo's nostrils flared as he blew out a deep breath. "You sure it's safe? We've been using it a lot lately."

She snapped, "Of course it is."

Because her little pet Steve said it was. "They're pretty rough with the animals there." Memories of what he'd seen the last time they dropped off a load of cattle at Brackston made his stomach turn, and he wasn't easily sickened.

She snorted. "Follow me."

Rondo dropped his phone in the passenger seat and fumed. It was dangerous to work this part of Missouri anyway, with Lana's nephew working at the Diamond J. He shook his head. That's why she suggested they hit the ranch tonight. Lana convinced him it was a way to throw the authorities off the scent. He'd gone along with it.

Everything Lana wanted, Lana got. It had been that way since him and her hooked up. She knew how to work him. The woman was flexible as hell and up for anything when it came to sex. He ran the family, and enjoyed having a woman at his side.

But she was forgetting her place.

Raindrops splattered against the windshield, blurring the road. He flipped the wipers on and listened to the rhythmic squeak as he followed Lana and Steve. Might as well settle in. Brackston was a good two hours away.

By the time they reached the turnoff for the Brackston Meat Company, his eyes were gritty and dry. Lana slowed the rig as they drove down the narrow blacktop. The trees nearly touched overhead. Lightning streaked across the sky every few minutes, throwing shadows across the road.

The glow from the huge processing plant was visible long before the buildings were. That place was lit up like broad daylight 24 hours a day.

Lana pulled into the graveled lot and the semi shuddered to a stop. Rondo alongside her and put the transmission in park, but left the engine running. Normally, he'd turn the truck off to save gas, but the BMC gave him the willies. If anything went sideways, he planned to throw gravel and lay rubber.

He watched through the rivulets of water on the window as the passenger door of the semi opened and Steve dropped to the ground. The little weasel lifted his jacket over his head, glanced around the lot, then strolled into the building through a side door as if he owned the place.

That guy came out of nowhere, and ingratiated himself with Lana in no time at all. He seemed to know a lot of people, and Lana trusted him.

Didn't mean he had to, though, Rondo thought.

The big garage door of the building yawned open, then Steve stepped out and motioned to Lana. The semi rolled forward, swallowed by the building, then the door closed. They were in.

Rondo looked down at his watch. The whole herd would be unloaded in a matter of minutes. Open the gates and down they come, one by one. Three sections in the trailer. Five minutes max per section to unload. Fifteen minutes.

Steve and Lana'd bullshit with the guys inside. Then they'd close up the gates, roll up the door on the other side and Lana'd pull out. She should drive around the side of the building and be ready to head out in half an hour, tops. He slid down in the driver's seat and let his head fall back against the ripped vinyl of the headrest.

If Steve was such a great guy, why'd he drive a piece of shit like this? The old Ford had nearly 200,000 miles on it, the seats were worn and the transmission made a funny sound when it shifted sometimes. Rondo wasn't sure how he'd ended up driving the little prick's truck while Steve rode in the semi with Lana. It just ended up that way, somehow, when they had to take off quick.

A lightning bolt shot out of the sky, straight into the trees. Thunder shook the ground almost immediately. An involuntary shiver ran down his spine. That was close.

A mewling, sniffling sound caught his attention. He sat bolt upright, every sense on alert. His eyes swept over the parking lot. No sign of the cattle hauler yet. A quick glance at his watch told him it had been twenty minutes since Lana drove into the building.

Another muffled sound. It came from the back seat. He pushed himself up and peeked over the seat. The blanket in the back seat shifted slightly. He swung his door open, slid out and tugged the back door open. He grabbed the blanket and yanked, exposing a small boy with wide, frightened eyes set in a round face. His chubby cheeks were covered with bright red splotches, streaked with dried tears.

"I want my daddy."

CHAPTER THIRTY-FOUR
Rondo

The grinding of gears and low growl of the cattle hauler's engine told Rondo that Lana was rounding the corner of the building. He held his hand over his eyes to block the rain. She rolled across the lot and he waved a hand to flag her down. The semi jerked to a stop and she leaned her head out the window. "What's going on?"

Rondo jerked his thumb to indicate the back seat. "We got a problem."

Just then, the boy scrambled across the seat and dropped to the ground. Rondo hooked the kid's arm with a beefy hand and held on tight. "Where do you think you're going?"

Lana closed her eyes and cursed.

Rondo lifted the boy up and tossed him into the back seat, then threw the blanket over the kid. He looked over his shoulder at Lana. "We can't leave him here. We can't take him home."

Steve leaned across Lana and asked, "Who is he?"

Rondo's brow furrowed. "How the hell should I know?"

266

Lana said, "It must have been at the Diamond J. That's the only place we've stopped since we left the compound."

A blue pickup truck turned into the lot and pulled up to the front door. The driver stared at them when he got out, then spun and pushed through the side door. The kid started to yell, but Rondo smothered the sound with the blanket. He said, "We're drawing attention out here. What do you want to do?"

"Shit," Lana cursed again. "Let's pull the trucks over to the edge of the lot and take him inside. It's loud in there. I need time to think. To figure this out."

Rondo shoved the boy back roughly then slammed the door and climbed into the driver's seat. He threw the transmission in drive and followed Lana to the shadowy edge of the lot, where the big dusk to dawn lights didn't reach.

After he stopped, he reached in the back, wrapped the blanket around the boy, then threw the bundle over his shoulder like a sack of feed. The kid kicked and struggled and tried to yell, but the blanket muffled the sound.

Steve and Lana fell in step beside him. Steve eyed the blanketed kid and whispered, "Dump him off in the office and leave." He reached out to pull the edge of the blanket back.

Rondo spun away and snorted. "Not a chance. The kid saw my face." Easy for that know-it-all prick to say. He didn't have anything at risk.

Steve pulled his ball cap lower over his eyes and shrugged.

"Enough." Lana made a cutting motion with her hand.

Her gaze settled on a black extended cab Ford, a King Ranch edition. Her eyes narrowed. "We don't know how much he's seen and heard, and we aren't taking no chances."

They reached the side door and Steve tugged it open. Rondo followed Lana inside, and Steve took up the rear. The three of them shook off the rain. The bright glare of the interior lights made Rondo blink. His eyes were already tired and gritty. The kid struggled in the blanket, his feet kicking frantically. Smart kid. He knew he was in trouble.

They stood in a staging area, with a row of lockers against one wall. Keys hung from carefully labeled hooks just inside the door, and a scarred desk squatted in the center of the room, covered with an array of papers and forms, broken pens and stubby pencils.

A faded green door led to the deeper reaches of the processing plant. It pushed open and a tall skinny kid, maybe twenty tops, strode through.

He froze and his close-set eyes narrowed. "Who are you?"

The boy chose that moment to wiggle and kick, then a muffled cry sounded. Rondo shifted the boy and squeezed him tighter. He stopped fighting, but continued to sob.

The tall skinny kid focused on the blanket. "What's going on here?" he demanded. His hand shifted to the bulge on his hip.

Lana stepped forward, between Rondo and the nervous kid. "You know who I am, right." She reached out and tapped his chest where the name Matt was embroidered on a patch.

Matt's eyes slid to her, then back to the quivering blanket. He nodded once, his Adam's apple bobbing as he swallowed hard.

"We need a quiet place to . . ." Her voice trailed off and she hooked a thumb over her shoulder at Rondo. "Him and me need to talk to Brennan."

The kid's chest rose and fell as he sucked in a breath. "Don't think he's here."

"Oh, he's here. I saw his truck outside." Lana jerked her chin to the side.

Finally, the kid shrugged and turned, disappearing through the green door.

Rondo shifted the bundle on his shoulder. The boy didn't weigh much, but he wouldn't stop wiggling. What were they going to do with a rug rat? He knew what Lana likely wanted to do, but he needed to lay down the law. Lana was cold as ice when it came to protecting their little band of thieves, but they'd never crossed into cold blooded murder and he wasn't about to start now.

A short, stubby man with a balding head pushed through the green door. He was only slightly taller than Lana, but twice as wide. He wore a button up shirt, with the top button undone to expose a triangle of tangled gray chest hair. A thick gold chain sparkled at his throat. The broken capillaries covering his bulbous nose hinted at a life of heavy drinking. Right now, though, he was stone cold sober and the flush of his cheeks indicated anger, not drink.

He glared at Steve, then Lana, and finally, his gaze

settled on Rondo. His beady eyes narrowed. "What — or who? — is in that blanket?"

Lana stepped forward and put a hand flat on the stubby man's chest. "Brennan, we've known each other a long time. The less you know, the better. But we need someplace quiet and safe until we can figure out our next move."

Brennan's eyes flicked to the woman in front of him. "There's a storage room in the basement. You can use it."

He spun away, opened the green door and shouted, "Matt!"

The tall skinny kid appeared almost immediately. "Yeah, boss?" His eyes darted around the room, then lit on Brennan.

The stubby man waved a hand at Rondo and the other two. "Take them to the back corner storage room and make sure everybody knows that room is off limits to everyone until further notice." He crossed his arms over his barrel chest and watched as the three marched out of the room. Rondo glanced back at the man.

He'd never liked Brennan. The man had a cruel streak in him a mile wide, and Rondo didn't trust him as far as he could throw 'im. He swung the kid to his other shoulder. They walked through a maze of hallways. Fluorescent lights hummed overhead. The cinder block walls were plain, utilitarian, punctuated by cheap core doors. Cattle mooed and bellowed from other parts of the building.

Matt opened a door and motioned for them to follow him. Lana went first, followed by Steve. Rondo went last and walked carefully down the steps behind Lana and

Steve, gripping the cold metal handrail and placing his feet carefully on each tread.

They went down two flights of narrow stairs. At the bottom, the stairwell opened into a wide hallway with a low ceiling, punctuated with dangling bare bulbs every twenty feet or so. The only sound was the echo of their boots on the worn linoleum tile. Rondo followed the others and occasionally glanced over his shoulder. This place gave him the creeps.

The skinny kid stopped in front of a heavy metal door with a small window inset in it. He tugged a ring of keys from his pocket and tried several before the door swung open with a low creak. He swept his hand to indicate they should go on in. Rondo followed Lana and Steve, squeezing to get past the skinny kid.

The room was low and dark, lined with cartons and crates. Rondo had to duck to keep from hitting his head on the dangling industrial light. He lowered the kid to a pallet, and the brat immediately began kicking and screaming.

"Shut that kid up!" Lana ordered.

Rondo tightened the blanket around the kid, then sat on the edge. The muffled cries finally stopped, and the rug rat quit struggling. Try as he might, Rondo couldn't think of a good ending to this situation. Once they got back to the compound, he was going to set Lana straight. But first, they had to deal with the situation.

Lana crossed her arms and tapped her chin with her index finger. Her lips pursed and the muscles under her eyes tightened. "First thing we gotta do is get the vehicles out of here, back to the compound. They're like a flashing neon sign out there in the parking lot. Somebody's gonna spot 'em and wonder."

Rondo nodded. She was right. This place was full of crooks and thieves who wouldn't hesitate to make a call if they thought there was a reward. Or they might try to get a piece of the action. He glanced down at the slight form in the blanket. Could they hold the kid for ransom? The Diamond J was money. Maybe they'd be willing to pay to get him back.

He shifted on the pallet, gathering his feet under him. "You drive the semi and I'll drive the truck. I'll send one of the boys back here—"

Lana held up her hand, palm out. "No. Me and Steve'll go back to the compound. Then we'll decide what to do with him." She reached out a toe and poked at the blanket. The kid mewled pitifully.

Steve grinned and held out his hand. Rondo couldn't stand the little prick. Steve was too slick. Too sneaky. He was always going off on his own, his phone tucked tightly against his ear. And the way he wore his ball cap pulled low over his eyes. Steve wiggled his fingers, palm up.

Lana warned, "Rondo. Now. We ain't got time for attitude."

Rondo clenched his fists. He wanted nothing more than to wrap his hands around her neck and squeeze. He sucked in a deep breath and fought to control his temper. What mattered now was the family, and the first thing he needed to do was keep the kid safe, because if they crossed the line and ended up wanted for murder, the whole family would suffer.

He straightened out his right leg, then pulled the keys from his front jeans pocket. He tossed them to Steve, who snatched them out of the air with a flourish and grin.

Rondo ignored him and turned to Lana. "Want me to do some checking? Find out who he is?"

She looked at him and arched her thinly penciled eyebrows. "Why?"

Rondo gave a short laugh. "We could ransom him. Make some money off this clusterfuck."

Lana answered with a wry laugh of her own. "Sounds like a lot of trouble to me. Probably better if you dispose of it."

Rondo shook his head slowly. "Not a good idea." Murder wasn't their way. And he sure as hell wasn't going to be the one to do it.

She waved her hand to indicate the storage room. "Concrete walls. Basement. Wait until tomorrow when the business upstairs is in full gear and no one'll hear a thing."

He pressed his lips together and sighed. Whether he wanted to admit it or not, Lana scared him. She was crazy. He'd seen her slit a man's throat and leave him to bleed out in the dirt one night around the bonfire back at the compound. He wasn't even sure what Deke had said to her, but because Lana was Rondo's woman, he'd let her get by with it.

Lana opened the heavy door with a grunt, then followed Steve out. After the door slammed shut with a thud, her curly red halo of hair appeared in the small window. The diamond shaped mesh embedded in the glass looked like slashes across her pale face. She grinned, then disappeared.

The sudden silence was jarring. Rondo pushed to his feet and hurried across the cracked linoleum floor to lock the door. After he twisted the knob to make sure it was locked, he reached up and flipped the deadbolt closed too. He turned and stared at the lump on the pallet, then turned back to look at the door.

A deadbolt inside a storage room? That was odd.

He turned back to see the kid wiggling free of the blanket.

CHAPTER THIRTY-FIVE
He's Missing!

Aidan paced the width of the front porch, still clutching his cell phone. He rubbed at the furrows between his eyebrows. What had happened? How had the night gone so wrong? Gina had insisted on walking the backyard again, crisscrossing the field between the house and the pond with Charlotte. Aidan looked up the driveway again, searching for headlights. He glanced at his watch. It had only been fifteen minutes since he'd called the Sheriff, but he hoped one of the deputies was nearby.

Movement along the fence row caught his eye. Joe jogged across the yard and waved something in the air. Aidan peered at him, then hurried down the steps to meet the other ranch hand.

Joe held up a little toy horse. He breathed heavily with exertion, but said, "Found this by the gate."

Aidan took the plastic toy and held it up to the light. His shoulders drooped when he recognized it. It felt like the weight of the world was on his shoulders. "Damn." He turned on his heel and tossed over his shoulder, "You wait

275

here for the Sheriff. I'm going to go get Gina."

He strode around the side of the house, his long legs eating up ground. He spotted the two flashlight beams sweeping the edge of the field, and hurried toward the closest one. He waved his hands over his head and shouted to get their attention. The two shadows moved toward him, the slimmer one moving faster. He met Gina at the edge of the patio and grabbed her arm. "Joe found this out by the gate."

She blinked at the toy. "The gate?" She looked up at him, her eyes wide.

He nodded, but she didn't respond. It hadn't sunk in yet. "Where the cattle were taken."

Her jaw dropped and her whole body drooped. He caught her as she began to shake her head. "No. No, that's not — how did he get out there? Why would he have been out there?" She choked back a sob and wrapped her arms around herself, then began to rock back and forth.

He steered her toward the house. "I don't know. It doesn't matter. What matters is—"

"Finding my son." She pushed away from him and stomped across the patio.

He followed close on her heels. He could only imagine the pain she was feeling. Guilt nagged at him. "The Sheriff should be here any—"

"No time to wait." She jerked the kitchen door open and snagged her purse. She tugged her keys out of it and hurried across the living room and out the back door.

He trailed behind her as she yanked her car door open. She slid in and slammed the door. He leaned in and watched helplessly as she rammed the key into the ignition, missing her mark twice, but hitting it on the third. "Please," he pleaded as he ran to the passenger side and slid in. "The Sheriff—"

She twisted the key and the car sputtered and died. She slammed her fist into the steering wheel. "Start, you son of a bitch! Start!" She twisted the key again and pumped the gas. This time the engine caught and roared to life. She threw the transmission in reverse, hit the gas and spun the wheel.

Joe jumped out of the way as she shifted into drive and threw gravel. The little car fishtailed, then straightened out as she pointed it at the driveway. Headlights turned into the driveway and headed straight for them. For a moment, Aidan thought she wasn't going to give, wasn't going to slow.

"The Sheriff!" he shouted and pointed at the oncoming headlights. He grabbed the dash as she jerked the wheel to the side and roared past the cruiser, missing it by mere inches. He glanced back and saw brake lights. Lord help 'em if the deputy came after them, because he knew Gina wouldn't stop for anything. He turned back around as Gina jerked the wheel to the right and the tires squealed onto the blacktop. The little car raced forward, engine whining, and she didn't let up. Telephone poles flashed past, trees were a blur. He hoped like hell that no deer tried to cross the road.

When they reached the state highway, she screeched to a stop and her head swiveled right then left, then back again. She turned to look at Aidan, her eyes wide and wild with fear. "Which way?" she demanded.

He shrugged and said helplessly, "I don't know." He took a deep breath and tried to guess where the rustlers might be headed.

"Think," she hissed. "Which way would they go? Where would they take a load of cattle?"

He chewed his bottom lip. He thought out loud. "The sale barn wouldn't be safe. Everyone there knows our brand."

She made a rolling motion with her hand. "Okay, so not the sale barn here. Are there any others nearby?"

He shook his head. They always used Angell's place. He didn't know the others in the area. Sirens sounded behind them and Gina looked up into the rearview mirror as Aidan glanced over his shoulder. Flashing lights strobed across them. Gina clutched the wheel tightly and pressed her lips together.

"Don't do it," Aidan warned.

But she did.

Aidan braced his hands against the dash as she stomped on the gas and spun the wheel. The car leapt forward and the engine roared, then coughed and sputtered and they rolled to a stop.

Gina slumped forward and banged her head against the steering wheel. "No, no, no," she repeated softly.

Aidan reached over to touch her shoulders, and felt them convulse with her sobs. "We're going to find him," he promised. A cold chill passed through him. He'd find Toby, and he'd find the cattle. Whoever did this would pay.

Gina shook Aidan's hand off her shoulder. This was all his fault. If they hadn't been out at the Diamond J, Toby wouldn't have been caught up in this. It didn't make sense. Why was he outside? She had left him inside the house by himself watching television. The way the front door was standing open, he'd obviously gone looking for her. How long had she been outside with Aidan?

She'd been so excited, so relieved, by the offer from Signet. Then the night with Aidan had been perfect. They had strolled along, holding hands like they were in high school. Then they made out by the pond, under the moon as stars, like some fantasy.

Well, damn it, she didn't deserve a fantasy. She was a single mother, and her first priority was her son. Had to be her son. She never should have left him alone in a strange house like that. What had she been thinking?

She huffed and sat up straight. She hadn't been thinking. That was the problem. She glanced in the rear view mirror and watched as the deputy got out of his car. The strobing lights made her head throb, so she looked away, out into the darkness. The deputy walked up and tapped on her window.

"Roll the window down," prompted Aidan softly.

Gina shook her head. "Right." She cranked the window handle and took a deep breath. She had to get her emotions under control. Her son was depending on her.

The officer leaned down and gripped the door. "Gina Montgomery?"

"Yes, sir." She looked up, expecting to see a deputy. Instead, the Sheriff himself glared down at her. She gripped the wheel tightly, her knuckles white. "I'm sorry—"

"That's enough." He slapped his hand on the door frame as he leaned down. He looked past her. "Aidan."

Aidan nodded in response. "Sheriff."

The Sheriff's voice softened. "Ma'am, this isn't helping your boy. Why don't you let Aidan drive." It wasn't a question, it was a statement. An order. "You two can follow me back to the Diamond J and we'll work out how we're going to get your son home."

Gina swallowed past the lump in her throat that threatened to strangle her. Every fiber of her being was taut with the need to do something, to take action, to go out there and run as far and fast as she could until she found Toby. She pressed her lips together and nodded brusquely. Aidan reached over and wrapped his hand over hers and gently pulled it off the steering wheel. He squeezed her fingers in his and nodded to her. The depth of concern in his eyes was touching.

He probably thought she was out of her mind.

And he wouldn't be wrong.

Half an hour later, she sat across the plank table from the Sheriff, with Aidan close beside her. Charlotte filled their coffee cups, then hovered behind the Sheriff, wringing a tea towel in her hands.

The Sheriff said, "We don't know for sure the cattle rustlers have Toby. Is his father in the picture?"

Gina felt her hackles raise. Of course the rustlers had Toby, otherwise why would his toy horse have been out there? "I don't know where his dad is. He lives in town, but he didn't answer his phone when I tried to call him a few minutes ago." This was a waste of time.

The Sheriff flipped his notebook open. "His name?"

"Steve Potts."

The Sheriff's head snapped up. "Steve Potts? Local guy? On the thin side?"

Gina cocked her head and frowned. "Yes." Of course the Sheriff knew him. Law enforcement all throughout Cardwell County knew Steve. "But he wouldn't do anything to hurt our son. He may be a lousy criminal, but he wouldn't do anything to put Toby in danger."

"You said you don't know where he is." The Sheriff leaned forward. "When did you see him last?"

Gina shrugged. "I don't know. Last weekend, Toby's birthday, I guess."

"Have you talked to him on the phone?"

This was absurd. A waste of time. "No. He hasn't been answering." Hadn't she just said that?

The Sheriff sat back in his chair. "Try to call him now."

"I tried already. I've left a dozen messages for him since Toby disappeared." She squirmed in her seat. It didn't matter where Steve was. What mattered was her son.

Aidan leaned forward on his elbows. "What are you getting at, Sheriff?" His eyebrows pushed together as he stared at the officer.

The Sheriff shifted in his seat. "I may know how to get a hold of him, and he might be able to help."

Gina sat back. "What?" Her eyes narrowed.

"What I'm going to say here can't be repeated." The Sheriff looked around, making eye contact with everyone in the room. His gaze settled on Gina. He punctuated his words by tapping his index finger on the table. "I mean it. It can go no further."

"Sheriff?" Aidan asked.

"Aidan, please." The Sheriff held up his hand, palm out, then turned to face Gina. "Ma'am, I need your word."

Gina nodded and blinked. A tear slid down her cheek. She had no idea what was going on, or what this had to do with her son.

"Your husband is an undercover agent with the Rural Crimes Task Force."

Gina straightened in the wooden chair and shook her head. Had she heard him right? "Undercover?"

"Yes. He's been working undercover gathering information and evidence on a cattle rustling ring."

Aidan slapped the table. "Then that's it! Toby is safe!"

Charlotte murmured, "Praise the saints."

The Sheriff pulled his cell phone from his pocket. "I'll send a message to Steve."

"Be careful," Aidan warned.

Gina echoed his concerns. How could they alert Steve without giving him away, without putting Toby at risk? The Sheriff tapped a message out, clicked send and sat the phone in front of him. The Sheriff tapped his pen on the table while they all stared at his cell phone.

The grandfather clock in the hallway ticked out the seconds. The silence in the room was deafening. They all stared at the cell phone lying on the table.

Aidan asked, "So, you've been going after these rustlers for a while?"

The Sheriff nodded.

"Where do they take the cattle?"

The Sheriff took a sip of coffee and grimaced. "That's the problem. They've never taken Steve with them when they deliver the cattle. He's just been there for the theft itself, but tonight he was going in the cattle hauler with the leader of the gang."

"Let's think about this." Charlotte said. "They steal a herd of cattle, they aren't going to want to keep them around for long, so they'd take them to a sale barn, right?"

"First thing they do is strip them of identification. Cut off their ear tags, rebrand 'em, that sort of thing. Probably mix 'em in with legit stock blend 'em in." The Sheriff continued, "We think they were taking them out of state, based on how long the cattle hauler was away from the compound, but the last couple of herds have only been short runs."

Charlotte frowned. "Have you checked out the sale barns around here?" She shook her head and clucked. "I can't imagine Angell's doing anything untoward."

The Sheriff scoffed at the suggestion. "No. We're confident none of the sale barns in the tri-state area would take stolen cattle."

Gina asked, "So, if they don't take them to a sale barn, where would they take them? Are they hiding them at another ranch or something?"

The Sheriff clicked his pen several times as his brow furrowed. "The problem is, tonight they almost got caught. They'll need to unload those animals quick. No time to go through the usual routine."

Aidan snapped his fingers. "I think I know." His voice was cold and hard.

Gina swiveled to look at him. His face was ashen. "What?" She grabbed his hand and squeezed. If he knew . . .

"My father owns a huge meat processing company. They treat cattle like a product. It's all about volume. The BMC is run by a guy named Brennan, a scumbag who wouldn't care where the stock came from to get more pounds through the door." He pushed to his feet, scraping his chair back from the table. "As long as there were no inspectors around, he'd take anything."

The Sheriff pushed his chair back, too, but Gina held out a hand to stop him. "If you go in there guns blazing, Toby could get hurt." She didn't care about the cattle or the crooks. All she cared about was her son.

"But I can go." Aidan pushed his chair in and stood behind it, gripping the back. "I'll take a look around and report back."

Gina jumped to her feet. "I'm going with you."

"No. No, absolutely not." Aidan shook his head and wagged his finger at her. "Not a chance."

She glared at him. Like he had a choice in the matter. "I'm going and there's nothing you can do about it."

"Listen, son, I'm not crazy about letting you go in there, but I've got sense enough to see that might be the best way to save her little boy." The Sheriff put his hand on Aidan's arm. "I'll follow you, but hang back. You go in there, observe, then report to me. Got it?"

Aidan nodded once, then spun on his heel and hurried

out the door. Gina jogged to keep up with him as he strode across the driveway. He was already turning the key in the ignition of his truck by the time she climbed in. She buckled her seat belt as they reversed out of the parking spot. The Sheriff pulled out right behind them. Charlotte stood in the driveway and watched them, still wringing the tea towel gripped in her hands.

"This isn't a good idea," Aidan said as he glanced over at her.

She shrugged. It didn't matter what he thought was a good idea. While they drove, her thoughts turned to Steve. An undercover agent? And here all this time she thought he was a low level criminal, skirting trouble. She snorted. This was nuts. This had to be a dream. It was all so crazy.

She glanced at Aidan. The glow of the dashboard highlighted the set of his jaw. It seemed like hours had passed since she'd been in his arms. Goose bumps pimpled her skin and she shivered. She turned forward to watch the truck eat up the ribbon of gray highway, mile after mile.

The fact that Steve was involved gave her hope. Her stomach twisted with worry. Her biggest fear was that they'd use Toby to get to Steve. Would Steve take unnecessary risks? Would he do whatever he could to save his son?

Her chest rose and fell as she heaved a sigh. Yes, Steve would do whatever it took to save Toby. He'd always been a devoted father.

Time seemed to slow as they drove. She kept checking her watch, desperately willing the truck to go faster. She glanced at the speedometer. Aidan was already pushing the truck as fast as he dared. They wouldn't do Toby any good if they wrecked or were stopped by a highway patrolman.

Finally, Aidan pointed at a road sign. "That's our turnoff."

She nodded. "What's the plan?"

"When we pull in, hunker down in your seat so nobody sees you. I'm going to go inside and take a look around."

She watched his face. His teeth were clenched. "You said you don't have much to do with your father. Won't he think it's weird that you just show up, especially so late?"

He shrugged. "I've been thinking about that. Chances are, he won't be there. It's the middle of the night. But Lloyd Brennan might be. He's my dad's right hand. He's the one that does the dirty work. If I run into him, I'll have to come up with a reason for being there."

"Something about a family member?" she offered.

"I'll come up with something." He signaled and turned onto a narrow blacktop. After a couple of miles, he pointed ahead. "See that glow? That's the great Brackston Meat Company."

She remembered what he said about how bad the conditions were, and made a mental note to never buy anything with the Brackston name on it again. He turned onto a gravel road without signaling. "We're almost there."

She glanced in the rearview mirror and saw the Sheriff pull in after them and cut his lights.

He hissed, "Hunker down."

She unfastened her seatbelt, slid into the footwell and wrapped her arms around her legs. The truck slowed as Aidan applied the brake. As soon as the truck stopped, Aidan looked around and whispered, "I'm leaving the keys here with you. If anything goes sideways, get out of here. Don't wait for me."

She watched silently as he swung open the door and jumped out of the truck. She knew he was right, that she had no business going in, but she hated waiting here alone. She closed her eyes and reached out with her mind. Was Toby close? She was sure he was okay. He was alive. He had to be. She couldn't let herself think otherwise. Besides, she'd know if something had happened to him.

She'd feel it.

CHAPTER THIRTY-SIX

Smart Kid

Rondo reached for the kid, then shrugged and stopped. Not like the boy could go anywhere anyway. The kid wiggled and squirmed and threw the blanket off. His eyes were big as half dollars and snot ran from his red nose.

The kid swiped his arm across his face and sniffled. "Where's my daddy?"

Rondo said, "You just sit there and keep your mouth shut—"

Right on cue, the kid opened his mouth wide and screamed. A big, hearty, blood curdling scream.

Rondo dove for the boy and slapped his palm over the kid's mouth. The kid bit down hard, and Rondo jerked his hand away, cradling it against his stomach. The little snot opened his mouth again, but Rondo swung his hand hard, backhanding the kid hard enough to send him sprawling.

Rondo stood over the brat and shook his finger at him. "No more yelling. Got it?" This was what was wrong with the world. Kids didn't listen to their elders. They needed to be smacked around, taught to respect adults.

The kid's eyes blinked rapidly, but he nodded.

Rondo turned away and pulled his cell phone from his pocket. He held it up. No signal. Of course. He shook his head and started pacing. He poked around at the boxes stacked around the room, then glanced at his watch and sighed. What was he going to do until Lana and the golden boy returned?

The kid sniffled again, then started sobbing. "Oh, jeez," Rondo groaned. "Enough with the waterworks."

A stack of boxes caught his eye. He pulled a knife from his pocket and flipped it open with a quick flick of his wrist. The kid squeaked. Rondo looked at him and raised his eyebrows. The boy shrank into a ball. Rondo slit the box open and pulled out a handful of meat sticks. He shrugged. At least he wouldn't go hungry. He peeled back the plastic and bit off a piece. Mmmmm. Jalapeno. His favorite. He glanced at the boy, who smacked his lips hungrily.

"Ah, jeez," Rondo moaned. "You want one, too?"

The kid nodded. Rondo pulled another meat stick from the box and tossed it to the boy. The snack landed on the floor with a soft smack and slid across the floor. The kid scrambled forward, snatched the package up and retreated to his pallet. He fumbled with the wrapper, then ripped at it with his teeth. As soon as he discarded the plastic, he devoured the snack. Rondo shrugged.

It had been a long night for him. Probably seemed even longer to the rug rat. No wonder the kid was hungry. The brat watched him like a wary wild animal as he chewed, gripping the meat stick in his chubby hands as if he were afraid Rondo would rip it away from him.

Rondo ran his tongue over his teeth. His mouth was on fire. That's what he got for eating a jalapeno stick. He looked at the kid, then walked across the room and peered out the glass window. He turned back to the boy and said, "I'm going to go find us something to drink, okay?"

The boy nodded seriously and pulled the blanket around him.

"Don't move a muscle." Rondo held up his hand like a gun and pointed at the kid. Wouldn't hurt to put the scare into him. "Got it?"

The kid yanked the blanket over his head and whimpered.

Rondo nodded. Stupid kid was scared shitless. Rondo strode across the room, flipped the deadbolt open and unlocked the door. He glanced back at the mound under the dirty blanket. He went out the door and strolled down the hallway, looking in side windows as he went. Every now and then he glanced back. Though he was fairly sure the brat wouldn't try to escape, he wasn't taking any chances.

A sign on the door at the bottom of the stairwell was marked "Break Room." He pushed the door open and smiled when he spotted the soda machine. He dug in his pockets and pulled out a handful of change. He counted out enough for two sodas, and plugged quarters into the machine. He got a Coke for himself and a Sprite for the kid. The brat didn't need caffeine.

He popped the top on his soda and sipped the sweet liquid as he strolled back to the storage room. He grabbed the door knob and twisted.

Locked.

What the—? He peeked through the window and saw the brat sitting on the pallet, staring back at him. He pounded his fist on the heavy door. "Open up!" He jerked the knob, then put his shoulder to the door and pushed. He spun around in a circle, trying to think.

Outsmarted by a damned kid!

He looked over his shoulder toward the stairwell. He had to be in that room by the time Lana and the golden boy returned, or he'd never hear the end of it. He stalked down the hall, and looked into the rooms for anything he could use as a tool. Keys? Would there be extra keys somewhere? He jogged to the break room and yanked open cabinet doors and drawers, scooping stuff out, but he found nothing. He heaved a sigh.

Think.

He jerked the door open and stomped down the hall, when a bump in the wall at the end of the hallway caught his eye, just past the storage room.

A fire extinguisher.

He hurried down the hallway and yanked the big metal canister from the wall. He turned to the storage room door and held the extinguisher over his head, then swept it down as hard as he could. It bounced off the metal knob.

Shit!

He lifted it up and slammed it against the knob, over and over. The noise of metal striking metal echoed in the wide hallway. Finally, he stopped. He tossed the dented canister to the side and tried the door knob again.

Nothing.

He pounded his fist on the door again, then looked inside. The kid had pulled the blanket over his head again, a shivering lump of scared shitless. Rondo cast around for something, anything he could use.

Suddenly, he remembered the Sprite in his jacket pocket. He pulled it from his pocket and held it up to the window. "Hey, kid!" he shouted. "Aren't you thirsty? Open this door and I'll give it to you. You're not in trouble. Just open the door."

He peeked in. The kid's head poked out of the blanket like a turtle. He blinked his big eyes, but shook his head no.

Damn it!

A flash of reflection caught his eye. He stepped back to the niche in the wall where he'd gotten the fire extinguisher. An ax. That should take care of it. He pulled it from the wall and hefted the weight in his hands, then turned toward the heavy door.

If he had to knock that thing off its hinges or rip it to splinters, he'd get in there before Lana returned.

CHAPTER THIRTY-SEVEN
Mama Bear

Gina hugged her legs to her chest and listened to her heart thud wildly. This was crazy. She couldn't just wait here when her son was so close. She knew it. She could feel it.

She raised up and peered out the window. A couple of pickup trucks, several cars and a minivan were parked in the lot, but that was it. The night shift must be pretty thin.

The bright, glaring lights lit up the graveled parking lot like day. There was no movement, no sign of life. She pulled herself up onto the seat, but stayed low. The building was massive, a hulk of steel and concrete.

A mural depicting an idyllic scene of cattle grazing in a rolling meadow covered the entire front of the building. Aidan had parked in front of an unmarked door, next to a huge roll up garage door.

She couldn't stand it any longer. She carefully pulled the handle, slipped out of the truck and pushed the door shut as quick as she could. She winced at the loud sound, and froze. When nothing happened, she crept forward along the side of the truck then stopped to peek around it. No sound other than the muffled mooing of cattle. What now? Should she creep forward like a burglar, or walk in like she belonged? She took a deep breath, stood up and strode straight to the door. The knob was loose in her hand, rusted and dented. One twist and she was inside.

The smell was overpowering. Mud, muck, urine and shit. The sound was just as bad. The mooing wasn't like what she'd heard during her visits to the Diamond J. That sound was peaceful. This sound was distraught, bellowing and bawling. Mothers looking for babies. Underlying the cattle sounds was the hum of machinery, clanking and clacking. A quick glance around the room revealed a staging room of sorts, with keys and lockers and a time clock.

Which way to go? Where did Aidan go? There was only one door leading deeper into the building, a scratched up door covered in peeling green paint. It had taken a great deal of courage for her to walk into the building, and now she needed to go through yet another door.

She took a deep breath and immediately regretted it, nearly gagging from the stench. The thought of what might lie in wait on the other side of that door made her stomach squirm, but the thought of her son being in the building and needing her gave her the courage to move forward. She turned the knob and opened the door a crack. A narrow hallway ran to the left and right.

No sign of anyone, but she could she hear a forklift running. She stepped through and pushed the door shut behind her, then walked quickly to her right. A large freezer door was on her left. She glanced through a small porthole and saw sides of beef hanging on tracks running along the ceiling. The placard on the wall indicated it was Cold Storage 2.

Moving equipment meant people. She had to be close to the butchering area. She flattened against the wall and moved forward, then froze, her eyes pinned to a small camera set in the ceiling ahead of her. A flashing red light indicated it was on. She shuffled forward faster. Whoever was watching that camera had already seen her. If they were watching. This time of night, maybe no one was, if she was lucky.

At the next door, she ran her fingers along the placard. Cutting Room. She swallowed the lump in her throat, and swore she'd never eat beef again. Just as she rose up to peek into the room, the next door down swung open and Aidan appeared. She ducked down and hurried toward him.

His eyes rounded and his jaw dropped. "What are you doing here?" he hissed.

"I couldn't sit out there and do nothing."

He nodded once, but his expression was dark. She asked, "Have you seen anything yet?"

"No. But if I were going to hide a kid here, I'd sure as hell not be here on the main level."

She pointed at the door he had come from. "What's in there?"

His eyes narrowed. "Leads to the kill floor."

She opened her mouth, then closed it. She didn't want to know. He hooked his thumb of his shoulder. "The other side of the building is full of cattle. A bunch of paddocks, crisscrossed with catwalks. Nowhere to hide anyone there."

Gina looked back toward the first door. It had said cold storage 2. "There has to be more cold storage, right?"

He nodded. "What are you thinking?"

She knelt and touched the floor. "Feel that? Ventilation. Condensers, maybe."

Aidan looked down and seemed to mull it over. "The lower level has a mechanical room and storage." Then he pointed past Gina. She turned to follow his gaze. Just past her was a sign on the ceiling. Service elevator. She was right. There was another level to the building. Every nerve tingled, every muscle tensed. She needed to go, she needed to do something. Her son was here, close. She could feel it. But what would be waiting for them? It didn't matter. She had to go.

She turned to him and said, "Are you going with me?" She lifted her chin. Toby needed her to be brave.

He nodded and grabbed her hand. They walked down the hallway, ducking when they reached a door with a window. She whispered, "There are cameras. We need to hurry." She pointed up toward the corner, where another red light shone above a camera.

He shook his head. "I found the security room. Nobody there."

She felt a rush of relief. They needed every little bit of luck they could get. As soon as they reached the elevator, she punched the down button. Machinery groaned and creaked. Something was wrong, she could feel it. She grabbed Aidan's hand and pulled him to the side. The lift ground to a halt. She heard voices just as the door slid open. They dashed through the doorway into the stairwell. Aidan reached back and slowed the door, letting it ease closed. They pressed against the wall, waiting.

Who was in the elevator? What if they had Toby? Gina pushed past Aidan and very carefully pulled the door open. Metal creaked and she froze.

Aidan mouthed, "What?"

She mouthed back. "I need to know if they have Toby?"

He nodded and slumped. She didn't need his permission. Didn't want him to get in her way. Yes, it was risky, but she had to know. She poked her head out the door and looked down the hall. Two men walked down the hall, slowly, casually, like they had all the time in the world. She wanted to follow them, see where they were going. She strained to hear what they were saying, but all she could hear was muffled words.

Kid.

Her eyes brightened. They said kid!

Toby was here!

Somewhere in the distance, somewhere in the depths of the building, she heard a muffled shout. Aidan's head snapped around. He'd heard it too. She turned, ready to explode down the stairs, but Aidan grabbed her arm.

"Easy," he whispered. He pulled her behind him and peered over the metal railing. She squeezed next to him, keeping close, and looked down. Two flights, one landing. Another shout, then a crashing sound. She started down the stairs, but Aidan put his hand on her shoulder. He shook his head no, then motioned for her to get behind him.

She shook her own head in response and kept going. She went slowly, one step at a time. She peered over the metal railing, watching for any sign of the door below opening. Her ears tingled. If she were a wolf, they'd be pricked up straight, swiveling. She could feel Aidan right behind her. He kept one hand on her back, a reassuring touch.

At the bottom of the steps, she paused. The yells were louder, punctuated by sharp cracks. Aidan whispered in her ear, "Let me look."

She looked back, but he pushed her to the side and slowly turned the doorknob, then peeked out the door. He whispered, "Someone's trying to break in a door."

She put her hand on Aidan's back and leaned over him to see for herself. A man was raging at the other end of the hallway, screaming, yelling and slamming a fire extinguisher at a door. While she watched, he stopped, and she thought for a moment he had given up. Suddenly, he took two quick steps and returned to the door with something in his hand. Gina peered at the weapon as he raised it over his head. Light glinted on the blade.

An axe.

The man bellowed, "You little snot! Unlock this fucking door!"

Gina's eyes widened. Before Aidan could stop her, she darted out of the stairwell and pounded down the hallway, hell bent on taking that man down. There was no conscious thought, no plan of action, just adrenalin. The man turned and looked at her, his eyes wide with surprise, jaw slack. He lowered the ax just as she lowered her shoulder and hit him like a linebacker on Sunday.

He grunted as she connected with his stomach, knocking him off his feet. He landed on his back, with her on top of him. His face turned purple as he struggled to suck air into his lungs. Gina didn't let up. She straddled him, wrapped her left hand around his throat and squeezed with all her might. Her right hand balled into a fist and she drove it down with all her weight behind it, aiming for his nose.

Her knuckles connected with the bridge of his nose with a satisfying crack. The man cried out, a high pitched whine. She pulled her fist back, ready to drive down again, but Aidan grabbed her hand.

She looked up and realized Aidan held the ax the man had dropped when she hit him.

Aidan jerked his chin to the side. "I'll keep an eye on him. You see if Toby is in there."

Toby! In her blind rage, all she'd thought about was hurting that man. She leapt to her feet and grabbed the knob. Locked. She twisted and shook it, but it wouldn't give. She stretched up and looked through the small window. No sign of him. She pressed her face to the glass, but there was nothing but boxes and pallets.

She spun around to the man and screamed, "Where is my son?"

The man had scooted back against the concrete wall. He didn't respond, just stared at her sullenly. He held one hand to his nose, blood streaming between his fingers.

Aidan held her back with one hand. She was vibrating with anger. Aidan hissed, "Keep it down. He's not the only one we have to worry about."

She breathed in and out, short, quick breaths. Her son's life depended on her keeping her cool. What next? Where else could he be? Her head swiveled back and forth. One of the other rooms? But why was that man so desperate to get in that room?

She grasped the edge of the window with her fingertips and stood on her tiptoes. The blanket. It moved. She tapped on the glass. The edge of the blanket lifted, and Toby looked at her. His eyes widened with recognition, then he jumped to his feet and ran to the door. He fumbled a moment, then the lock clicked and the door knob turned in Gina's hand.

The door swung open and Gina swept Toby up in her arms, holding him tight and nestling her head against his hair. She breathed in that little boy scent, mixed with dust and dirt and sweat.

Oh, she never wanted to let him go!

Aidan leaned close. "I hate to break this reunion up, but we've still got to get out of here."

She nodded quickly and turned. Aidan grabbed the man on the floor and hauled him into the storage room. Gina watched as Aidan snagged a packing tape gun from a hook on the wall and quickly secured the man's hands behind his back, then his feet. Finally, he wrapped tape over his mouth and around the back of his head. She winced. That was going to hurt when it came off.

She cradled Toby against her chest. Before they closed

the door, she twisted the lock on the inside. She glanced back at the man and his eyes pleaded with her. Let his buddies save him. She pulled the door shut and they darted down the hall.

Gina reached out to punch the elevator button, but Aidan shook his head. "Stairs are safer."

She nodded and followed him through the doors and up the stairs. They were almost safe. Toby wrapped his arms around her neck and held on tight. A short hallway and they'd be home free. They stopped at the top and Aidan pressed his ear to the door. He held up one finger, then he pulled the door open and peeked out.

He pulled the door open and went out. Gina followed. He put one arm around Gina and they hurried down the hallway. She panted with exertion, but held on tight to her son. They reached the doorway to the break room and burst through, but slid to a stop.

A man and a woman spun to face them, shocked at first, but then their faces contorted with anger. The man pulled a gun. The woman was that pigtailed woman she'd seen at the truck stop.

Gina shook her head and pleaded, "My son is all we want. Let us go. We'll never tell anyone—" Toby buried his head tighter against her neck.

Aidan huffed out a breath and said, "Lana?"

The woman looked up at him and grinned. She looked absolutely manic, eyes wide and wild. "It's over. Shoot 'em and get it over with, Brennan."

The door behind them burst open and Steve strode through. Lana turned to look at him and tilted her head. It was a look of endearment. Of fondness.

Gina stared open mouthed at her ex-husband. He looked at her, eyes wide. His jaw dropped. His gaze flitted from Gina to Aidan to the boy in her arms, then back again, then he gathered himself and his face went blank.

Lana hooked her hand in the crook of Steve's arm and turned him toward the door. The door exploded open and two officers in full riot gear burst through and slammed Brennan to the floor in seconds. Lana stared at them blinking in surprise.

Steve jerked one arm behind Lana, then the other and held them there while he tugged a pair of handcuffs from the back of his pants.

Lana twisted around to look at him, her face twisted in an ugly sneer. "You double-crossin' twit. You're gonna pay for this."

Gina watched as her ex-husband turned the woman over to one of the officers. As soon as the officers had taken Lana and Brennan out, Steve rushed to Gina and cupped his hand against Toby's face. "You okay, buddy?"

Toby nodded gravely. Gina couldn't take her eyes off of Steve. "You're a cop?"

He grinned. "Sorry. Undercover."

Aidan stepped forward and stuck out his hand. "Thank you, man."

Steve took his hand and shook it. "Thank you for saving my boy." He nodded toward Gina. "And Gina."

Aidan nodded solemnly. "Happy to do it. Gotten kind of fond of both of them."

"Easy to do." One corner of Steve's mouth twitched up.

He turned to leave. "Y'all are going to have to give a statement."

"Wait!" Gina said, reaching out for Steve. "There's another guy in the basement. He'd locked in one of the storage rooms."

Aidan added with a grin, "And he might need medical attention."

CHAPTER THIRTY-EIGHT

Home

After Steve's captain was done talking with them, they were exhausted. Gina put Toby in the back seat of Aidan's truck and buckled him in, then climbed into the passenger seat. As they drove back to the Diamond J, Gina listened to the hum of the tires on the blacktop and mulled over the events of the night.

The relief at finding Toby was overwhelming. In all the excitement, she'd forgotten about the incredible offer from Signet. She was going to be able to keep the store.

And Steve . . . Wow.

An undercover agent!

Who would've ever guessed that?

At least now she knew why he often disappeared without warning.

She glanced at Aidan. This man dropped everything, risked everything, to save her son. She grinned at him. He reached over and wrapped his fingers around hers.

He nodded toward the east, where pink was just beginning to hint at the coming day. "It's late."

"Or early," she offered.

He snorted in agreement. "You guys want to stay at the Diamond J? Get some sleep?"

She squeezed his hand. Could she? The idea of being able to just collapse in a bed felt really good.

He released her hand and picked up his cell phone from the console. He punched a number with his thumb. After a moment, he spoke. "Charlotte. It's me. I've got a whole lot to tell you, but it can wait. Can you set up a spare room for Gina and her little boy?"

He pressed the end button and dropped the phone, then splayed his hand on the seat between them. Gina reached out and placed her hand on top of his, then tucked her fingers between his and settled back in the seat. She'd never met anyone as chivalrous as Aidan.

She'd found her knight in shining armor.

THE END

DEAR READER:

I hope you enjoyed this novel, the second in the Diamond J Series (the first was Denim & Diamonds).

Stop by my website and sign up for my newsletter. I won't ever sell your name and I won't bombard you with info - I send out updates a few times a year.

lorilrobinett.com

I'm happy to connect with you on Facebook, Goodreads and Twitter, too.

And if you are so inclined, I would be thrilled if you would pop over to Amazon, Barnes and Noble, or Goodreads (or all 3!) and leave a review. That makes me jump with joy.

Lori